LADY IN THE LAKE

Further Titles by Jason Foss from Severn House

BYRON'S SHADOW
SHADOW IN THE CORN
SHADESMOOR

LADY IN
THE LAKE

Jason Foss

This first world edition published in Great Britain 1996 by
SEVERN HOUSE PUBLISHERS LTD of
9–15 High Street, Sutton, Surrey SM1 1DF.
First published in the USA 1996 by
SEVERN HOUSE PUBLISHERS INC., of
595 Madison Avenue, New York, NY 10022.

British Library Cataloguing in Publication Data

Foss, Jason
    Lady in the lake
    1. English fiction – 20th century
    I. Title
    823.9'14 [F]

    ISBN 0-7278-4892-5

Typeset by Palimpsest Book Production Limited,
Polmont, Stirlingshire, Scotland.
Printed and bound in Great Britain by
Hartnolls Ltd, Bodmin, Cornwall.

For Kate

PART ONE

Chapter One

Excalibur! Its glittering point broke surface to the tones of Seigfried's 'Death March'. A hand appeared from the water and the Lady of the Lake held the sacred weapon aloft. In his black gown and polished cap, Merlin stood by the shore, waiting. He would deliver the sword into the hands of Uther Pendragon to symbolize that he was the true king of Britain. Uther was doomed to die in a thicket of treachery and his name be remembered only by scholars and by Hollywood. Not so his son.

A remote control was aimed at the video recorder, and the action stopped part way into the siege of Tintagel Castle. Jeffrey Flint yawned and went into the kitchen to collect his tandoori-for-one from the microwave. He'd eat at the table before going back for the rape of Igrain and the bloody bit where king Mark of Cornwall is impaled on a spike.

Alone in his cottage at the edge of the Yorkshire moors, the archaeologist crunched at an onion bhaji and read the letter again. He'd never taken King Arthur seriously, yet here was a request that he give a lecture on the subject of Arthur and Excalibur to the staff of a Leeds insurance office. To warm to the mood, he'd started watching the John Boorman epic, realizing how little he knew about Arthur; too little to deliver an authoritative lecture.

Given only a few days to prepare his talk, Flint was

stumped as to what he could actually say: did the insurance men want the facts, or the fantasy, erudite discussion or light entertainment? It had to be the latter; Arthurian romances were packed with death, disaster, fire, theft and Acts of God, but fifteen hundred years on, an insurance company would hardly care. Flint felt too relaxed to be suspicious. Perhaps he should just take the video of *Excalibur* along for the grey suits to watch.

His meal over, he glanced at the clock. It was folk night at the Green Man Free House, a few minutes' walk down the hill. If Arthur had ever existed, he was long dead. The remainder of the video could be watched another day; Arthur could wait until the morning.

"What's the latest dirt on King Arthur?" Flint folded his arms and leaned against the wall of the sunlit office. His tweed jacket had patched sleeves, his off-white shirt was open at the collar and he wore nearly new jeans. For a university lecturer, it was a kind of uniform.

Tyrone Drake was at his desk, well ordered with desk-tidy, memo racks and red designer lamp. The young man was square-set and square-jawed, not letting his career in archaeology stand in the way of a sensible haircut, or a sharp jacket. When he gave a question deep thought before he answered, it was to impress, and to make the other wait for a pronouncement.

"Arthur has wasted more research grants than any other historical character," Tyrone replied, after the expected pause. "You read my thesis: you know what I think. Arthur is dead, so why the interest?"

Flint raised a restless finger to his close-trimmed straw beard. "Believe it or not, an insurance company want me to give a seminar about Arthur to their employees."

"After-dinner cabaret?"

"Not quite: next Tuesday at eleven, followed by nibbles and plonk."

"London? Can I come?"

"Leeds. Still want to come?"

"Nar."

"I'd appreciate being able to quote a few bits of your thesis."

"No problem, quote away. It only took me three pages to kill Arthur off. He wasn't a king at all, only a battle-leader under Ambrosius Aurelianus, operating around the turn of the sixth century. I'm writing a paper on it. Do they want to know the truth, or do they want all that sword and sorcery crap?"

"I checked, and they want the truth, hard as it comes. Could you be a hero and run me up an idiot sheet? I'm lecturing in ten minutes and I've got all those first year essays to mark."

Tyrone made 'my-project-is-running-behind' type faces, then acquiesced with a shrug of his padded shoulders. "Sure thing."

The Polytechnic of North Yorkshire had recently been elevated to the status of University. It hovered in a geographical no man's land east of Leeds, west of York and north of everywhere Tyrone considered civilized. Dr Jeffrey Flint had moved back to his native Yorkshire to take up his post and at thirty-four had been made Reader in Archaeology. His departmental head was only four years from retirement, so the odds were shortening on him making professor before he hit forty. Not that Flint was ambitious, but he reasoned that the higher he rose, the fewer people could mess around in his life.

For half his time, he was lecturing, writing papers and avoiding administration, the other half was spent running

UNY-DIG, an archaeological consultancy operating from the University. It had been established to generate income to subsidize the archaeology department, but in its first year, the subsidy had run the other way. Contracts were hard to win and payment was harder to secure, so the money-juggling went to Tyrone, who claimed an enthusiasm for capitalism. Meanwhile, Dr Flint was the front man and it was his opinions that Northern Consolidated Assurance PLC wanted to hear.

Matt Humphries was a straight six-foot tall, topping Flint by a couple of inches. He had round, marble-sucking cheeks and chose a trendy city crewcut to top off his suit of powder grey. Flint had abandoned his usual Oxfam and street market fashion, in favour of an almost new charcoal grey suit he reserved for impressing businessmen and interview panels.

Only five men and one woman, all under forty, attended the twenty minute seminar on the 'Real Arthur' in the side-room of the insurance office. Flint found them a serious, almost humourless bunch, who took notes in their filofaxes at intervals. He suspected they were pencilling-in lunch windows, not recording the date of the *Adventus Saxonum*.

He delivered the lecture with his usual bouncy cynicism, stripping away the layers of varnish added to the Arthurian legend in successive centuries. By the time he had reached the sixth century and the 'real' Arthur, almost everything was gone; Camelot, Guinevere, Lancelot, the Holy Grail, the Round Table and shiny knights in plate armour. A little like skinning an onion in the hope of finding a sweet fruit at the centre, the entire flimsy mythology was taken back to its insubstantial core. His audience were either stunned by the hot news from

6

the sixth century, or were stupefied by boredom. Flint suspected the latter.

Nibbles were substantial and the Chardonay delightful.

"I envy you, Flint," Humphries said, waving a heavy-duty canapé.

"Jeff, everyone calls me Jeff." Flint grabbed at a vol-au-vent between sentences.

"Archaeology sounds so exciting."

"Discovering lost civilizations, unearthing crocks of Inca gold, fighting off hordes of screaming natives? In reality it's rather dull: *Indiana Jones and the Local Authority Planning Procedures*. Most of our time, we excavate paper and fight off redundancy."

"But not you," Humphries said, with purpose. He half closed his left eye. "A little bird told me that you liked to dig in places others fear to tread."

A strong wave of deep foreboding swept over the archaeologist. King Arthur may have been little more than bait to lure him out of his ivory tower. Flint set down his wineglass, sensing he would need a clear head. A free lunch and a modest cheque were not so easily won.

Too clumsily for an executive of his potential, Humphries made a show of working his way around to the crux of the meeting. "My um, my colleagues, don't actually know why they are hearing about King Arthur . . . sorry, *Artorius*."

"I share their sense of mystery."

"Come this way." Humphries led the way across an office subdivided by dwarf walls, behind which his staff beavered at computer screens, setting up policies, handling claims, paying off the dead, the maimed and other victims of life's random cruelties. Shirt sleeves and ties, squeaky chairs and ever-buzzing phones dominated this enclosed nine-to-five world. Even if his salary were

7

tripled and his job were secure forever, Flint could never hang up his trowel and settle behind a workstation.

Humphries drew out a key and unlocked a plain door. Flint was ushered into the darkness of an unlit room and heard the key turn again in the lock.

The light snapped on. At the centre of the room was a single table, bearing a wooden crate, over a metre long. It had the appearance of a small coffin constructed of crude pine planking. Humphries beckoned, and Flint helped him lift the lid. The box was half full of moulded styrofoam. Resting in a preformed nest was a sword.

"We would like your opinion on this."

Its metre-long blade was polished, but not bright, damaged here and there by nicks and pits of corrosion. It was ancient, there was no doubt, but had obviously been cleaned by a professional conservator. The cross-guard curved forward, each arm had the form of entwined dragons picked out in silver and gold. The grip was black and smooth and partly collapsed – possibly aged ivory. A gilt sphere made up the pommel, a number of small, empty sockets had once held precious, or semi-precious stones and were arranged in cruciform pattern.

Flint was immediately curious, indeed, suspicious.

"How old would you say it was?" the insurance man asked.

Such a question had red-hot implications and needed handling with care. "I can't give a spot assessment, anything I say would be guesswork. What was its context?"

"Pardon?"

"Where was it found?"

"I cannot reveal that, I'm afraid."

"It would help me if I knew . . ."

"Sorry."

8

Flint sighed heavily: he'd have to make at least a few guesses to maintain his credibility as a consultant. "OK, it's got a Christian motif and therefore is likely to be European and dating to after the fourth century or so. These dragons are fun; they look Scandinavian, or Saxon. You really need to team up a weapons expert and an early medievalist: I'm strictly Romans and Celts."

"There's an inscription," Humphries said.

Flint leaned in closer and ran his finger just above the incised Roman lettering.

Humphries referred to a piece of paper, *"Deuce Nobiscum,"* he pronounced the Latin with difficulty.

"Deus Nobiscum?" Flint queried. "God is on our side?"

"Yes, that's what she said it read." Humphries was unaware of the slip he'd just made. Flint gobbled up this crumb of information without betraying himself.

"Deus Nobiscum is, I believe, the old Byzantine battle-cry."

"Who are they?"

"The Byzantine Empire was based on Constantinople: it was what was left of the Roman Empire after the Goths sacked Rome. By that date, your typical Roman legionaries had been replaced by armoured cavalry called Cataphracts; kind of prototype knights."

"Ah." Humphries had the smile of one who has just solved the crime at a murder-mystery dinner party. He was drawing conclusions.

"I'm not saying it is Byzantine," Flint warned him. "The Vikings also inscribed their blades, and they became christianized after they'd grown out of freelance raping and pillaging."

"So, what would you say its value is?"

"You're insuring it?"

9

Humphries nodded.

"Can I do a little more research; I'd like to get it right before putting my head on the block?"

"It needs a value today."

Flint was allowed a pause. He cared little for the trade in antiquities and found it repugnant to put a cash price on the past, but recalled a recent treasure trove decision on a Viking sword. "Twenty thousand, in case it turns out to be Viking."

"What if it turns out to be Excalibur?"

The words had the effect of a blow on the head with a rolled wet towel. Flint was stunned. "It can't be Excalibur," he stated.

"Why?"

Facts were needed instantly to quash the insane suggestion, but as there were no solid facts about Excalibur, Flint could use none of them to debunk the idea.

"Simple mathematical probability," he said after a few moments, pacing away from the box to construct his argument. "Excalibur, if it ever existed, would date to round-about AD 500; the end of Sub-Roman Britain and the beginning of Saxon domination. Now, we have very little pottery of that date, fewer metal objects such as coins or brooches. Swords are one of the rarest classes of find: any sub-Roman sword would be incredibly rare. The odds against finding a particular sword are millions to one."

The insurance man nodded. If he'd studied actuarial practice, he'd understand long odds.

"Next; we have very few objects dating to Roman Britain, or to the Dark Ages, which we can definitely say belonged to a famous historical character. We have a pencil-holder which may have belonged to King Alfred, but that's about all. The chance of finding anything we could prove was owned by Arthur is minuscule. The discovery of Excalibur must be as close to impossible as you can get."

"But people found Tutankhamun . . ." Humphries objected.

"But he was a real person, known to have existed and known to be buried in a relatively limited location. King Tut was bound to be discovered sooner or later. It was no big deal."

In shrugging off the most famous archaeological discovery of all time, Flint was overplaying the facts. Humphries was becoming confused.

"No big deal?"

"It's not Excalibur," Flint stated, in the soothing voice he applied to fraught students after examinations.

"But we still have to insure it."

"Ten quid – it's a fake."

"How much if it wasn't a fake?"

With no academic witnesses present, Flint had little to lose by playing the game. "The true Excalibur, correctly and exhaustively verified, would be Britain's premier cultural artifact. Forget the Crown Jewels, we're talking serious millions. Take whatever the Mona Lisa is worth and add a nought."

A smile came to the insurance man's lips. "So we could say it was priceless?"

"Or worthless."

"Could you investigate further?"

Flint was in no doubt that the sword was antique, probably ancient and probably had a story of its own well worth investigating. A paper was waiting to be written, somewhere at the end of the investigation.

"I'll need to sub-contract some of the research to specialists. That means the sword may need to go to London."

"Fine, we have the resources."

Tyrone would like that word 'resources': Flint would let him do the accounting on this project; the more creative, the better. It was money for old rope (or old iron). Flint knew several specialists who would welcome a cheque for services rendered.

"The sword will need to visit a lab: I'd recommend the Archaeometallurgy laboratory at Central College London."

"Do whatever you must, but the sword has to be returned to its owner by the twenty-fifth of March at the latest. I think they're planning some kind of press launch."

"Who?"

"The owners."

"They'll be murdered," Flint said.

"What?"

"Metaphorically speaking, but then that's their affair." He imagined ranks of academics lining up to ridicule the existence of Excalibur. A career was about to be destroyed and he hoped it wasn't one he respected.

"Who told you this is Excalibur?"

Humphries shook his head. "It's part of the deal that we don't disclose any names."

"Sooner or later, I'll need to know where it was found, and by whom: its the only way I can verify its authenticity." By 'verify' he meant 'debunk'.

"Work with what you have, but be discreet. You must not tell anyone it's Excalibur. To you, it is just a sword. Make up a cover story."

"Cover story?" It took only moments to devise, being already at the front of his thoughts. "OK, I'll tell people that the sword is unprovenanced, it could be Viking but it's probably a fake."

Humphries murmured satisfaction. "Then that's what we'll tell people."

Keeping his business face to front, Flint congratulated himself on his instant cover story. He could rehearse it before any expert, he could use it in any laboratory without feeling fraudulent. Flint was convinced it was true.

Chapter Two

Postgraduate archaeologists can largely be split into those who read the *Guardian* and those who prefer the *Independent*, but Tyrone Drake had deliberately avoided becoming a stereotype. In a quiet corner of the tea room, he was checking share prices in the *Financial Times* when Flint sat beside him at the morning lecture break and told him of the sword-in-the-box.

"Somebody is seriously deluded." If the Footsie Index had fallen a hundred points, Tyrone could not have sounded more disgusted. "If I were to claim I'd found Excalibur, they'd lock me away."

"Well somebody has." Flint raised a finger to his lips. "And it's hush-hush."

"Who?"

"Also hush-hush. I thought you might be able to advance a postulate."

"There are so many Arthurian loonies, I couldn't even start to guess."

"Could you try?" Flint spoke quietly, aware of having added his signature to a contract demanding absolute confidentiality. "For a start, when speaking of the discovery, the insurance man used the feminine pronoun. That should cut down the number of possibilities. If we're taking on this contract, we should find out who our mystery patron is, just for interest's sake. My mind would be easier if we knew."

A pair of female overseas students chose this moment to choose the next two soft chairs. Tyrone twitched his paper, but the students were oblivious to the furtive nature of the discussion.

"I bet she's in the Pendragon Society," Tyrone said, barely moving his jaws. "I'm speaking to their conference at Easter."

"Are you?" This came as news.

"Yes – you signed my application form. March 26th to 28th, Bath."

It wasn't news, it seemed, simply something Flint had done whilst his mind was elsewhere. "Are we paying for your jolly?"

"I like to think of it as professional development."

"Sorry."

The two overseas girls were now talking loudly in Spanish, drowning any need for conspiracy. Tyrone continued to expand on his plans. "I'm calling my paper 'The Death of Arthur'. I'm critically revising the sub-Roman origin of the legend. I've reforged that chunk of my thesis and sharpened it up for the kill."

"You're going to stand before a hundred Arthurian enthusiasts and deliver a hatchet-job on their fabled King? They'll hate you for it."

"Did you ever flinch from reading a thought-provoking paper?"

"No, just be well prepared, or they'll skin you. Remember what happened when you tried the same on the Romanists at Bradford?"

Tyrone was only just feeling his way into writing and delivering academic papers. The content was often brilliant but his style of delivery would be more suited to selling discount carpets. His abrupt dismissal of long-cherished notions won him more enemies than admirers.

15

Britain has a large number of semi-amateur societies, each devoted to exploring a specific, often obscure slice of the nation's heritage. Several focus on the Dark Ages in general or Arthur in particular. "Who's the secretary of the Pendragons these days?" Flint asked.

"Patrick Hewitt."

"Never heard of him."

"He's a retired dentist, or chiropodist or something equally glamorous." Tyrone had his nose turned up at the slightest whiff of amateurism. "He's into Arthurian poetry."

"Could you hunt him out and see if you can get hold of a membership list, plus an advance copy of the conference programme? I can't imagine any scholar turning up to his Society's main conference without dropping a quiet hint that he'd found Excalibur. It's not something one could easily keep quiet about."

"Will do."

In the early afternoon, Flint was in his own office, working his way through a pile of undergraduate essays on 'The development of the northern frontier system'. Twenty down, twelve to go. He hated marking almost as much as he hated attending committee meetings. If he had to read the term 'black burnished ware' once more, surely, his mind would suffer core meltdown.

After only a formal knock, Tyrone thrust the door open and strode in with two metres of fax sheets rolled over his arm.

"Got it!"

Tyrone unrolled the fax sheets over the top of the essays cluttering Flint's desk. It was the membership list of the Pendragon Society, some three hundred members long, with perhaps one hundred being female. The provisional conference programme advertised twelve lecture slots, nine already filled with erudite papers with titles such as 'A reappraisal of the Breton tradition' and 'the search for Mount Badon – new evidence'. Flint allowed his finger to fall on one name, scheduled to open the Saturday morning session.

'Lady H. Dunning – title to be announced'.

"Harry!" Flint said.

"Do you know her?"

"I met her on a field trip many moons ago."

Tyrone had long experience of the manner in which Flint and his lady friends could become acquainted. His square jaw twisted into a smirk. "Oh yes?"

"She must be well past sixty now – a bit batty as I remember her, but a decent old stick all the same."

"Could she be the one?"

" 'Title to be announced'. Doesn't that sound intriguing? Wouldn't you just like to swan into an unsuspecting Roman conference and announce you'd found Pontius Pilate's diaries? It would be much more fun than advertising it on a duplicated sheet a fortnight in advance."

As he was speaking, Flint lifted the telephone receiver and began to tap in the number for Central College, London, where he'd previously worked. He found the all-knowing departmental secretary and within a few more minutes, obtained a phone number in Somerset.

A well-educated, patrician woman's voice answered his call.

"Dunning."

"Harry, it's Jeffrey Flint here, remember me? Avebury, about ten, fifteen years ago?"

A prolonged silence would have been embarrassing, as would the reply 'Jeffrey Who?', but archaeology is a

17

small world and its inhabitants are attuned to remember times long past. Harry paused for just a few moments.

"Jeffrey, of course! I've followed your career; are you a professor now?"

"Sadly no."

"Ah, was it you that left lecturing to become a private detective?"

"I'm still an archaeologist, but I've acquired a habit of stumbling on other people's secrets."

An absence of sound from Somerset implied that Harry immediately realized the purpose of the call.

"You're still hot on the trail of King Arthur?" Flint asked.

"Yes, yes." Harry sounded flustered now.

Tyrone mouthed the word 'book', grabbed a cheap biro and began to scribble the title on the corner of the fax sheet.

"I hear you've written a new book," Flint said, bending his head to read the words, *A Guide to Arthur's Britain.*

"Yes," said Harry, now obviously on her guard.

He couldn't tease out the call for a moment longer. "Tell me, Harry. You wouldn't have found anything particularly unique recently?"

Harry made a curious gagging sound.

"Something in the sharp and shiny line?"

"Did you hear that I have?"

"I've seen it."

"Ah."

"The insurance people were very discreet, but as you say, I've become something of a detective; eminent Arthurian scholars are thin on the ground and I immediately thought of you."

Tyrone winced at the phoney flattery. Flint made

winding motions with his hands as he spoke. "Could we meet and have a chat?"

"I can't talk about it. Please understand, I've signed legal documents."

"So have I. I'm afraid we're bound together on this one."

"I'm very busy at the moment. I don't drive, and I don't get up to London very often."

"Nor do I: I'm in Yorkshire now."

Harry tried to change the subject, asking about his career, his research, praising his last paper.

Flint found a pause. "I understand you're going to be speaking at the Bath conference . . ."

"Yes, why not come along? Then you'll be able to hear all my splendid news."

"I'd prefer a private talk, we may have a lot to say. I've had the sword sent to London for examination."

"We've had all the tests done."

"Yes, well, this is for our client's peace of mind."

"I hope to goodness you're looking after it. Do you know what its worth?"

"I can guess." This sounded like a truthful answer.

"We will need the sword in Bath, by the date of the conference, without fail, do you understand? Have they let you have the replica too?"

"I understand that has also been sent to London."

"Well we'll need the replica at the conference – Saturday morning at the latest."

"My assistant is giving a paper – perhaps he could bring it with him, save all that bother with security companies."

Harry made grumbling, troubled noises. Flint impressed her with the reliability of Dr Drake and she ceased fighting the idea. "You will need proper security for the genuine sword, mark you! Promise me you'll use a proper company, who will take good care of it. I hate not having it in my sight, I never wanted it to travel up north."

"It's safe, don't worry." Flint pressed her on a date to meet. "Say Friday, before the conference."

She gave a heavy sigh "That Friday is going to be difficult. If you must come – come Thursday evening, that would be more convenient. I live near Glastonbury." Harry's tone had gradually shifted away from reluctance. "It's a long drive from Yorkshire – you could stay overnight and meet my family. Would you like that?"

"Love to."

"Don't forget the replica."

"No."

"And the security."

"Yes."

When he'd taken directions to her house, Flint put down the phone and rubbed his ear. Harry had become strident at the end. Spinning around in his chair, he beamed at Tyrone.

"Are you a cider drinker?"

"I can be."

"Good – I'm joining your West Country jaunt. Charge the expenses to Northern Consolidated Assurance. There's an old saying about fools and their money."

Grey-uniformed men from Stronghold Security delivered 'Excalibur' into the care of the Archaeometallurgy lab at Central College, London. Flint's northern University had no such facility and he wanted to be able to call in experts at short notice. Being back at his old college enabled him to chase up many friends, trade drinks and return

20

the odd library book which somehow had been packed in his move north.

With her white coat and huge, thick spectacles, 'Doc' Savage, head of Archaeological Science supervised the unpacking of the crates. In the first was the fabled sword, caressed by protective packaging. In a second, purpose-built case lined with velvet, was a second sword. This was glitteringly new, its blade bright and sharp, its handle wrapped with silk, its crossbar and pommel rich with gold and (hopefully fake) gems. Within the fuller, the blood-channel, the Roman letters DEVS NOBISCVM had been engraved, then filled with silver wire.

"This is very nice," said the scientist, holding the replica flat across the palms of both hands. "Did you say it is Viking?"

Flint made a vague affirmation.

Attention moved to the original sword. "This must have been found in a waterlogged deposit, such as a bog," she said. "Apart from the pitting, it's in very good condition and it's been well cleaned; do you know which lab did the conservation work?"

"No. Perhaps you could ask around, I'd be interested to know."

Doc Savage and her staff set about their work. The sword was photographed, measured and drawn and a tiny sample was removed from the back of the grip, which was revealed to be of walrus ivory. A friend from the Tower Armories dropped by and promised to send a batch of comparative drawings of the dragons on the hilt. Archaeologists love to identify such 'parallels' between objects of diverse origin; they are the things which spawn dating sequences and portentous essays about the diffusion of cultural influences.

All Excalibur's secrets were laid bare by the combined

onslaught of art-historians and physical scientists. Later that week, a green-jacketed pair of college guards escorted Flint and the sword by taxi across town to the British Museum laboratories. Here it was X-rayed and various experts of Flint's acquaintance wandered through and delivered their verdicts. All the work confirmed that the replica was as accurate as could be. No report or opinion contained the word 'fake'.

The insurance company had forwarded details of the first carbon-14 test on the walrus ivory; the result was 1470 BP ±80, giving a date roughly between AD400 and AD560. A second test had been prepared, but the results would not be known for some weeks. Flint became uneasy, and even despondent. He'd wanted an easy victory, a quick affirmation of his prejudice against the sword. It would have been nice to be able to save Harry from public humiliation.

Her breasts distorted the logo of a Yale sweatshirt and her arrival in the laboratory altered Flint's sense of mission. Tania McAuley stood a muscular five-feet ten inches tall, her auburn hair was worked into a wild mass of curls, her deep blue-green eyes never lacked the sparkle of distant waters and she needed no make-up to accentuate her vivacity. She burst into the lab as if onto a stage, pausing for applause.

"Tania!" Flint hugged her close (though not so close as he'd once hugged her).

"Jeff," she hugged back. "How are you, it must be ages!"

For three years the bubbly Canadian had sat through his lectures, freckled nose turned up towards him, with those wide, all-absorbing eyes following every detail of his movement. For three years he had resisted the clichéd staff-student affair, remembered his position, concentrated on the seven-year age gap until the night of her graduation party, when his vows had been broken.

One distant morning almost two years past, lying back in a sleeping bag on the floor of his office, Tania had blinked her eyelashes and curled up her mouth as if to say 'this was a mistake'. Expectation had spoiled the reality. The unobtainable lost its mystery once attained. Since that morning, a few postcards had crossed the oceans, and they had met once, briefly, as she passed through England *en route* to a marine archaeology conference. One day, thought Flint, he'd like to start anew, grow to know Tania the woman rather than Tania the devoted student.

Still with an arm half-around her waist he guided Tania to the table.

"Wow!" Tania's Canadian accent varied with her mood. Today it was strong. Her degree had been a lower second, her efforts having been diverted by a succession of fencing or swimming competitions. She picked up the replica in two hands, examining the details.

"I thought fencing, antiques – right up your street. As you were passing through . . ."

Tania jerked the grip into the palm of her hand, lowered its point and lunged into the air. Next, she held the blade upright, sabre fashion, and made three cuts in Flint's direction. Right, left, then a cut to the head. He stepped back, she giggled.

"Coward."

"What do you think?"

"The balance is wrong," she said. "The handle is too heavy for the blade."

"Try it in two hands."

She grasped the hilt as suggested, then made a violent

downward sweep towards some polystyrene packing. With an indignant, teeth-grinding squeak, a v-shaped chunk flew off the carton in a shower of white.

"Steady, it's insured for five grand."

"Oops, sorry." She rubbed a few balls of polystyrene off the blade. "For that much money, you should be sure that it works."

"It works."

Tania squinted at the pommel. "It looks like they used real gold plate, but these gems are paste."

"Thank God. Do you want to see the original?" He showed her the sadder sword in its box. "Without swinging this one, could you hazard a guess at the date."

A long, relaxed purr came from her lips, as if her fingers were dangling over a box of luxury chocolates. "Well, let me see. It's a slashing sword with parallel edges, so its happy in the Migration Period. It's what the Vikings called a 'svaerd'."

"So it's Viking?"

"The cross-guard has a north European look, Anglo-Saxon perhaps."

So many learned friends had ventured similar opinions, but this consultation carried an added bonus and Flint quickly worked his way from conundrums of the sixth century to the possibilities of the immediate future.

"Look, how about lunch? Call it your consultancy fee, I'll stick it on my expense account."

"Super, I want to ask you what I should do about Jake."

"Jake?"

"Mmm, you know Jake, I wrote you about him?"

"Oh, he's the Vancouver whale-watcher? Bushy beard, six-foot-two, check shirt."

She wrinkled her freckled nose. "That's the one. He keeps asking me to marry him, but I don't know what to say. You'll have to give me some male insight, you were always good at analyzing characters."

What could he say? Tania, married. His most attractive, eligible and vivacious ex-student was going to be married to a hunky Canadian boatman. Long-cherished fantasies vanished in an instant and the world looked very unfair.

Sea-green eyes flashed at him with wild anticipation. "So, lunch. Where are you treating me?"

Almost offhand, he came out with the name of the most expensive bistro in walking distance. Like Lancelot escorting Guinevere to her wedding, he had to smile, hide his feelings and do his duty. If he was losing any hope of a new start with Tania, he may as well do it in style.

She hardly seemed to notice his pain and had returned to talking about the sword. A delicate finger ran along the wrinkled black grip.

"Have you had the grip identified?"

"Walrus ivory."

"Never! What bastards those Vikings were."

"No Greenpeace in those days."

"It's jolly rare, even so."

Flint looked again at the replica; whatever the modern craftsman had used to imitate walrus ivory had been covered by red silk and bound about by a golden wire.

"Vikings usually went for grips of wood," Tania said. "Horn or leather is less common. The Romans were into leather."

His heart was no longer in the quest, but he continued to ask mechanical questions. "It can't be Roman, but what about Byzantine?"

"Byzantine?" Tania rolled her eyes from Flint to the sword and back again. "It's always possible. The

25

inlay and the inscription are acceptable for any date between the sixth and the thirteenth centuries, so you might be right. Otherwise, dear Jeffrey, your sword is a mongrel."

Inwardly, he cursed. Flint wanted certainties, but the experts had all ventured different opinions, all hedged around with doubt. The sword in the box had an amalgam of histories, not quite Roman, almost Byzantine, nearly Saxon or Viking. It was the sword one would have designed for King Arthur.

Chapter Three

Some years before, Tyrone had painted his Triumph Spitfire in green-and-brown camouflage, with RAF roundels on the doors. The car was aging less well than the ancient sword, one rusted wing had been replaced and undercoated a dull grey. The engine grumbled rather more than in its younger days, wind howled through gashes in the hood and Somerset was a long day's drive from North Yorkshire.

In the glove compartment lay a newly-purchased book. *A Guide to Arthur's Britain* by Lady H.N.E. Dunning.

"Is Harry an archaeologist?" Tyrone said to his passenger.

"Not strictly," Flint replied. "She's one of that dying breed of all-round amateur academics; bit of folklore, bit of history, bit of epigraphics and she burrows into the odd site when she comes across something interesting."

"People like that should be banned from digging."

"Perhaps, but amateurs are the lifeblood of archaeology at a local level. We feed off their discoveries, remember that."

"So has she got a big stately home?"

"No, the 'Lady' bit came quite late on. Her husband was General Sir John Dunning, don't ask me what heroic deeds he performed, he's been dead for eons. He was significantly older than her, she was a widow when I first knew her and that was ten years ago. I always thought it was a nice touch for Harry, finding a knight to sweep her away."

"Was she a King Arthur nut when you first knew her?"

"Oh yes, and her father before her."

Glastonbury stands aloof from the Somerset levels, its name means the Isle of Glass, for it was once surrounded by an inland sea. Winter rains could still turn parts of the levels into swamp and to either side of the road, field drains overflowed onto the margins of pasture and water-meadows. A grey bleakness was emphasized by a low sky and charmless English drizzle.

Some miles to the west, occupying a slight rise, was the small village in which Lady Dunning lived. It had grown into the shape of a letter T, with the Dunning house being last on the left arm of the T, set back from the lane. An estate agent would have described it as a stone-built character cottage with slate roof, granny annexe, outbuildings to side and rear, cobbled driveway and paddock with long views over a broad mere. Tyrone quickly priced up the place and was commenting on leaking gutters and rotting windowsills within moments of turning off his engine.

A substantial figure in small gold-rimmed spectacles came out of the house, a young Alsatian jumping at the sleeves of her tweed jacket. To social climbers, the ruddy-cheeked woman was Lady Dunning. Ever since the day at Avebury when she had taken the youthful Flint in hand, he had known her as Harry.

The car door was only half open when Flint slammed it shut again. Barking frenziedly, the Alsatian launched itself against the car, jumping against the windows, then

28

dropping back to bark anew. Harry seized its collar, chastizing the animal.

"Rimmy, Rimmy, behave! Friend!"

Once certain the beast was firmly under control, Flint ventured to open the door again.

"He won't hurt."

Some old wise saying about barks and bites came to mind as Flint took a few steps onto the cobbled yard.

"If you let him sniff you, he'll calm down."

Gingerly, Flint offered the back of his left hand to be snuffled and licked. Harry released the dog and it bounded up to Flint, planting two muddy pawmarks on the breast of his greatcoat.

"Down Rimmy!"

Harry was so full of apologies, that greetings and introductions were completely overlooked. Dragging the dog by its collar she invited the two young men into her house. Tyrone accepted a cup of tea, then explained that he would be staying with an old public school friend in Taunton.

It was possible that Harry had deliberately created the gloomily authentic west country interior of the dining-kitchen, but Flint doubted it. Little fundamental change had taken place in that room since the war. The switches were bakelite, the cord from which the ceiling light dangled was yellowed and wound about with spider's webs. Harry owned a pine dresser, a sideboard and a farmhouse table, but these were original, not freshly aged from a country pine warehouse. Her enamel stove-top kettle and the copper bed-warmers were at home amongst an assemblage of quasi-antiques still obviously in daily use. A middle-class couple would require years of scouring flea markets to replicate such a collection.

Across the stained pine table sat the tousle-headed

son, just short of forty, but still playing an angry young man. With his deep brown, curly, chin-hugging beard, he resembled Todd Armstrong in *Jason and the Argonauts.* Not even Harry could have called her son 'Gawain', but Gavin was close enough. Such reserve was cast aside for his twin sister, christened Guinevere, but talked about as Gwen. She was 'coming down' from Bath the next evening, as her husband would be travelling.

A dank March afternoon turned into evening as they talked over the old times (such as they were) and filled in the missing decade. Harry was wreathed in an enormous home-knitted Guernsey and she was one of the over-sixties who felt comfortable in jeans. She served stew and dumplings from an enormous two-handled aluminium pan, of the sort Grandma Flint once used to boil the washing in. Gavin brewed his own beer, so Flint drank a pint and chose polite words of appreciation which did not include 'thin', 'flat' or 'drainwater'.

"I've never heard of the University of North Yorkshire," Gavin said, whilst Flint was chasing a dumpling with a heavy pre-war spoon.

"It's new, it was promoted from a Poly three or four years back."

"Ah. A Polytechnic." His tone was condescending, even sympathetic.

"And you went to?"

"Oxford."

"Of course."

"Gavin and Gwen both matriculated together," Harry added.

"So you're down here to find out if the sword is a fake?" Gavin had finished eating and slouched back into his chair, a pewter tankard of homebrew in his hand.

"We've had all the tests done, valuations, carbon-fourteen dating, you name it. You're wasting your time."

"Blame the insurance company."

"But the local office were happy," Harry said.

"The head office is in Leeds – for whatever reason, they want a second opinion."

"What do they know?" Gavin snorted. "Kids in suits with shiny teeth. Overpaid and undereducated, what do they know?"

"And what is your line of work?" Flint asked.

"Gavin deals in antique books," Harry said with a deep, proud smile.

Gavin nodded, a look of unremitting distrust in his face.

"Good trade?"

"Can't complain."

Ah, but he did have patches on the sleeves of his cardigan and the russet tie had known happier times. Gavin was not at the leading edge of the great British recovery, his occupation need be no more than a dalliance.

"I assume you help out with your mother's quest for Arthur?"

"Oh, Gavin is invaluable!" Harry trilled. "Although he's no archaeologist, are you dear? I have my own little round table of helpers who help me with my work."

"And so who made the great discovery? One of your helpers, or was it you yourself?"

Harry drew herself back, a flick of her eyes demanding support from Gavin.

"You have to understand that this is sensitive information," Gavin said, in his most patronizing tone.

"What about academic freedom? You can't just sit on a discovery of this magnitude."

"Look, we have to, understand?" Gavin snapped.

31

"Its business, I don't expect you know much about business."

"I am actually a director of a company," Flint said, although with its two-and-a-half employees, UNY-DIG was hardly a multinational corporation. The bluff served to baffle Gavin, allowing Harry to press her own case.

"I sense, Jeffrey, that you have come to destroy my discovery. You have been charged with pouring scorn on Excalibur."

"I have an open mind."

"But they want you to disprove that I have found Excalibur."

A wince of disgust may have crossed his face as he sipped at the homebrew. Laying the beer mug carefully on the ring-marked table, he attempted to sooth the pricking pride of both mother and son.

"Look Harry, I don't want to pour scorn on anything. Like the TV cop in the raincoat, I just want the facts. You have an intriguing discovery, people want to know more. Presumably, they'll hear it all at the press conference."

"No," Harry said sharply. "I cancelled it."

Gavin made a slight intake of breath, then said, "It was going to be tomorrow, but we've rescheduled it for Monday."

"Gavin: I've cancelled it."

"Ah, so you have your doubts," Flint said.

"No, quite the reverse. I'm going to reveal my discovery in front of my peers, not live on television! I want to give those old fools in the Pendragon Society something to remember. I'm going to make them wake up on Saturday morning. If you keep the replica nice and safe until my lecture, you could play a part in the little surprise I'm planning for the Society."

"Mother . . ." Gavin objected.

"No, no, Gavin, I've looked forward to this for so long."
She turned to Flint with a look of childish glee. "Now,
at the appropriate moment, I shall give you a signal and
you would bring out the replica sword, with a flash and
a sparkle!" The flash and the sparkle was all within the
woman's eyes.

Such a dramatic role sounded more like Tyrone's
line.

"Maybe," Flint replied.

"I'm simply dying to see their faces; all those Welsh
fanatics and that ludicrous woman who claims Arthur was
French."

"And have you written a book?" Flint asked.

"Not just a book," Gavin chipped in. "We've worked
on this for a year; we have prepared a whole mobile exhibition; display boards, video, models, period dummies.
We've produced leaflets . . ."

"'I found the Grail' T-shirts?" asked Flint. "Excalibur
pencil sharpeners?"

"You can mock all you like!"

"No, no, no!" Harry said, more to Gavin than Flint. "My
discovery will not be devalued. Excalibur is the story of
the decade."

"Like the Hitler diaries?" asked Flint. "Or the last
resting place of Noah's Ark, or cold fusion? Don't you
worry that people will be a mite sceptical?"

"We have the proof in our hands," Harry said with
urgency.

"He has the proof in his hands," Gavin echoed. "Dupli-
cating our effort when we have everything documented to
the last detail. We have no time for cynics, you'll only
look foolish, Dr Flint."

No chance, thought Flint, secure in his own conviction. He hated it when people used 'doctor' as a

form of sarcasm. That PHD had cost him a chunk of his life.

A superior grin had settled on Gavin's lips, whilst Harry was unrepentant. If the pair across the table were going to hang themselves, Flint decided he may as well run out a little more rope. "So where will the public be able to see your great exhibition?"

"As soon as the press conference is over, we'll be taking bookings," Gavin stated. "I've invited some people I know from the Metropolitan Museum of New York."

"It has to be the British Museum," Harry said.

"Everyone will want Excalibur," Gavin added.

"At a price?"

Gavin merely blinked.

Money and archaeology never mix, Flint repeated to himself. Any mention of cash and the harmless intellectual pursuit becomes tainted. Gavin was aggressively defensive, Harry was clearly out on a limb and somewhere, someone in the insurance business was worried. Flint cast another eye over the blistered paintwork and the line of damp creeping up the kitchen wall. Harry had inherited the cottage from her father and then been comfortably maintained by her late husband. A general's pension would be impressive; what did she do with it all?

"What do you do when you're not snooping?" Gavin asked.

It was the kind of remark to be attacked obliquely, with superior grace. "I'm writing a coffee-table book about the way Hollywood depicts the ancient world. I wanted to call it 'Hollywood BC', but I need to go at least as late as the fall of Rome, perhaps into your territory. Have you seen John Boorman's *Excalibur*?"

"It's rather violent," Harry mumbled through a frown.

34

"But it's terrific stuff," Flint said, "Cornish accents and all. Every time I watch it, I want to believe the Arthurian legends, but I know that as you strip away the fantasy, Arthur grows smaller and smaller until he's nothing more than a name. Parade your sword in public and the scholars will descend like vampires, sucking every drop of life from your theories."

Harry banged a spoon on the table, then waggled it towards Flint. "No, no, no, you don't understand. I have at last got to the truth behind the real Arthur."

"Why search for the real Arthur? The fantasy is better." Flint had his arms crossed, gripping the patches on the sleeves of his jacket as he held tightly to his own position. "Why spoil people's neat and cozy view of history? I don't think the public is ready for the dull reality of sub-Roman petty chieftains."

"That is why I've kept silent until the time was right. Just think of the stir, remember Arthur was 'Rex Futurus', the Once and Future King." Harry was in a state of high animation now, preaching to the heathen who refused to believe. "Remember the prophecy? When Excalibur is found—"

"Arthur will arise again?" Flint asked.

"What would our wretched Royal family say?

"Surely you don't believe the Breton Hope nonsense? Arthur is not kipping under some hill waiting to be woken from sleep."

"No, of course not, but it's an intoxicating legend." Hands weathered by decades of probing the earth for its secrets clenched tight before him, seizing the past and refusing to let it loose. "Arthur has a hold on the imagination of the nation, you cannot deny that, Jeffrey Flint."

Harry's voice became more measured once more. She

relaxed her fists, sat back in her chair and took a few shallow breaths to calm her excitement. "Tomorrow I'll take you down to the lake and I'll answer any question you like. Then you will believe."

Chapter Four

The mere was mirror-still. About its margins lay a low film of mist which ebbed onto the meadows beyond and swirled around the feet of bare trees. Beyond the village, the sun peeked amongst banded cloud and a pair of ducks broke the waters. The level of the water was high, almost reaching the top of a jetty of warped planks that jutted ten metres out from the bank.

Flint shuffled around on the thwarts of the rowing boat, pulling the skirts of his RAF greatcoat out of his way and trying to control the oars.

Harry filled much of the bench opposite, with her broad green fishing jacket, her deerstalker, her granny glasses and ruddy cheeks. Rimmy the Alsatian had been abandoned by the boathouse, it barked and howled as they pulled away from the shore. For an awful moment, Flint feared that Harry would be bringing the brainless animal aboard the boat and he would be rowing in constant fear of attack.

Progress was slow and not always in direct line. "I'm not very good at this," he admitted.

"It's easy, that's right, let your back do the work." Harry was enjoying the ride. It would be a fine morning once the mist rose. She beamed at her own slice of England and began to reminisce. "My father bought the house when I was eight, and he taught me to row the very first summer. After he died, I brought Gavin and Gwen here when John was abroad. We would row about this lake for hours, swimming, fishing . . . do you fish Jeff? No? I hazard you would call it cruel."

"Right on."

"You always were a funny boy."

"Are we going anywhere in particular?" Flint grunted.

"Over to the far side."

"Is that where you found the sword?"

"Always to business, ah well."

"Harry, I've dragged in every expert I could find to look at this sword. Some say Saxon, some Viking, some Byzantine."

"Ah," she intoned, with deep significance. "In Byzantium lies the answer to the puzzle. Arthur appears from nowhere, he has an exotic lineage, he has won renown in foreign lands, he is a Christian knight before such things were heard of."

"You're saying that Arthur was a Byzantine Roman?"

"Yes! Why not? The pagan Saxons were ravaging Britain and the Britons appealed to Rome for aid. Arthur embodied the hope of the Christian Britons, charged by Rome to save the province. He brought with him armoured horsemen from Byzantium, who became the original knights of the round table. Imagine the effect just a few such knights would have on the Saxon rabble!"

"So he would have a Byzantine heavy cavalry sword . . ."

". . . and call it Caliburn."

Flint peered over the side of the boat into the grey, slightly rippled waters.

"Yes," said Harry. "My father spent his life proving this lake is Camlann, the site of Arthur's fatal battle with his nephew Mordred."

Flint suspected that the research conducted by Harry and her late father would not meet the modern standards of proof. "If this is Camlann, is there a goddess in a swimsuit lurking down there?"

"Are you alluding to the lady in the lake?"

"She didn't just pop up her hand and toss you the sword one evening?"

"Do I detect some ridicule Jeff? You should listen to what I am saying, it has profound importance for the heritage of this nation!"

Flint liked the idea of a Byzantine Artorius, simply for devilment, but the missionary zeal of his lady companion unsettled him. "Come clean, Harry, where did you get the goods?"

"This lake was Camlann," she stated. "My father proved it to me twenty-three years ago and I've been searching its shores ever since. This is the lake into which the sword Caliburn was cast."

"As far as I understand it, correct me if I'm wrong, but that whole episode was invented by Thomas Mallory in the fifteenth century when he wrote *Le Morte D'Arthur*."

"Ah, but what were his sources? You credit him with too much creative talent. The Celtic west had a practice of throwing swords into lakes and streams two thousand years before Mallory was born. It was a mystical, sacred act, quite natural for Celtic survivors fighting for Arthur, but completely outside the experience of a medieval novelist."

Gosh, that was a cracking argument! Flint had never encountered it before and would need time to find a loophole. He needed another way to object. "These meres move, it wouldn't necessarily have been here in the sixth century."

His companion smiled. "It was much larger, it extended

39

for half a mile in that direction, where the trees are now. Last year, we found a wooden chapel . . ."

"– you found a sixth century chapel! Take me. Look, I'm making a right pigs-ear of this – can you row?"

She shook her head and clenched her right hand. "Arthritis, the curse of the English archaeologist. I've had it since I was thirty-five, how about you?"

"No, I'm surviving." Flint put his mind to the oars again, working out how to make the boat turn a half-circle. "So you never row out here any more?"

"Not alone; my knees are worse than my hands. I would be fish food if I fell in. Gavin usually acts as my boatman when I can't find any other young men to escort me. Merlin can be quite helpful at times."

Flint tried to keep rowing. "Merlin?"

"Yes, he's very sweet. I'll introduce him this week-end."

Flint was speechless, growing more convinced he was sharing an open boat with a madwoman. It was depressing how archaeology and folklore tended to attract the lunatic fringe. A glance over his shoulder confirmed that he was close enough to swim to shore if Harry suddenly began to froth at the mouth, or started to call upon the sleeping Arthur.

He rowed a little harder, tried to keep the boat straight until softly, it ground into soft mud on the far side of the mere, where gaunt birch trees were waking to the first touch of spring. Both his shoes were soaked wet as he stepped over the bow. Harry squelched ashore in her short green wellingtons, instructed him to tether the painter to a birch, then led the way into the trees. She would point at intervals to open patches where she'd dug, or wanted to dig. Much of the ground was waterlogged and they crossed a score of streams hidden beneath a carpet of sodden leaves. Flint's socks and the bottom of his jeans were black and dripping before he was brought into a wide, treeless space.

A ruined farm building lay a hundred metres away, on the edge of higher ground used as pasture. Harry pointed across the clearing, which was scattered with tree stumps and opportunistic weeds.

"See how the ground rises? That's the island."

He could see that the far corner of the clearing was perhaps a metre higher than the rest. In times when the mere had stretched this far, an island might have stood proud of the water. Damaged vegetation had not recovered from Harry's excavation. Even an inexperienced eye could see the scar left by three trenches which had been cut across the island. Unless Harry had the budget to hire experienced diggers, her methods of excavation and recording would probably fall short of accepted professional practice.

As Flint was assessing what he saw, Harry had forged ahead, mounting the low rise and turning to encourage him to join her. "Here was my chapel," she said. Harry opened her arms to indicate its size. "You're at the west corner right now. And just below where I'm standing, we found a cist under the floor."

"And in the cist was the sword?"

"No."

"So what? Pottery? Coins?"

"Yes, yes, the usual things."

"Could I see them?"

"Is that necessary?"

"I need to see the associations."

"The Chapel floor is the *terminus ante quem* which dates the artifacts found beneath it."

41

"Fine, yes, but what dates the Chapel? Don't tell me the sword."

"No, the sword was over here." Harry led onwards for another forty or fifty metres, finding another patch of ground which bore evidence of being hacked about during the past few years.

"Associations?"

"None, of course, it was thrown into the lake. See, we're about twenty yards from where the land would have been. How far could you throw a three-pound sword?"

She was right, of course, the scenario was perfect. Too perfect.

"There must be half a square mile of woodland here; you were very lucky to stumble on the very spot the sword was hidden."

"We have been looking for three decades."

Seek and ye shall find, thought Flint. Perhaps the analogy with the hunt for Tutankhamun's tomb was not inappropriate. It could explain the drain on the family fortune.

"I finally found it using a metal detector," Harry explained. "You have no idea how many ploughshares and rusty nails I've found since I bought that clever little machine."

"How deep was the sword?"

"Oh, three and a half feet, buried in black peat."

"Waterlogged?"

"Certainly."

Yes, that explained the lack of deep corrosion on the blade and the well-preserved ivory hilt. Flint began to be excited. He believed none of the Arthurian nonsense, but to find a sixth century chapel and a Byzantine sword was a feat which a professional might wish for but never hope to achieve.

"Were you on your own?"

"No, I had my circle of helpers, but it was I who turned the turf and I was the first person to touch Excalibur. You can never imagine how magical, how, how sensational it was. I went without sleep for days, I just wanted to be with the sword, look at it, touch it."

Caution still held back Flint's growing enthusiasm; wish-fulfilment could be highly dangerous. One of his former postgraduates had failed his PhD thesis for doctoring the evidence to fit his outrageous theories. Many academic careers had been ruined by the same excess of zeal. Harry was clearly inured to the risk. She enjoyed a deep lungful of Somerset air, then stood with hands on hips, as full of life as if she were a third her age. "Do you know Jeffrey? I am the luckiest person in the world."

After a lunch of cold pork, Flint was collected by Tyrone and driven to the conference venue. On the half-hour drive to Bath, he re-told the confused tale of Harry's delusions of immortal fame. Tyrone had been to visit a vintage vehicle warehouse that morning and spouted endless details of classic sports cars, surplus jeeps and derelict tanks. He probably knew that as a firmly anti-materialist, anti-militarist and anti-motorist, Flint would be unmoved by his experience.

It was conference season, a time of year which held a special place in Flint's calendar. New places to visit, old friends to greet, new ideas to encounter and exchange. As an excuse to travel on expenses, it was one of the few perks of his chosen career.

Set in rolling country south of Bath, Edgar Jenkins Hall was sufficiently isolated from the real world to host the annual meeting of the Pendragon Society. Like most learned societies it was itinerant, shifting between competing Arthurian homelands for each of its meetings: one year Wales, the next the Scots borders, this year, the West Country.

The venue had been a stately home, built in the middle Victorian period, but was now a teacher training college. After signing in at the door, the hall warden led them along corridors, up and down short flights of stairs, past kitchenettes, showers and toilets and deep into the architectural pot-pourri that was Edgar Jenkins Hall. If fire broke out, Flint was convinced he would die before he ever found a way to the exit.

In Flint's experience, accommodation at academic conferences normally consisted of bare and draughty student rooms stripped of all their posters for the vacation. Surprise! He touched the radiator and found the heating was working. At many conferences past he'd shivered under thin blankets whilst the occupant of the next room entertained 'til four and the elderly delegate next along banged on the wall to complain about all the noise.

The window in his room gave a view of budding trees, hillsides and a distant lane. Flint loved this life. He slipped off his wet shoes and watched the unchanging scene across the fields. He listened to the cackle of rooks through an open pane until the damp bottoms of his jeans prompted him to unpack a change of clothes then went seeking the shower.

On his return he tried to close the top pane of the window, but found it was jammed open. This proved fortunate, as the radiator was full on, with its valve broken and pumped heat mercilessly into the atmosphere. With clean jeans and clear head, Flint walked two rooms along the corridor to where Tyrone was staying.

"Enter!" Tyrone called as he knocked.

Flint pushed open the door, then stopped dead. The muzzle of a very large gun was aimed at his nose. Some ten seconds elapsed before Flint overcame his shock.

"What you been up to my lad?"

"Shopping – it's a Bren gun. Brilliant isn't it?" Tyrone was seated on the bed, holding the elderly machine-gun, with its butt between his knees and its distinctive curved magazine part-masking his boyish glee. The muzzle was still pointing at Flint.

"You bought a machine-gun? How much?"

"Three hundred quid. It's original, 1944."

"A bargain. I hope it's not part of our equipment budget."

"No, it's for my jeep – to mount on top."

"You haven't got a jeep."

"No, but this guy I stayed with is going to hunt one out for me. Only four thousand."

Tyrone allowed his arms to rest and propped the gun up on the window-ledge, covering the car park.

"Don't you need a licence for a monster like that?"

"It's decommissioned."

"I think you still need a licence."

"I'll look into it."

"Do so, quickly. And hide it: we don't want the management to suspect we're terrorists. Three hundred quid! I'm paying you too much. Speaking of concealed weapons, where's the sword?"

Tyrone pulled back the pink candlewick bedspread to reveal a familiar box beneath his bed. He folded the bipod of the Bren gun, then slid it next to the box containing the replica sword.

"I'll strip it down later."

"OK Biggles, dinner time."

There are societies and societies. Some are full of

dynamic, excitable graduates, primed with the latest socio-political perspectives and ready to debate any point. Others are composed of ageless scholars, where youths of twenty and veterans of sixty mix freely and intently. The Pendragon Society was middle-aged and middle-class by composition, amateur by persuasion. Over dinner, after the keynote speech, in the coffee room and in the bar, Flint and Tyrone met a score of teachers, retired civil servants and white-collar workers, most amateur historians or self-taught literary critics. A few academics tried to hold court amongst the crowd, but none had names which Flint recognized. Tyrone had read a few of their papers whilst researching his thesis, so offered his opinion of each in turn, taking pains to say nothing complimentary.

Only one other delegate was younger than Flint and Tyrone. He was a slight, dark-haired figure, dressed exclusively in black: slacks, roll-neck pullover and aged blazer. The young man stood close to the bar until someone bought him half a cider, then stood nodding through a conversation. With his long brown hair and beard, he stood out from the crowd of grey and balding heads. Tyrone made a direct line for the newcomer, hoping to find some source of debate to set the evening alight. After a few minutes, he returned, head down, to where Flint stood alone.

"Train-spotter!" he sneered over his cider glass.

"Takes one to know one."

"Oi, Jeff!"

"You judge people too quickly."

"Yeah, but that kid's a real loony. And he's in good company."

"Just watch it tomorrow. They're all dedicated Arthurian loyalists. You may need your toy gun to cover your retreat after you give your paper."

46

"I can take criticism."

"Yes, but Harry is convinced she's found Arthur's sword. She's going to hate you if you crap all over the legend. Rub it in too deeply and they'll have your head off with the replica."

"We've wasted our time coming down here." Tyrone looked a little morose. "There's no disco, no talent and this cider's like gnats' pee."

Flint had grown out of discos but tended to agree about the cider. "Early night then?"

Tyrone drained his glass. "And tomorrow: the king dies!"

It appeared that the Pendragons did not deal in midnight antics. Everyone seemed to come to bed early, with little more noise than a polite 'Good-night' echoing down the corridor. So the plumbing rattled, but this was *de rigueur* in student accommodation. Conference breakfasts can be excellent, as it takes institutional cooks of a special calibre to spoil muesli, fruit juice and toast, so it was a rested and contented Jeffrey Flint who wandered in to hear the first lecture of the day.

A magnolia-painted drawing-room had been furnished with eighty red plastic chairs of bucket design. Harry was due to speak first, with Tyrone filling the final slot before lunch. Six papers in three hours threatened to be heavy going. Tyrone put his box of slides and his notes beneath a chair in the back row, then went for breakfast. Initially sceptical, he'd been persuaded to take part in Harry's dramatic unveiling of the replica. It was a bit of fun, Flint had said, a little pantomime to amuse the crowds.

The arrangement was that Tyrone was to meet Harry in the vestibule at 9.20. Following her plan, she would begin her lecture at 9.30: the lights would dim, then he would

47

slip out and bring down the replica sword in its box. The surprise could not be spoiled by having the thing lying at his feet, eliciting questions. At 9.50, Harry would look his way and Tyrone would bring the box to the front. Lights up, sword drawn from box, gasps from audience and ten minutes of breathless questions before the next speaker. The drama would steal the conference.

In his plum jacket and wild, Tasmanian-devil cartoon tie, Tyrone loitered with intent, increasingly edgy. It was 9.27 and there was no Harry. By 9.35 some seventy delegates were in place, muttering, coughing, rustling notebooks and squeaking back in their chairs. Tyrone worked his way into the lecture room and slumped down into a creaking bucket seat beside Flint. A man dressed in a blue blazer stood at the front, wringing a sheaf of notes in his hands. He was overweight, flabby-cheeked and held his head backwards, looking down his nose like a Roman Emperor, regarding the crowd in the Circus. If Flint were a Hollywood director, he'd give this man a curly perm, and cast him as Nero.

"Ah," Nero began.

The room fell a little quieter.

"Ah," he repeated, as close to achieving silence as he ever would be. "I'm afraid Lady Dunning hasn't arrived yet," he spoke with hesitation, almost a stammer. "Ah, so with your indulgence, we will proceed straight to our second paper. The Reverend Timothy Allsop will be reading his paper entitled 'Aspects of the Grail mythology'. Reverend Allsop? Has anyone seen Reverend Allsop?"

A pattern of gradually developing chaos engulfed the morning session. Lectures fell out of sequence, slides became mixed and were projected upside down. All the speakers waffled in excess of their allotted half hour, allowing little time for the obligatory questions and causing tempers to fray amongst old-timers who insisted on voicing their own opinions after each paper. Tyrone began to fidget, looking for Harry every few minutes. She had not appeared by the end of the coffee break, engendering more schedule-juggling by the conference organizer.

"Who is this guy?" Flint whispered to Tyrone.

"Patrick Hewitt, the secretary."

Nero had a name. "Ah," said Patrick Hewitt, playing with his glasses case. "As we still have no sign of Lady Dunning, perhaps we could move the programme on once more and ask Dr Tyrone Drake of the University of North Yorkshire to deliver his appraisal of Mallory's 'La Morte d'Arthur'?"

"It's nothing to do with Mallory," growled Tyrone, taking up his script and slicking back his hair. Confidently, he marched towards the lectern and clicked his fingers to indicate he wanted the lights turned down.

"The death of Arthur," he stated loudly. "The paper I shall deliver has no connection with the medieval fantasy entitled 'La Morte d'Arthur', rather it is the concept of Arthur as a King which I intend to kill . . ."

A rising noise at the back of the room brought Tyrone stumbling to a halt.

"Excuse me," said a figure who had walked into the light of the lectern. "Could I perhaps interrupt?"

Tyrone stepped back, ruffled and tense. Patrick Hewitt took his place. "Ah, could we perhaps have the lights turned back on?"

Half of the lights came on, were turned off, then on again. Hewitt was bathed in the stark white glare of a pair of spotlights as someone at the back fought with the light switches.

"I'm afraid I have some rather terrible news," Hewitt managed to stutter. "We have lost an old and very esteemed colleague. Tragically, Lady Dunning died last night."

Chapter Five

A shock wave rippled through the audience. Tyrone flinched, his mouth falling open. Flint felt his heart skip a beat or two. The secretary continued to stammer over the hubbub.

". . . in the circumstances . . . long-standing member . . . much respected scholar . . . suspend the session . . . coach tour . . . perhaps when we resume this evening, Dr Drake?"

"No, I'll withdraw my paper." Tyrone gathered his notes and solemnly walked out of the room, Flint shot off in his wake. Once Tyrone was almost at the front door of the hall, he spun around, clutching at his lecture notes.

"Dead?" Tyrone said, crunching the notes in his hand.

"Poor old girl. She seemed a little over-tense, but . . . poor old Harry."

Lectures on mythical heroes were now superfluous. Tyrone fidgeted on his feet, casting his eyes around for guidance as to how he should feel and act.

"Shall we pack up and go home?"

Flint thought for a few moments. "No."

"What's to stay for?"

"Dunno – perhaps I've got a hunch."

"It could be removed surgically." Tyrone forced a laugh.

"Don't horse around, I'm trying to think!"

"You're thinking there's something fishy about Lady Harry's death?"

"Maybe. It is a somewhat unlikely coincidence that Harry happened to die on the night before her greatest triumph."

"Ironic – so what are we doing next?"

An immediate response was called for. "You stay here and keep your ear to the ground." That seemed a good starter, Flint continued to compose a plan as he spoke. "Meanwhile, if it's OK, I'll borrow your car and drive up to Harry's place. She was hardly my long-lost aunt, but she was a decent old girl. I'll give you odds of ten to one on that she didn't die in her sleep."

Flint made only one wrong-turning on the half-hour drive. Rain had fallen during the night and he had only just driven clear of a shower when he passed through Glastonbury. His detour led him into Harry's village from the west, meeting her house first. Activity could be seen around the mere as he drove past.

As he approached the open gateway, he counted three cars, two police cars and a van filling the yard of the Dunning house. Flint's eyes and mind were fixed on the police cars, not the gateposts. A deep grinding crunch informed him it was too late to concentrate on steering.

He braked sharply, cursed, then stalled the engine. Flint suffered a few moments of self-accusation, before getting out and inspecting the damage. The nearside back wing of the Spitfire had been scraped to the metal, the wheel arch was buckled and the rear bumper dangled just clear of the ground. Tyrone would not see the funny side, and neither could Flint.

"Had a bump?" A strong-jawed woman in a jade ski jacket came from around the police van.

"It's not my day."

By the manner in which she asked his name, he knew she was a policewoman. Her blonde hair was turned into a tight bun, accentuating the severity of her expression. After he'd answered, she checked her notepad and said, "Dr Flint, yes. We were coming to find you next."

"Was Harry murdered?"

"Harry?"

"Lady Dunning."

"What makes you say she was murdered?"

It was the kind of gaffe which landed innocent men in custody and Flint had ten seconds to waffle his way free.

"Her death was so sudden, she was so healthy – and you wouldn't be here if she'd passed away peacefully."

"You'd better come and speak to Inspector Roper."

"And you are?"

"Detective Sergeant Chaff."

He could never resist trying to sweet-talk stern women. "What do your friends call you?"

"Sergeant." She rebuffed him without even a hint of a smile. "Could you come with me?"

It was three hundred metres downhill to the mere, where a cluster of figures could be seen gathered around a polythene tent at the water's edge, not far from the boathouse. A thin, cold wind came from the west, tugging at the plastic, rippling the silver surface of the pool. Another shower was due. With each step Flint took, the scene became clearer and he consciously began to look and listen and learn.

A man in a green anorak stood facing the water. Another, wearing a Burberry and holding an attaché case was speaking with measured, precise words.

". . . at least twelve hours, perhaps more, as she's well

wrapped and quite heavy. It is unlikely to be this side of midnight."

As the cold wind struck straight through Flint's great-coat he sensed his own proximity to death. Yesterday the luckiest person in the world, today, Harry was a waterlogged corpse hidden by a plastic tent.

Detective Sergeant Chaff addressed the back of the green anorak. "Sir!"

A hawk-nosed man turned to face Flint. He was introduced as Detective Inspector Roper.

"Was she murdered?" Flint asked immediately.

"You tell me. When did you last see Lady Dunning?"

Flint made an inquisitive glance towards the tent. "About two, half-two yesterday afternoon. I stayed here on Thursday night, I went boating with Harry in the morning and my assistant picked me up after lunch."

Detective Sergeant Chaff asked for the name of his assistant.

"Would you say Lady Dunning was in a sound state of mind?" the inspector asked.

"Ah." Flint had to think hard on that point. The curse of genius, or obsession led many academics to totter towards lunacy at times. He recalled her rather wild claims regarding Excalibur, but kept them in perspective. "She seemed lucid."

"She didn't strike you as being depressed or suicidal?"

"No, she was as chirpy as could be."

"Chirpy enough to go for a moonlight swim?"

"No, she had arthritis. She told me she couldn't swim properly."

Flint was asked to expand on his boating trip. He omitted the Excalibur story, not wanting to sound like a lunatic, or give away all his cards at once.

"Did you make any arrangements to see her again?"

"Yes, at nine-twenty this morning. She was giving a lecture to the Pendragon Society at Edgar Jenkins Hall."

"Oh yes, you're one of them, are you?"

" 'fraid so."

The reply seemed to disqualify him as a rational human being. He could have explained that he was not actually a signed-up member of the Pendragons, but sensed the police were hardly interested.

"Well, thank you Dr Flint. I don't think I have any more questions. Have you any Chaff?"

"No sir," said the sergeant, chin held high and back straight to maintain her profile amongst taller men.

"I have," Flint said.

"I'm sorry?" The Inspector sharpened his bird-of-prey expression.

"I mean, how did she die? And when?"

"You will have to wait until the inquest." By his tone, Inspector Roper clearly dismissed the idea of Flint playing any further role in the enquiry. He shouted a farewell to the man in the Burberry, who had begun to trudge up the greasy track towards the house.

"Can I go then?" Flint asked, already making steps up the hill. "You know where I'll be if you need me again."

"Yes, thanks for your help."

Flint nodded a polite farewell to Detective Sergeant Chaff, then set off in a brisk walk, heart pounding. Half-way up the slope, he caught up with the man in the Burberry, at least twenty years his senior and moving with less urgency.

"Hi. You the pathologist?"

"Yes. Are you Press?"

"Good God No: Dr Jeffrey Flint, University of North Yorkshire." He stretched the truth just a little. "I'm a forensic archaeologist."

"You are?" The pathologist swapped his case from right hand to left, then shook Flint's hand, all without breaking his stride. "That's a fascinating line, I almost went into archaeology myself. I was tempted to study Egyptology, all those papyri and temples half buried in the desert sand . . ."

Flint jumped in before the romantic image of archaeology spoiled the impression he wanted to make. "Forensic science is only a hair's breadth away from my field of research. Your bodies are a little fresher than ours, but we all want to know who and why and when."

"Yours is the more pleasant career," the pathologist said.

"Hmm, but what you do must be utterly intriguing, for example, you are the only one, I presume, who knows how Lady Dunning died?"

"I'm hedging my bets until after the post-mortem."

"Was she murdered?"

The pathologist stopped just short of the Dunning house. "Now whatever made you say that?"

"All this activity is a little dramatic if she died in her sleep."

"Oh, this is just routine. Lady Dunning only died in her sleep if she was sleepwalking."

"Drowned?"

"She certainly spent time in the water, but she was found on the bank, clear of the edge. She must have crawled out and collapsed of exhaustion. I'm performing the post-mortem this afternoon; there are clear signs of drowning but I'm expecting heart failure. I say, as you're a fellow scientist, would you like to come along?"

For a moment he hesitated, then Flint's investigative nerve failed him. "No thanks."

A grim smile came to the other man's lips. "I don't

56

blame you – it takes a strong stomach if you're not used to it."

"I'd like to see the site photo's when they're done," Flint added hurriedly.

"Site? Do you mean the scene of crime? They show very little. The lady was dressed in a long wax jacket and wellingtons: devilishly hard to swim in. She was about a metre clear of the water, lying on her back, arms across her chest." The pathologist put his free hand across his coat front. "It reminded me of the way Egyptians mummies are portrayed. She looked very serene."

Laid out, thought Flint. But by who? Or was the posture simply a reaction to a heart attack? He wished he knew more.

"You seem troubled," the pathologist said.

"And why not? One of my colleagues is dead."

"Ah sorry, I didn't realize you were close. It's the inquiring mind, you see, I always detach myself from the case, otherwise one becomes awfully morbid."

"I know what you mean. We're terribly irreverent with our skellies."

"If you're interested, the inquest will probably be on Tuesday – Glastonbury Guildhall. I'd say about ten o'clock, but I'd ring to check."

A pathologist's fees bought a large red BMW estate. He climbed inside and reversed out of the yard. Flint's eyes fell on a dangling rear bumper, a tragedy of such minor proportions that he could hardly be concerned. Poor Harry had been reduced to an object to be photographed and recorded by a parade of specialists, with no more dignity than if she were a Saxon skeleton unearthed from one of her own hurried excavations. Within the next twenty-four hours, that nice pathologist was going to remove his Burberry, don a surgical coat, saw open her brain case, slit her torso from crotch to sternum and drop her internal organs into jars. No wonder the man had been attracted to study mummies.

The indignity of post-mortem practices was too disgusting to contemplate and Flint needed a whirl of fast-moving air to blow away his nausea. He took down the hood of the Spitfire, then used his belt to strap up the bumper. As quickly as he could, he left the yard and the village behind, seeking and finding a garage on the edge of Glastonbury. A young mechanic bolted the bumper back in position and made an effort to push out the dented wing. Flakes of rust dropped from inside the wheel arch.

"It's falling apart as we watch," he drawled with a heavy rustic accent. "You need new tyres all round. I'll give you a price if you want."

Even with his limited driving experience, Flint had grown wise to that old ruse. "Another time perhaps – how much for what you've done?"

The mechanic checked that he was alone. "It be me tea break. Twenty pounds fer cash."

Two notes passed into the back pocket of the overalls and Flint cursed the invention the motor car. He drove back towards Bath, found Edgar Jenkins Hall, parked the car and surveyed the damage once more. Spirits low, he ventured towards the porch just as Detective Sergeant Chaff emerged from the front door.

"Hello again," he said, his voice full of familiarity.

"Dr Flint," she gave him a token smile of recognition, but was not stopping to talk.

Tyrone's face was at the window. He was watching Chaff walk to her car, paying little attention to Flint's arrival.

"Nice isn't she?" Tyrone said as Flint came into the lobby. "She's called Stephanie."

"Ah, but intimate friends call her Sergeant."

Tyrone normally fell for classically pretty students, fresh and unworldly, often American. If Chaff had caught his eye, his tastes were maturing.

"So what did the maiden in uniform want?"

"She's plain clothes – she's a detective. She was checking up on you. I told her your hippie image was a front and you were really a hit man for the London mob."

Somehow, Flint regretted smashing the car slightly less than he had before.

Tyrone ceased trying to tease. "She wanted to know where you'd been, and when you last saw Harry. I told her."

"Did you make her day?"

"It's hard to tell, she'd be good at playing poker. I had to take her upstairs and show her my weapon."

"Crude *faux pas*, Tyrone. I assume you mean the replica sword. What did you do about the machine-gun?"

"I hid it on the ledge outside my room – you'll have to help me get it back."

"First things first. I think I ought to show you something." It was time to confess the damage. "Forgive me, for I have sinned."

Gravely, Flint followed Tyrone to the car park. Tyrone said nothing as he walked around the Spitfire. Flint pointed out the repairs funded from his own pocket and aroused only a quiet sigh.

"Sorry old chap."

On the day of a tragic death, damaged paintwork became a trivial concern and Tyrone obviously knew it. He would complain at any opportunity, except in adversity. Hard knocks only made him harder to knock.

Back in his room, making bad jokes to lighten the

mood, Tyrone dangled from the window, with Flint holding his belt. The Bren gun was hoisted back into the study-bedroom.

"Did you learn anything useful whilst I was gone?" Flint asked.

"Nar, the old folks all went on a coach trip after lunch."

"Bad taste."

"It keeps 'em occupied. Some have even bugged out. Are we zooming off now?"

"No, we've paid for the weekend and I want to hang around until the inquest on Tuesday."

"How did she die?"

Flint had been relieved that Tyrone had taken the damage so well, but the question served to depress his spirits once more.

"It looks like she fell in the lake and drowned, or died of exhaustion climbing out, or suffered a heart attack, or all three. I'm not sure it matters to her."

"Did she slip or was she pushed?"

"Maybe she jumped, who's to know?"

Here was the crucial question, the one that had begun to nag his conscience.

"She wouldn't jump – this was the biggest day of her life."

Flint had begun to recall the way in which Harry had cancelled her press launch, then splashed cold water on her son's enthusiasm for promoting Excalibur. Harry had a very good reason to dive into the lake and swim away from her cares.

"When I was talking to her, Harry would not shift an inch from her assertion that she'd found Excalibur. Now suppose that once she was alone, she had a last minute crisis of conviction. She was going to drive over here today, stand in front of her peers and make a complete ass of herself. Then sooner or later her vulpine son was going to drag her in front of the TV cameras so she could make an ass of herself all over again. Serious historians would stick in the daggers faster than you could say 'Julius Caesar'. A lifetime's dream would last what, a few days, before it was destroyed. Perhaps she realized that she'd wasted her life chasing an illusion."

Tyrone nodded. "That's true."

"What is also true is that I spent Thursday evening and Friday morning telling her this." Flint paused, finding it hard to admit his darkest fear. "If she committed suicide, it was my fault."

Chapter Six

Dinner was a sombre affair. Men and women who had travelled the length of the country to indulge in arcane debate were subdued by the harsh impact of reality. Even those who had disliked Harry, or disagreed with her views felt they should be reserved and respectful. Of course the conference would go on: ". . . it was what Harry would have wanted", but the edge was taken off the arguments as whispered conversations around the tables reviewed her life and work.

A few had felt the mood soured and had abandoned the conference: the survivors sat around five long tables in the darkly-panelled dining hall, eating the over-boiled chicken with over-boiled green beans and over-roasted potatoes.

Of sixty-two delegates, forty-eight were at dinner. Patrick Hewitt, now a much saddened Nero, delivered the after-dinner speech. With many an 'um' and 'ah' this grew into a panegyric for Lady Harriet Dunning, doyen of the Pendragons. At the end of the speech he alluded to the importance of the lecture she never delivered; the audience rippled with agreement. It was obvious that many already knew – or suspected – Harry's great discovery.

Veteran of many conferences, Flint habitually sat close to the exit. He could sneak out if a debate became tedious and he could avoid the clatter and crush of the formal end of session. He could also be first into the bar.

A lunate counter curved across the corner of the lounge and a mature student stood behind it, arms folded, buttocks resting against the till. Reluctant, lethargic movements brought up two bottles of Mexican beer from the rack – cider was to be avoided. Backs turned on the barman, who would hardly care, Flint and Tyrone leaned against the counter, watching the Pendragons filter towards them.

Deep in his own thoughts, Patrick Hewitt would be their first target. He walked in slowly, even guiltily and was startled to be apprehended.

"Mr Hewitt, what are you drinking?"

"Ah, that's very kind of you. A Glenfiddich please."

Out came the money, out came the information. Hewitt took his whisky and swirled it around the glass as Flint and he exchanged the expected meaningless expressions of shock and disbelief. Flint cast appreciative comments on the dull and long-winded after-dinner speech.

"Everyone seemed to know Harry's secret."

"Yes, I think it leaked out. Only myself and perhaps one or two others were actually told the truth; I had a devil of a job persuading the committee to chose this location for the conference without being able to tell them why. Harry made a great thing of being able to visit Glastonbury, she was going to lead us around the Arthurian sites and end up where she found . . ." he gave a paranoid look over his shoulder, ". . . It."

"But someone let the cat out?" Mexican beer was sipped slowly from the bottle. "Do you believe she found the true Excalibur?"

More gloom seeped into Hewitt's expression. "No, and I urged her not to deliver that paper, it would ruin her reputation, but she was insistent and she was within her rights. Our society must encompass a wide range of viewpoints and a minority of our members believe passionately in the truth of the Arthurian legends. Some have spent years or even decades researching the true location of Camelot, or the Holy Grail, but for most of us, the search for a real Arthur is a fool's quest. You and I know that if he existed, he was probably not even a king. My interest, and that of most of the Society, is the mythology, the literature and the traditions which have grown up around Arthur. He is not so important because of what he was, but in what he has become."

"So you tried to talk Harry out of it? Couldn't you have simply rejected her paper?"

"That would be censorship. I took a dislike to Dr Drake's paper when I read the synopsis."

Tyrone was about to intervene, but Flint laid a light hand on his chest. Hewitt gave a gesture of apology. "Who am I to act as censor? I must let the audience decide on the value of a contribution."

"High principles."

"Yes, and I regret them now. This was one occasion when I should have put my foot down. I may have lost her friendship, but I may have saved her life."

"Saved her? Was she suicidal?"

"Could one predict who is? A neighbour of mine came home from the office one evening, about two years ago. He drove his car into the garage, closed the door and ran the engine until he suffocated. Why? He had a wife and three charming daughters, a well-paid job . . . why? We will never know."

Never knowing was a sensation Flint could not bear. He had to know, he had to discover. In his world, the unknown was an endangered phenomenon.

"So you think Harry had second thoughts about Excalibur?"

Hewitt rolled up his Nero chin and gave just a suggestion of a nod with a faint hum of agreement. His thoughts clearly ran deep and the conversation barely distracted him.

"I had this," how could Flint phrase his guilt? "I had this awful nagging feeling that it was my intervention that changed her mind."

"You flatter yourself if you think that Harry would be swayed by a single interview. Many of her closest friends advised caution, as did some whom you would not count amongst her friends."

"Such as?"

"Oh!" Hewitt was caught by his own slip, and was pressured into justifying himself. He looked from face to face in the growing crowd of scholars. "Valerie, over there; they fought like cat and dog." Another scapegoat was sought. "Charles, poor Charles, he's here somewhere, he ran our coach trip this afternoon. Harry actually sued him last year for what he wrote about her *Guide to Arthur's Britain*."

"That shows she was going off the rails," Tyrone intervened. "We've all got to take the flak."

"In a sense, I agree," Hewitt said. "Charles overstepped the mark, of course, but Harry . . ." He finished with a shake of his head, unwilling to criticize her further.

"Do you know at what point Harry cancelled her press launch?" Flint asked. "To me, that was the clearest indicator that she was having cold feet."

"Publicity was never Harry's style; she may have seemed larger-than-life, but she was a very private person. She never threw her title around and she'd be very modest if anyone ever mentioned her husband's war decorations. The only thing she ever boasted about was her children – and they hardly warrant it. They're still going ahead, with the launch, I understand. It was postponed, not cancelled."

Flint was sure Harry had used the word 'cancelled' – only her son Gavin had disagreed.

"I hope they put it back until after the funeral. Harry called that crowd her 'round table', but I don't like what that crowd is doing, what I know of it. Ah here's Charles now."

Charles Evans was stooping his way towards seventy. He paid little attention to his hair which wandered in a white cloud around the back of a bald pate, and his hand-me-down brown suit was even older than Flint's ex-Oxfam tweed jacket.

"Could I buy you a drink Mr Evans?"

Pale and puffy blue eyes had begun gazing at the bar tariff, possibly in the hope someone would say just that.

"Half a Guiness please, Dr Flint." He spoke in a hoarse, hesitant voice.

Flints' memory verged on the photographic and he quickly recalled the faces in the dining-room.

"We missed you at dinner."

"Did you?" He seemed not to want to dwell on the subject. "It's Dr Drake, isn't it? Let me shake your hand. I very much regret not hearing your lecture."

Tyrone shook the hand and shrugged the wide shoulders of his plum jacket. If the drinkers in the bar were put into a competition, he would easily have won first prize for dress sense. Patrick Hewitt excused himself and turned to make some point to the indifferent barman.

A line of Guiness-froth now ran along Charles Evans' upper lip.

"I'm sorry we missed your coach tour," Flint said. "Other things on our minds."

Evans nodded in sympathy. "It was quite successful, in the circumstances. We visited Glastonbury Abbey and Arthur's tomb, then the Tor, then on to the hill fort at South Cadbury. Do you know it?"

"It's reputedly Camelot."

"More than reputedly – there are Arthurian remains at Cadbury."

"Did Harry believe that?"

"Not in the sense of the grand chateau of Camelot, as in the Chretien de Troyes stories, but Cadbury had a place in Lady Dunning's personal mythology. She had developed a very strange idea about Arthur and his knights being Romans. But what she missed – and we argued the point many times – was that Arthur was part of a Celtic revival." His short sentences became interspersed with short panting intakes of breath as his excitement rose. He raised his forefinger and thumb when emphasizing his words, as if gripping a chalk. "Celtic revival!" he repeated. "When the Romans left, it was as if they had never been here. The hero-chieftain of ancient Britain was revived in the face of new invaders."

Tyrone had drawn himself back. By the way he was preparing his jaw, Flint knew he was about to savage the old gent. Quickly he pressed on. "Did you know what Harry was going to speak about today?"

Evans bowed his head. "That damnable chunk of rusted iron." When they flicked up again, his eyes almost accused Flint of complicity. "Someone said you brought it here."

"Not the genuine sword, the replica," Tyrone said.

"There is no genuine sword," growled Evans.

"So if she'd stood up here this morning and delivered her lecture, you'd have given her a rough ride?"

Charles part closed one eye and nodded warily.

"I imagine you wouldn't have been alone. Who else disliked her theories?"

Evans released a finger from around the handle of his half-pint glass and pointed it. "Valerie Chastel: now she's my idea of a lady."

The Frenchwoman was tall and had superimposed an image of elegance on the advancing years. She gripped the obligatory Gauloise Blonde and spoke with the earnest conviction of one who knows she is right. Three older men hovered about her, detecting perhaps a glint of former glamour.

"Miss Sorbonne, 1968," Tyrone said.

"Uh?" Charles Evans missed the jibe.

"You didn't see Harry yesterday?" Flint quickly asked.

"No." Evans suddenly sounded wary.

"What's the story behind the libel writ?" Flint would have continued to explain that he'd heard such a rumour, but Charles Evans cut him short, like some precocious fourth-former.

"That's not the sort of thing one asks, is it? Poor Harry has passed on, you can't tittle-tattle about her now, not on the day after she died!" His tone had changed swiftly and without warning.

"I was just wondering why she sued you?"

"You are presumptuous, as if buying me a Guiness buys my soul. I don't like your manner, Dr Flint."

"Few people do, I'm sorry. I like to get to the truth and it makes people uncomfortable."

"We're not that kind of society. Good-evening, Dr Flint." He made his exit with an archaic nod of the head. "Dr Drake."

"God, what a fossil!" Tyrone sneered at the brown jacket shambling away. "And why was he so cagey?"

"Drs Flint and Drake lack a bedside manner. Before we make any more enemies, we should perhaps have another early night."

"No, don't be boring, let's insult someone else." Tyrone set his mouth into a thin, thuggish leer.

The young man who Tyrone had described as the train-spotter chose this moment to brush past them. Flint glanced his way, caught a whiff of body odour, then decided against offering the lad a drink. Tyrone was still selecting a victim: he'd been robbed of his chance to deliver his damning lecture and was keen to cross intellectual swords with anyone who would fight.

"What about the old French tart?"

"Racist, sexist and ageist in one sentence; that must be a record."

"Coming?"

Flint acquiesced. "Lead on, Lancelot."

The chronicles of Geoffrey of Monmouth describe how Arthur's Saxon foes would habitually fight in a wedge. One warrior would lead, the rest formed a vast triangle behind him. The whole would forge forward, driving apart the opposition to break through to the objective. Flint and Tyrone effected a similar manoeuvre against the Frenchwoman, pressing their way into her company, excluding two of the hovering gentlemen.

Her nose was gallic, her cheeks shrunken, her accent was cultured, but heavy. She spoke quickly, with almost angry insistence.

". . . take the lost island of Lyonesse, it is obviously a reference to the Isulae Lenuri: the Channel Islands, which lie off the coast of Brittany."

". . . so Arthur was a Breton?" Flint interrupted.

"Of course, there are many place-names in Brittany and there is the great history of Chretian de Troyes. Why else would a Frenchman concern himself with an English legend?"

"Quite," said Flint.

"Lady Harry would have disagreed with that theory," Tyrone began his attack.

"Oh, poor Lady Harriet! It made me so sad this morning."

"She wouldn't like your Breton Arthur."

"No, I could never convince her."

"Or me," said the surviving older man, just before Tyrone moved in front of him. Valerie Chastel's eyes glowed slightly. She was now occupying the attention of the only two under-forties remaining in the room. Flint introduced himself and Tyrone, titles and all. Titles seemed to count in this company.

"Valerie Chastel," she said, then hunted out another pungent Gauloise. "Do you have a light?"

Flint apologized, but Tyrone produced a disposable lighter from an inside pocket. Ever resourceful, ever prepared, ever hopeful. Frisk him and Flint would expect to find a packet of condoms in the other pocket and a Swiss Army knife down his socks.

Between Tyrone's attacks on the idea of a Breton Arthur, Flint repeated the question he had put to Charles Evans.

"Lady Harriet's talk?" Valerie's expression shifted from charmed animation through doubt to disapproval. "Pooh! Some silly story."

"Excalibur?"

"She was . . ." Valerie grimaced, then waggled her cigarette hand near to her ear. "A little, you know?"

"Mad?"

70

Valerie nodded as she sucked. Flint found the effect nauseating.

"It's all very sad, but . . . pouf!" Valerie dismissed Harry's life's work in a wave of her hand.

"But some people in the society must have supported her."

"Oh Euan Treppeek," she struggled with an unusual name. "And that, er, child, and . . ." she listed a few more members who were clearly deluded, or senile, or who had read too few of her papers.

Valerie began to describe how her own research undermined the bedrock of Harry's theories and Tyrone began to object with counter-arguments. Flint felt depression creeping up on him again. He had been far from alone in wanting to crush Harry's dream, but this knowledge made him feel no better. He extracted himself from the progressively deeper debate surrounding the Breton Arthur. Valerie had the intellect and the determination to resist Tyrone's scorn and counter-attacked his theories with vigour.

Two more bottles of Mexican beer were bought and paid for. Valerie was still in full flow and Tyrone was nodding, if gradually retreating before the gallic onslaught. A beer bottle was inserted into the debate, then Flint walked out of the bar, through the lobby and out onto the porch of Edgar Jenkins Hall.

Someone was leaving: the tail-lights of a car turned across the gateway and vanished. Someone had the right idea. Waiting for the inquest would be futile and masochistic. The verdict 'suicide' would only ram home the point. He would go home tomorrow, prepare the Easter field course and arrange himself a wild birthday party for the coming Thursday. Thirty-five: half-way to three-score years and ten. Harry hadn't even made that.

71

Time slid past as Flint spent a little more of his life's remaining balance breathing the damp night air. When the novelty of the deserted porch wore thin, he went back into the hall, winding up and around, following the maze of passageways to his room. To occupy his mind, Flint plonked his suitcase on the bed and threw his conference notes inside, quickly followed by the few possessions not needed in the morning. He put on his plain blue pyjamas, gave his teeth a good, hard, Calvinist scrub, then slipped between the thin sheets and took up a paperback: Philip K. Dick's anthology *Hope I Shall Arrive Soon*.

Someone hammered on the door.

"Doc!" Tyrone's voice sounded urgent. He'd stopped calling Flint 'Doc' the day he'd won his own doctorate.

"What?"

The muffled voice tried to explain as Flint padded barefoot across the room. He jerked open the door. "What?"

"It's gone," Tyrone said. "Someone's nicked the sword."

Chapter Seven

The shock of the news was greater than the shock of cold linoleum on Flint's bare feet. In moments, he was in Tyrone's room, kneeling beside the tired iron-framed single bed. Tyrone pulled out the Bren gun.

"At least they didn't take this."

"So we have a very picky weapons freak."

Tyrone lay the bulky machine-gun onto the bed. "I've got this awful feeling."

"And me."

"Lady Dunning died, then someone took the sword. It can't be coincidence."

"And the insurance company was already jumpy, they must have known something was amiss. Was your door locked?"

"Yes, but it's a Yale. You could do the credit card trick."

Rising to the window, Flint pulled aside the curtain, as if to see a thief running across the lawns with a sword tucked under his arm. The night was dark, misty and lacked any such scene.

"Thank God we didn't have the original here, but even still, that replica is worth five thousand pounds – so you'd better report it to the police PDQ. Find Hewitt, if he's not gone to bed and get him to take a roll-call, find out who's

missing. I'll get the warden to organize a room search –
it may still be here."

It was doubtful if the Pendragon Society could take much
more excitement. The police did not arrive until after
midnight and two uniformed men accompanied Patrick
Hewitt around the bedrooms, taking brief statements
from distinguished, and disgruntled delegates. Flint and
Tyrone were left firmly without a role, drinking coffee
in a kitchenette and passing time with a succession of
bemused men in dressing-gowns and carpet slippers. At
one a.m., the trail was as dead as King Arthur, leaving
bed as the only option.

Neither Flint, nor Tyrone slept well, and both supported
the grumbles of the other over breakfast. Amongst the
pile of paper they had been given on registering for
the conference, was an attendance list. Tyrone had
already picked Patrick Hewitt's brain and crossed off
three delegates: two being sick and one dead. Hewitt
had tried, and failed, to remember which residents he
was unable to find when accompanying the policemen
on their rounds.

Each delegate was supposed to wear a name tag. It
saved the embarrassment of accidentally insulting some
erudite scholar by asking who he was, or worse, by
criticizing a particular theory unaware that its arch-
proponent stood at your elbow. The Pendragons had
issued tags with a black-and-white Holy Grail at the
right-hand end from which handwritten names tailed
away in black. Tyrone sat close to the door and ticked
off names one-by-one as delegates came yawning into
breakfast.

A married couple from Lancashire took interest in the
project.

"I'm spying," Tyrone said, not wanting to engage in small talk.

"Is this to do with your sword?"

"It is."

"Isn't it terrible? Whatever next?"

"Whatever next?" asked Flint, as the delegates moved on.

"Alien invasion?" suggested Tyrone. "This hasn't been your typical dry and dusty conference, has it?."

"No – it's more like one of those murder mystery weekends."

"You know, boss, I bet the same person who swiped the sword is the one who did Harry in."

"Let's soften our terminology, shall we? We don't know that anyone 'did her in'."

"I bet the events are connected —"

Tyrone broke off as Patrick Hewitt came into the dining hall. He stopped to confer over the breakfast list. Six people had paid for a meal they had not eaten:

Pauline Cook

Charles Evans

Lydia Goatheland-Hoare

Hugh Goatheland-Hoare

Manfred Smith

Euan Trepennick

"The Goatheland-Hoares went home before lunch yesterday," Hewitt said. "Lydia was at school with Harry and they were quite close. I think she was very upset and Hugh took her home. Manfred and Euan, too, they were very close to her way of thinking. In fact I don't think I've seen Euan at all."

"Did he know what Harry's paper was going to be about?"

"Who knows? Nothing makes sense this weekend. How some thief could have broken in is beyond me."

"A common thief wouldn't have known the sword was in our possession. If Harry had been alive, the sword wouldn't even have been here by Saturday night, it would have been back with her people. Our thief was either very lucky or very well informed."

"Ah," Hewitt puckered his flabby cheeks, "which brings me to my conversation with Gavin Dunning on the telephone just now. It was his sword you lost, apparently."

"Is he spitting mad?"

Hewitt blew air, as if cooling a red hot telephone. "Well, it's understandable. First his mother, now this, and their press launch was going to be tomorrow."

"I'd have thought he'd have had other things on his mind."

"One would have thought so."

A reporter named Vikki had taught Flint all the secrets of her trade. "They say you should never let bad taste spoil a good story. Do you know Gavin Dunning well?"

"I've seen quite a lot of him over the years." Hewitt was clearly trying to be diplomatic, but Flint had a limited use for diplomacy.

"Gavin was barely civil to me the first time we met – did I merit special treatment, or is he always like that?"

Hewitt opened his mouth as if to disagree, then changed his mind. "He's quarrelsome – a little difficult. He doesn't share his mother's sense of purpose."

"Yes, there's often something disappointing about the sons of the great and good. I assume he's unmarried?"

"Divorced, rather traumatically. He has a little daughter somewhere in Bristol."

"So he lived with his mum and they tried to run each other's lives?"

"That's rather an astute observation, I couldn't have phrased it better given the whole morning to consider it. That's exactly how they were. I remember one summer when we held a barbecue at Harry's farm and Gavin was trying to organize everyone, including his mother. Now Harry was never organized and could never be organized. If you can imagine the scene: Gavin was fussing and trying to usher the guests to where the food was being served and Harry was, well, busy being Harry.

"'Come on mother!' he said, but Harry was in mid-flow and determined to finish her anecdote. She turned around and spotted he had wine on his shirt and she ticked him off as if he were a twelve-year-old. Gavin simply stood and looked like a naughty schoolboy as she took a hankie and dabbed at the stain."

The mother-son relationship could be odd: the plot of Hitchcock's *Psycho* flitted through Flint's mind. "Where's this press launch going to be?" he asked.

"A hotel near the British Museum, at ten. Gavin wants you to telephone him about it."

What could Flint say? Sorry we lost your sword and p.s. isn't it sad that your mother was washed up on the lakeside yesterday morning? Which expression of remorse would Gavin want to hear first. Flint followed his own heart (and conventional etiquette). Gavin said little other than "yes" as Flint explained how terribly shocked and saddened he had been. All the adequate words had already been turned into clichés by umpteen TV soap operas, and Flint could invent nothing which sounded new, or fresh, or genuine.

"The funeral will be on Thursday, if the coroner gives

the go-ahead," Gavin said. "I can't see any reason why he shouldn't."

"No."

"About the sword. I've spoken to the police and they gave me the details. You could have telephoned me last night, Flint, it would only have been right."

"I assumed you had other things on your mind."

"It would have been the proper thing to do."

"OK, sorry, so any idea who could have swiped it?"

Silence, then Gavin said, "That's not relevant now, what I want to be sure of is that the genuine sword will be at the hotel an hour before the press conference begins."

"We haven't completed our tests . . ."

"Fuck your tests Flint, we need that sword at nine o'clock tomorrow! If we don't get it, you'll hear from my solicitor. Make the arrangements today, and don't for God's sake lose the sword in transit!"

Remaining cool, Flint asked, "Can we have it back afterwards?"

"No."

"What if the insurance company insist?"

"They won't."

Flint nodded to himself: they'd insist.

"Now keep away from the press until tomorrow; some of them are already beginning to guess what we're going to announce."

"OK." Flint was planning to spend the night in a reporter's flat. It would be fun trying to keep the story down until after her copy deadline. If he felt really evil, he might just let enough slip to spoil Gavin's day.

By late afternoon, Flint and Tyrone were back on the motorway, driving to London after exhausting the

78

patience of the Pendragons with their oblique questions and by persistently cross-checking the word of one august member against another. Tyrone owned a flat in Earl's Court, which he rented out to students, reserving one room as his own London 'pad'. Flint was dropped at the underground station, with an hour's ride across the city allowing time to think ahead and plan his week. He had already abandoned hope of returning to Yorkshire before his birthday.

In the East End of London lived a reporter named Vikki who had once shared Flint's life. Her dark angular looks and schoolgirl figure had not made compensations for hard edges to her character. She wrote freelance for a number of tabloid newspapers and spent three days a week researching and presenting *True Life Crimes* for a satellite TV show. She was the dinky girl filmed in so many alleys and deserted copses, gleefully describing the discovery of the body for the benefit of camera and microphone.

Vikki had once been charmed by the laid-back, fun-loving Jeffrey Flint, but had never broken through the barrier into the intimate world of the academic. A few too many women inhabited his world and his feet had never been firmly anchored to the ground. Together for eighteen months, they had now been apart for twenty.

Flint arrived at the flat bearing a Chinese dinner, neither presuming on hospitality nor trusting Vikki's cooking. Whilst her washing-machine and tumble-drier worked on his clothes, he sat at her tubular steel-and-glass kitchen table in a red kimono and chased beansprouts with chopsticks. Vikki was full of 'her' TV show, running through the hack-and-stab of studio politics, shaping up her move into the presenter's chair.

Flint kept away from mentioning the sudden death of

Lady Dunning, lest Vikki plus film crew materialized in Glastonbury to compromise him. Instead, he told her the news about Jules' and Sasha's separation and Vikki retold the story of how her old photographer Vince had walked on a landmine in Bosnia. Each little world had its casualties.

Sexy, yes, sexual, no. Vikki had never shared his need for frequent carnal indulgence. Flint slept on the sofa-bed and in the morning gave Vikki a functional peck on the cheek and asked her to take care. She'd shown little interest when he'd finally mentioned Excalibur – some rusty old sword, she'd called it. Without the drama of a bizarre death and dramatic theft, the story would be buried on the inner pages of any newspaper, or be reserved for the 'roller-skating duck slot' at the end of the TV news. Perhaps this said something about society.

An early start found him at Central College, where Tyrone was dispatched inside a Stronghold Security van to nursemaid the 'true Excalibur' towards its destiny. Flint waited until nine, then telephoned the insurance office in Leeds.

Matt Humphries ran through the whole range of reactions; shock, rage, outrage, disbelief and confusion. Flint held the phone slightly away from his ear. Sitting in the corner of 'Doc' Savage's office, he was retelling a succession of bad tidings.

"How could you let it happen?"

"How could you let it happen to me? You must have known something was afoot! Come clean, Matt, what the hell is going on?"

Humphries did not respond directly. Flint drained a coffee cup, then continued. "Let me float an idea past you. You have this heavy commitment to insure these

80

swords and you felt uneasy, so you engaged me to check out the authenticity."

"Yes."

"What was it that made you nervous?"

"I'm afraid that's our business."

"How much are you in for? I mean the whole deal, not just the replica?"

"I can't tell you, our business is confidential."

"Your boss is going to have your balls for this. I imagine it sounded like a big coup when you won the business."

"It wasn't my business, it came through the Bristol office."

"So you were checking up on them?"

"That's —"

"Confidential, OK. So tell me, Matt, who gets the pay out?"

Breaking confidence was perfectly in order when it suited Humphries' purpose. "The insurance contract for the swords was proposed by her company. They're called Museum Projects Plus, based in Bath. Have you had any contact with them?"

"Briefly: they're exhibiting the sword today. If you believe their hype you'll see the blessed thing on the lunchtime news. This press launch is going to cause us a problem, though. Gavin Dunning seems keen to lay his hands on it for keeps. Can you ring them up and make sure the sword stays in my care? I've not finished all the tests yet." Flint told a partial truth. He'd finished all the planned investigation, but could always devise more.

"You'll keep it secure?"

"Locked, controlled-environment store inside a locked room: CCL is a Central London college: we've got security guards, video monitors, anti-rape alarms, you name it."

81

OK, so Flint knew that anyone scruffy enough to pass as a student could waltz right into CCL, but Humphries wasn't to know. It took a few more words of encouragement, plus a few strenuous pledges to convince him.

"Right, you keep the sword, at least until we understand what happened at the weekend. I may have to go to the inquest tomorrow – it's a bit of a bugger, but we're not talking peanuts, are we?"

"I thought we were," Flint said. "I mean, the replica was only insured for five grand, that's less than most cars."

"Flint, Flint, we do more than just insure cheap swords."

"You insured her life?"

"And loans taken out in her name. New contracts, of course, all taken out in the past year."

Ghastlier and ghastlier, thought Flint. "How much are you in for?"

"You don't want to know."

He did, but clearly was not about to find out. "And the beneficiaries?"

It served Humphries' purpose to tell. "Her children."

Chapter Eight

One television team, three pairs from radio stations and at least a dozen newspaper reporters swelled the invited audience of forty. Several of the Pendragons were present: Patrick Hewitt, the train-spotter, the Reverend Allsop, but not the flamboyant Valerie Chastel nor the cynical Charles Evans. Flint arrived late and joined Tyrone in the back row. At the front of the hall, surrounded by a selection of display panels, four people were dressed in hypocritical black, with one pair of bright red lips the only flash of colour.

The woman with the red lips was leading the briefing. A slightly-built young man with a ponytail worked the visual aids whilst Gavin played the quietly grieving son. A big-boned woman, quite likely his twin sat silently at his side, whilst their backs were watched by a giant head-and-shoulders photo of their mother. Just once, Gavin caught Flint's eye and glared.

Blown up to triple life-size, a 3D photo cut-out of the sword was suspended behind where red lips spoke of a miraculous find, an untimely death and a baffling theft. Bathed by bright lighting, 'the true Excalibur' nestled in regal velvet, its display box propped at an angle for all to admire.

Every image counted and every word was swallowed by the press, even the pointed revelation that Dr Flint had care of the replica sword when it had been stolen. He felt a little warmer below his beard, crossing his arms and sinking ever so slightly lower in his chair.

On cue, a linked pair of television screens showed a video of the sword, and the replica and of Harry, still alive, holding and enthusing over them. The effect was eerie, as if she was speaking from beyond the grave. An urge to call out "Whodunnit, Harry?" was strong.

"I'll finish now," said the sticky, seductive PR voice. "As this is a story of such importance to the national heritage, you must have plenty of questions."

Yes, Flint had plenty of questions. He'd only half listened to the delivery, his brain now fully engaged. This was the Once and Future plot, part had already been lived through, but more was to come. He'd once thought the whole affair farcical, treated it as a joke and easy money. Now it was serious, and it involved big money, hard-won. Clues he'd stumbled across began to combine and make some kind of sense; more surely lay waiting to be revealed.

A voice came through the hubbub of question-and-answer. "Trevor Gregson – the *Guardian*." A hack in a raincoat stood up, pen poised. Red lipstick spread into a smile, wrinkles rose up to the woman's hairline and possibly beyond.

"If you don't mind, as I came in, I noticed we have Dr Flint in the audience. I wonder what he thinks of the discovery." The reporter turned to nod towards where Flint lurked in the back row.

Flint awoke from his introspection. Yes he'd met the reporter at some party Vikki had dragged him to. He said nothing, keeping his head low, with arms firmly crossed.

"Would you say the sword is genuine, Dr Flint?"

He raised his head so slightly above the parapet. "Er, difficult to say." His career was on the line, his credibility was about to die and several million TV viewers were waiting.

"No," he added. "It's ancient, but it's not Excalibur."

Breaths were exhaled, papers rustled and the audience reacted with a simultaneous purr of interest. Flint felt himself pierced by venom-tipped glares from the platform. He was already on his feet, making for the door.

"Dr Flint's opinion is not relevant," the red lips called from the podium. "He has been paid to undermine this discovery."

The atmosphere bubbled as pens began to record the scene of two academics squaring up for battle.

"How do you answer that, Dr Flint?"

Dr Flint had no intention of answering that – not yet. He would escape quickly, before any of the pack managed to cross-examine him. Within moments he was out of the room, free of pursuit. Tyrone shot to his feet and physically blocked one reporter who tried to pursue.

Once outside the hotel, Flint jogged fifty yards along one side of Russell Square, before allowing Tyrone to catch up.

"You need a minder," Tyrone panted.

"Stick close, kid, you'll do." Flint's adrenalin was up, he was at the centre of something he felt he should understand. "I didn't see Vikki," Tyrone said.

"No, she'll be in Brussels, by now – not enough blood in it for her."

After a few moments by his side, Tyrone stopped walking. "I'm going to have to go back in there. Someone has to make sure the sword gets back to the CCL lab."

"OK – but keep quiet about where its going – tell nosy parkers it's going to the British Museum, that will throw them off the scent, I don't want reporters making the college untidy."

"What are you going to do?"

"Go back to CCL and trawl the library. When you get back, drag me down to the Union Bar: we'll have the odd pint and pop our thinking caps on."

It was late afternoon before Tyrone, plus 'Excalibur', returned to Central College in the security van to be met by a pair of green-jacketed men who helped him into the Mezzanine laboratory with the sword. College employed its own, highly unselective security force to patrol the buildings against petty thieves, vandals and the perverts who think college girls make easy targets. Almost all the force were recruited from ethnic minorities, not to advance positive discrimination, but so the college could pay rock-bottom rates for long shifts. Students had dubbed the underpaid green-jacketed men 'The Khyber Rifles'.

A few floors higher up the building, Flint was in the library; he had worked his way around the offices of the staff who had yet to go home for Easter, culling their knowledge of Museums Projects Plus. Once in the library, he sped through the glossier archaeological magazines looking for articles about past exhibitions. Tyrone found him amid a pile of *Current Archaeology*.

"One fake Excalibur, all present and correct. The Khybers did their duty and protected it to the last man." He saluted.

Flint lolled his glazed eyes skywards, making sheep-like noises. "Bar . . . Bar."

The Union Bar was all but deserted. On one barstool sat Dr Stewart Paxman, the astrophysicist whose dark-matter theory was within an ace of the Nobel shortlist when it had been disproved by a twenty-two-year-old Vietnamese

86

postgraduate at Arizona State University. For the past year he'd done little other than subsidize the college bars. It was a fate that had awaited Harry once Excalibur had been thoroughly debunked.

"Poor sod," Tyrone commented, bringing his beer to join Flint in one corner.

"The fragility of dreams," Flint mused. "He spent eight years on that project, you know?"

"He should have got his sums right. At least he didn't do a Harry."

"But did Harry do a Harry? The more I think about her, the less convinced I am that she killed herself." Flint replaced his innermost hope with more solid conviction.

Tyrone was so eager to disagree he slopped his lager down his tie. "Until the inquest, any theory is just a guess: we might learn something tomorrow."

"I doubt it; it's too soon, they'll probably just run through the formalities then wait until after Easter before we get the gory details."

The two archaeologists were now just visitors at their old college, with no office to work from, no computer password and only day reader's tickets for the library. Tyrone was over two hundred miles from his laptop computer, his mobile phone and the other toys he liked to use in problem solving.

Flint had always liked to think on paper. He spread a pair of A4 notepads on the table in front of him, and by his side lay a pile of scrap computer printouts retrieved from the recycling bin. Whilst in the library, he'd started to draw charts and tables on the green-striped side. He ran through what he'd learned about Museum Projects Plus, or MPP as they were known in all the glowing accounts of their work. Other than Harry, the directors seemed to consist of Gavin Dunning, Alison Wright (she of the red lips) and Ivor Pulleine (possibly the one with the ponytail who had worked the visual aids). Their former glories were minor glories: a museum exhibition here, a living history display there. Several other staff had been mentioned and a few names rang distant bells.

"Have you heard anything about this crowd before?" Flint asked.

"Yes, I thought they'd folded up – everyone in the heritage industry is having a tough time."

"Just like good old UNY-DIG. I haven't looked at our books lately, how is the unit doing?"

"We're still in the red, technically speaking."

"Times are hard," Flint said in his broadest Yorkshire accent. "We've had it rough, lad, but MPP are still holding their heads above water."

"That's a bit of a sick joke."

It wasn't funny, but they both laughed anyway. Half the pint pots were empty already and the night was young.

"You know MPP nearly went bankrupt last year?" Tyrone said, once the horseplay had died away.

"Did they?"

Tyrone nodded. "So rumour has it. I rang a few people last night."

"So could that be another reason for Harry to go for a final dip?"

"No, I think she used her dosh to bail them out of trouble. It's probably where her money went. She saved them, if anything."

Flint leaned down to the floor and brought up one of his green-striped charts. "OK, let's not dabble with Harry – at least until we've heard the coroner's side of things. I think that we should examine the theft of the replica sword. I've started to run through possible motives. Number one is the obvious ordinary theft."

"No – it's too unlikely. Your usual yobbo would have taken the gun too, he wouldn't have known it was decommissioned."

"OK, two – someone wants to foul up the Arthur Roadshow."

Tyrone nodded, then added a third idea. "Someone wants to make the Arthur Roadshow more exciting than it is."

"Ooh," Flint scribbled on his chart. "Paranoid conspiracy theories abound."

"Four," Tyrone added. "Professional art thieves."

"Not stealing a replica sword."

"Stupid art thieves – they thought it was the real one."

Reluctantly Flint wrote down 'S.A.T.' as motive number four. "Ransom? Blackmail?" he suggested.

Tyrone turned up his nose. "Four guesses without any evidence is enough to work on. We know the suspects if it's number three, otherwise we've got nothing."

Whilst Tyrone liked to eat at times of crisis, Flint liked his comfort in liquid form and pint-shaped. He was looking through the bubble-stained bottom of the glass as an idea began to grow. He lowered the glass slowly, talking along one line whilst his mind was exploring other directions.

"If I know the police they won't want to link the death and the theft, so that's our task. Once they take the theft seriously, they'll look again at the circumstances of Harry's drowning."

That idea was there, worming its way forward from the muddy depths of his mind.

"We can't afford to work for free," Tyrone said. "Someone's got to pay for the petrol."

Flint looked at his empty glass. "And the beer."

"Can I work on Humphries? I'll talk him into funding us for another week. I'll make up some new test we have to perform, there must be something we haven't tried."

"Ha!" The idea struck home with the force of a swinging broadsword.

"What's wrong?"

"If you were the culprit behind plots two to four, what would be the next logical thing to do?"

Tyrone was still forming an answer when Flint placed his pen on the list of motives. "Two – foul up the Roadshow more. Three – enhance the glamour. Four – perhaps our art thieves won't be so stupid next time. Whatever their motives, they're going for the real sword next."

Chapter Nine

Neither the second, nor the third pint of beer helped clarify the faintly bizarre situation. It was public knowledge that Flint had lost the replica sword, but few people knew that he was still in charge of the original. After a pint-and-a-half he believed the secret was safe in a small number of hands. Tyrone, however, began enumerating the specialists and curious students who had wandered through the lab whilst the anonymous sword had been analyzed. Now the sword had a name, simply dozens would know of its exact location. By the time the third pint had been drained, Tyrone had convinced him that the thief would also share the secret: up to date he'd proved well-informed.

"We have to get rid of it," Tyrone said. "Let's take it to the BM."

It was the most logical move to make. Harry had wanted the sword to find a home at the British Museum. "Yeah – I'll ring around this evening and get someone to agree to receive the blessed thing in the morning."

"Insurance – they won't want it unless its covered."

"OK, I'll ring Humphries first thing tomorrow, get that squared, then arrange a security van."

"What about tonight? We can't trust the Khybers."

"Racist remark."

"Yeah, but race apart, they're still pathetic."

Flint felt his temper rising. "Point taken – OK?"

"We can't trust them," Tyrone repeated.

"OK, then apply the old saying, Tyrone. If you want a job doing properly, do it yourself."

"Me?"

"Young, fit," Flint paused, "white."

Tyrone frowned, a blush coming to his cheeks. "That's not what I meant."

"It's how it sounded. Now I suggest you pop down the road and get us a couple of kebabs from Mick the Greek, I'll see Gerald the caretaker, then we'll snuggle down for a cozy night in the Conservation lab."

The library at Central College, London, closed at eight. The caretaker locked up sharply and came down to the Mezzanine where Tyrone and Flint were settling in for the night. Tyrone was just rolling the TV unit into position in front of two soft chairs brought in from the rest area.

"What do I do if something happens?" the caretaker asked from the door.

"Nothing in the slightest bit heroic, Gerald. Somebody died at the weekend and they might not be the last."

Gerald used some suitably choice words of alarm. "Is this sword worth that much?"

"I don't know what it's worth, but its value seems to be growing by the day. You lock us in and go back to your flat. If the alarms start ringing, call the cops and get college security off their backsides."

Gerald hunted through a ring full of keys and handed out one for the lab and another for the conservation store. He'd heard some story about Flint and fires.

"In case you need to get out," he offered the keys. "It'd make me happier. Don't tell the bursar, though, you're not on the staff any more."

"Cheers, Gerald – I'll buy you a jar sometime."

As he left, Gerald began whistling. The shrill tones echoed along the deserted Mezzanine even after his footfalls had faded. It emphasized how empty the college could be in mid-vacation. Two men in green manned the main College gate, or to be precise, they manned the television within the gatehouse which served as their base of operations. The main task, as the 'Khybers' saw it, was to stop people from parking in spaces reserved for the senior administrators. At this they were very proficient.

One porter was based in each college block, one in each hall of residence. An occasional perimeter patrol of two would wander through the maze of rat-runs which ran between and beneath the buildings, surprising the odd graffiti artist or entwined couple. The college was not a compact, self-contained unit, but wandered over several blocks of the city, interspersed with buildings belonging to private persons and other institutions. For anyone with the nerve, or the knowledge, it was easy to penetrate.

Perhaps Flint was on a fool's errand, but he would make no more mistakes. He'd deliver that sword straight into the hands of the British Museum, then he could sleep easily – in a real bed. From the plate window along the side of the lab, he looked out into the sodium-tinted darkness beneath the Engineering block, the opposite side of a deep canyon which cut into the college. Out in the gloom of inadequate lighting he could distinguish silvery wheelie bins, a pile of empty gas cylinders, a great mound of black plastic rubbish sacks and the obligatory abandoned supermarket trolley.

Upstairs, the porter named Ralph would be in the ground floor lodge, watching the lights on the intruder board. His nearest green-jacketed ally was across in Engineering, with his own lights and TV monitors to watch. Flint locked the door of the room, with himself and Tyrone inside. After an hour spent browsing a heap of papers and magazines, they settled down to watch Martin Scorsese's *Goodfellas*. It was not a good choice. Within moments of the film's opening, one hoodlum had been kicked, knifed and shot to death. Over the next two hours, men were bludgeoned, killed, chopped, wasted, whacked and blown away in the pursuit of crime. The black humour scarcely helped.

Some time after midnight, the film ended and Flint unlocked the room at the back of the laboratory. This had controlled humidity and temperature for storing delicate objects and was always kept locked. The original sword was still where it had been left, in its padlocked wooden box. Such was his state of mind, Flint found himself checking for alternative entrances, grilles, ventilators, loose panels, anything to convince him that the sword was safe. He came out again, locked the door and put the key on top of the television, lest it fall from his pocket whilst visiting the toilets, just four paces from the lab door. Flint paid a call, quietly humming to himself. To hope for something came naturally, to hope for nothing demanded a certain philosophy he couldn't manage. Perhaps airport firemen or the crews of nuclear submarines became used to it.

One more glance along the fully-lit corridors, one more walk as far as the fire doors, then Flint could try to make himself comfortable. All four soft chairs had been dragged in from the waiting area beside the lifts, but the night proved long, cold, and tedious. The tang of chemicals worked their way into Flint's nostrils and he fought hard against identifying them: Acetone? B.T.A? Cellulose nitrate? Working his way through to Xylene was like counting sheep; very smelly sheep.

Hour after hour was marked by the absence of incident,

absence of noise or alarm. Slowly, he imagined it was becoming light.

Tuesday, 5.58 a.m. and dawn was sticking her fingers down the chasm between Archaeology and Engineering. The necessity to pretend to be sleeping had gone, so Flint abandoned the effort and took down *First Aid for Finds* from the Conservation bookshelf. Tyrone continued to snore, bundled up on one of the soft chairs, with his feet on another and his coat as a blanket. At nine, Flint would ring Stronghold Security and book one of their vans. Then he'd let Humphries in on the plan to move the sword to the British Museum.

Tyrone's first words were, "I'm starving."

"Café Albert is closed for the vac.," Flint said, stretching himself. "We might get breakfast in Leopold Hall."

"Their food's inedible."

"I'll go and do some hunter-gathering."

Flint unlocked the laboratory door and looked down the silent corridor. His paranoia had been misplaced: the night had been fruitless, the stiff neck pointless. He volunteered to go up to the concourse and pump coins into the machines. Tyrone eased himself upright, grumbling.

Leg muscles welcomed the stretch as Flint walked along the corridor and up half a flight of the back staircase. He passed a minute's conversation with Ralph, the Indian porter, then wandered along to the machines outside the main lecture theatre. From one machine came a Kit-Kat and a Mars Bar, then from another he bought two coffees with sugar. Hot water squirted into the powder, churning it into a familiar muddy brown liquid. The bitter aftertaste was one of Flint's least tender memories of CCL. Gingerly he lifted the second overfull cup.

A distant hollow thumping sound stopped him. Intruders? In daylight – it was daylight. Every door was wired, but no alarm sounded. None of the accessible windows could be opened more than a few inches. Flint was confused until the moment he thought of the dustbin men, who usually reversed their truck down the rat-run and collected two department's garbage. They had wakened him before, when he'd slept on his office floor after a party. He smiled, thinking of one particular party and one particular Canadian student.

"Grow up, Flint," he said to himself and began to walk sedately back past the porters' box, half ignoring the continued thumping and crashing. He cursed the way the coffee machine seemed deliberately calibrated to scald fingers.

A muffled cry joined the thumping. He was at the top of the back staircase when a crash followed. He quickened his pace to a fast walk, cursing as hot coffee slopped over his right hand. Stairs were taken as quickly as he could manage, splashes of brown marking his progress towards the Mezzanine. He reached the turn of the stairs, then a green figure flashed past the window of the fire doors.

"Hey!"

For a crucial second, Flint hesitated, then let the coffees splatter onto the stairs, leaping down to the fire doors and punching them open. Down the corridor to his left, rapidly vanishing towards another set of doors, was a green parka and a rucksack, propelled by a pair of white trainers. Flint sprinted after the green parka, past the environmental lab, past Archaeobotany, past Sasha's office, past the photocopier, then through more fire doors into the heart of the building. How had he got in? What had happened to the alarms? What had happened to Tyrone?

Flint battered the swinging doors apart to see the figure

96

vanish up the main staircase. Stairs were taken two at a time. His quarry was out of sight, but he could hear feet slapping on the mock marble, up, up, up. Past the ground floor, past Flint's old floor. That was all the main exits missed. Past Classics, past the Library, top floor, what a maniac!

In twenty seconds, the green parka was going to run out of building.

Chapter Ten

At the very top of the Archaeology building was the Classics lounge and Staff Bar. Flint kept trying to compose a strategy for when he ran his prey to a dead end. The green parka had avoided all the locked doors, was now too high to jump from a window and stood no chance of calling a lift and dropping back to ground level, so what was his plan?

The problem was solved before Flint guessed at a solution. Green parka knew exactly where he was going. At the far side of the Classics lounge was an emergency exit leading to the fire escape. He threw over a trail of chairs, then hit hard against the crash bar. An alarm sounded at last, but the door was slammed closed. Flint was five or ten seconds too late. He battered the crash bar to no effect. He shouldered the door and it grated open, but only by two inches. This had been planned. He put his slight twelve stones behind his shoulder and the door slithered another inch. Protruding below it was a tiny slither of wood: the burglar had come equipped with door wedges. Flint pulled the door sharply towards himself, then worked it back and forth until the wedge was knocked free.

A minute later, standing at the top of the fire escape, he could see a green figure sprinting across towards the Life Sciences block. He could only watch as it vanished under a concrete walkway.

With his pulse rate still racing above normal, and his brain in a state of complete confusion, Flint slowly made his way back through the building. He met Ralph outside Classics, then Gerald the caretaker on the stairs, then the porter from Engineering, just rushing into the lobby. Group impotence gripped the men; hands went into pockets, shoulders shrugged and each sought some positive action he could take.

Flint trotted down to the Mezzanine, thinking now of Tyrone, who should have been standing between the intruder and the sword. He was found unharmed, sitting on one of the work benches in the lab, swinging his feet, with a look of total bewilderment on his face.

"What happened?" Flint asked. "Where were you?"

"In the toilet – and so was he. The bastard locked me in."

"You soft sod! How did that happen?"

Tyrone showed him the outer door to the gents toilet, now badly damaged. The intruder had allowed Tyrone to adopt the position, trousers down, then sneaked out of his own cubicle. Once free of the toilet, he'd hammered a six-inch nail into the door jamb with three blows.

"Three? You counted?"

"I was in the middle . . . yes three. And he'd taken the handle off the inside, there wasn't even any leverage."

Flint stayed close to the door, taking undue interest in the damage, not wanting to venture into the lab.

"It was a professional job," Tyrone said. "He must have heard everything we said last night and known exactly where to look. He was just waiting for his chance."

"And he knows this building," Flint said. "Or has friends who know this building."

The toilet was directly opposite the lab. It had taken Tyrone several minutes to wrench the door free. It had taken the intruder only a fraction of that time to smash open the door of the lab, spot the key on top of the TV and unlock the store. Flint looked at the plank box, now cast on the floor, empty.

"By gum, lad, we're up shit creek now."

Owl-like Sandra Savage made Flint a real cup of coffee as he sat and fretted by her telephone. The police had already been and gone. A group of ivories from Iraq, a Roman bronze hoard and miscellaneous precious finds from the wreck of the *Holy Venture* had been ignored by the intruder, intent only on taking the sword in the box. At least Flint's Motive One (casual theft) had been finally disproved and Motive Four (art thieves) was highly suspect.

"Matt, I've got some bad news for you . . ."

"Hey, Matt, you'll never guess what happened this morning . . ."

"You know bad things happen in threes, Mr Humphries . . ."

It was no use. Flint could procrastinate for as long as he might, but sooner or later he was going to have to confess to Matt Humphries. Deep breath, dial, say hi, then plunge into the bad tidings.

The insurance man did not immediately die of heart seizure, but for a few moments, Flint could not be sure.

"It was a professional job," Flint said, in his best matter-of-fact voice. He felt a complete fool and his ego had shrunk to the size of a pinhead.

"Sorry we lost you half a million quid," muttered Tyrone from the other side of the office.

"It was a big mistake getting you people involved, wasn't it?" Humphries said at last.

"Whoever you had hired, I don't think it would have stopped the theft. Someone is pretty determined."

"To do what?" echoed Tyrone.

"You've been set up, Matt. We've all been set up. We're bound together on this one."

"Are we?"

Long silences were always awkward. Anything Flint could say would sound insincere. A torrent of abuse could be expected at any second.

"Keep the media away from the story," Humphries said, with obvious, measured consideration.

"That could be difficult," Flint said.

"Motive Three," Tyrone observed dryly. "Add to the glamour."

"Don't tell them about it!" Humphries said, his tone becoming authoritarian. "It's simple; I'll talk to the police, have them sit on the story. You keep it to yourself."

A glance through the morning papers showed the media were already confused by the Excalibur press launch. The discovery had been presented in a variety of ways, and with variable accuracy. One report even stated that it was the original Excalibur, not the replica which had been stolen at Bath.

"We might be able to keep the lid on it for a few days."

"Good." Humphries sounded sobered, but not panicked by the drama.

"Are we sacked?" Tyrone hissed.

Flint nodded, without having to ask.

"Ask!"

"Look, Matt, our brief was fairly limited and now

the sword has vanished . . . I hope we retain your confidence."

An explosion of long-distance derision came from Leeds.

"It's why you employed us, after all. You know we investigate, you know we dig deeper than the surface. You got us into this, you can't just sack us."

"No," Humphreys said carefully. Another long silence, full of potential evils followed. "OK, you lost it; you can help us find it."

Tyrone whispered, "How much?"

"My colleague is asking about expenses. Are we still talking standard rates of payment?"

"As written in the contract, but this time I only pay by results. No find, no fee. I want to know where you are each day and what you're doing. Take down my home number."

Flint scrawled a number on the corner of a handy copy of the *Independent*.

"Don't leave messages, don't send faxes, don't call me at work."

That serious, huh? Flint should have backed away at this moment, but UNY-DIG needed every pound to stay afloat and his own pride had been wounded by the triple disaster. A memory of a robust Harry stomping through the woods haunted his mind.

"You're on."

"Advance?" Tyrone hissed, but Flint waved him down.

"We'll drive back to Bath straight away."

"I'll expect a call," Humphries said, and put down the phone.

Flint yawned heavily, putting one sleepy eye on the clock. It was not quite nine-thirty and the day had already contained more drama than he could handle. It would be possible to be back in Bath by the early afternoon. He wanted to find the company called MPP, before they found out he'd lost another of their swords.

"You should have insisted on an advance; we're broke," Tyrone insisted.

"Don't push it, I wouldn't blame Humphries if he sued us for losing the damned swords."

"How mad was he?"

"Livid, but he quickly calmed down. Too quickly, if you ask me. I think our insurance man isn't showing us all his cards; he knows more than he's letting on."

The manner in which Tyrone's jaw tightened and the way his chin was visibly thrust forward gave warning that he was dissecting the facts. He eased his chair back onto two legs. "Motive Five: insurance scam. I bet Humphries fixed up the whole thing himself."

"Then why engage us?"

"As a cover-up operation, to make it look like he's straight. To make it look like he's been trying to unload bad business. He can take his cut on the side, and then can go back to his boss and demand a raise because he was the one who spotted the scam."

It was a worrying idea, until given a moment's reflection. "It wouldn't be worth it, not on his salary. He's a thrusting executive hacking his way to the top; he'll make more money by screwing people within the law, he doesn't have to break it." Unsettled as he was, Flint had to take Humphries at his word, for now. He always disliked the enthusiastic way Tyrone would tear people's characters apart. "You suspect the worst in everyone."

"And I'm usually right."

As they drove from London to Bath in the Spitfire, Flint and Tyrone talked Road Movies: *Vanishing Point, Wild at*

103

Heart, Thelma and Louise. Flint regarded it as continuing education for his ex-student; wean him away from pulp fiction into classic cinema. It also served to keep the driver awake.

At the Leigh Delamere service station on the M4, Tyrone rang the telephone number he'd extracted from Detective Sergeant Chaff. In a few moment's conversation he learned the results of the opening session of the inquest into the death of Lady Harriet Dunning. Her son Gavin had formally identified the body and the pathologist's report stated that the cause of death was by drowning. The Coroner had issued a certificate to allow cremation of the body, then adjourned the inquest for ten days.

Still without revealing the overnight drama and hoping that the police wouldn't inform them before they arrived, Flint had made an appointment to visit Museum Projects Plus at 3.30 that afternoon. Tyrone proposed they simply turn up to 'catch them out', but Flint wanted allies, not enemies. MPP rented a pair of classrooms in a redundant Victorian school on the outskirts of Bath. Tyrone parked in the old school yard beside a pair of Peugeot 205's.

"Thus far, we've not been digging deep enough," Flint said. "We've focused on the death and on the theft of the damned swords, and we've overlooked the original puzzle: how did Harry come to make the billion-to-one discovery? She hardly used state-of-the-art fieldwork techniques and I still haven't come across one professionally-trained archaeologist in her whole 'Round Table'."

Flint would not normally decry amateur archaeologists, as few excavations could function without them, and they made major contributions to the field. Their role was threatened by the increasing complexity and conformity in the discipline, with the creation of written manuals and agreed standards. Many unqualified amateurs proved unequal to these new demands.

"Harry was a sweet old thing, but she belonged to a past age. They don't make them like her any more."

"But the hype is state-of-the-art," Tyrone said, "the medium is the message. The story is a hoax, but it's a very well-presented hoax."

"You're casting aspersions again."

"I am. I spent a morning with the MPP people in London and I don't trust them at all."

"You don't trust anyone." Flint yawned.

Tyrone yawned in sympathy. "Someone's up to no good."

"Yes, some*one*, but not everyone."

It was time to test Tyrone's all-embracing distrust. One doorway of the school had the word BOYS carved on its lintel, the Bath Stone now grey and rotted by pollution. The logo MPP was painted on a blue board, with a finger pointing the way inside.

Bright red lips spoke the welcome, "Dr Flint, hello." The woman pushing out her hand was dressed in a dark blue artist's smock.

"I'm Alison Wright: I'm afraid we got off to rather a poor start yesterday." Her face owned too many creases for its size, or her forty years. Black hair fell about it like a carefully controlled mop. Too much make-up, Flint decided.

"I'm sorry about London," he said. "Reporters have a habit of landing you in it."

"They live by controversy. I'm glad you didn't stay to give them a show – it was very good of you to bow out gracefully."

"Saving red faces all around."

"Yes, we have to be on the same side, don't we?" Alison gave a nervous laugh. "Well, now we're here, come and meet the others."

Paintbrush-thin legs carried Alison across the high-roofed classroom, now converted to a design studio. Draughtsman's desks were supplemented by the obligatory computers and graphics plotter. The walls were festooned with artwork portraying the past work of MPP, an Irish castle, a Roman villa and of course the Bog Lady; a gruesome, twisted face in grey and blue whose death agony had been preserved, and presented in award-winning style.

A meeting had been in progress behind a set of hessian-backed screens.

"Right, who do you know?"

Gavin was seated. He grunted acknowledgement of their presence. By his side sat a woman, almost another Gavin minus the beard, or a Harry minus a couple of decades.

"And this is Gwen," Alison said.

Keeping his eyes on the visitors, Gavin inclined his head towards his sister. "This is the illustrious Dr Flint."

"Hi," said Flint.

"Dr Flint doesn't believe that Mother found the true Excalibur," Gavin spoke more for the benefit of Flint than for his sister.

"And this is Ivor," Alison said, with a hint of hasty nerves. "He's our graphic designer."

"Ivor the ink." The young man with the brown ponytail stood to gently shake Flint's hand. His welcome had a natural, friendly warmth that the others lacked. His smooth, boyish cheeks carried a genuine smile free of distrust.

106

"Splendid AV display," Flint said. "It was very impressive."

"We try to please." Ivor could have been speaking serf-to-squire, with his courteous dip of the head and Gloucestershire accent.

"So what do you want?" Gavin asked. "We're very busy."

"We thought —"

"You thought you'd carry on snooping, even though Mother is dead, and you've lost the replica. Well you've no right."

"Gavin!" Gwen spoke.

Alison intervened instantly. "So, why don't you let Ivor show you the graphics."

It was a place to begin and Flint hated interviewing committees; people on their own were better sources of information. Ivor made the expected expression of grief for Harry, then led on to demonstrate his own work. In the adjacent classroom, the Arthur Roadshow was almost complete. Display boards stood concertina-fashion along one side. Maps, photographs and artistic reconstructions were interspersed with gobbets of text. A group of four fully-dressed waxwork dummies portrayed historical (or mythical) characters. The first was the Hollywood Arthur, replete in fourteenth-century plate armour, the second was a comely Guinevere, decked out as a Romano-British lady, the third was a wild-haired Merlin and the fourth, the 'Real Arthur' in thigh-length chainmail shirt with a Gothic 'spangelhelm' on his head and a shield with an image of the Virgin painted upon it. His right hand was raised, and open.

"Guess what went in there," Ivor teased.

"Our replica? What are you going to do now? Make a new one?"

"It would take too long: we just have to trust the police to find the thing." An ironic wriggle of his nose accompanied the word 'police'.

Flint went back to reading the text, taking his time over the story of Lady Dunning's long search for the site of the battle of Camlann. Photographs showed the excavation of her sixth-century chapel. Tyrone peered close to them, trying to find extra information that the narrative omitted. Hands in pockets, he began to read snatches of text aloud, then yawned.

The story differed in detail from the one Harry had told Flint in the rowing boat. She had excavated the chapel, then prospected the area around the little islet. Diagrams showed a pseudo-scientific method of surveying with metal detectors. The text next said Harry *went back* to a previous area of excavations and uncovered the sword, 'deeper than they had first thought to dig'.

Sure enough, there were the photographs of the step-by-step excavation and recovery of the sword.

"Disturbed ground," whispered Tyrone, close to Flint's ear.

In the first photograph, the sword was one-third uncovered, its hilt messily surrounded by uncleared loose mud. Tyrone had to comment again. "I'd kick a digger off the site if he cleaned up that badly."

Ivor was still hovering. "I'm not an archaeologist," he said. "But I'd have liked better photographs to work up."

Revealed in its full length, the sword was shown being packed for lifting, then unpacked again on a laboratory bench. Its grip was shown being removed for separate conservation and a sequence of stills showed the rust-coated blade in various stages of cleaning.

"That's whatsername." Tyrone pointed to a woman in

a white coat who was dabbing the blade with a paintbrush. Archaeology was a small world; familiar faces cropped up all the time.

"Lucille," Flint said. "I'll remember where she works in a minute."

Ivor pointed to pictures of the grip being cleaned. "That's walrus ivory," he said, "I was amazed when I learned that."

As casually as he could manage, Flint slipped in a question. "How long have the Dunnings been part of your team?"

"We went into partnership after they asked us to do the graphics work on the sword."

"So how many of you are there?"

"Just Alison and me at the coalface."

"I thought you were bigger," Tyrone said, rather too bluntly.

"We were; there used to be six of us, it's the recession."

"I blame the government," growled Flint.

"Ah, we're organized now." Alison had crept up unnoticed.

"Ivor was just saying he was trusting to police to bring back the swords. Any idea who nicked them?" Flint suddenly realized his gaffe, but Alison failed to notice. She was too anxious to impress.

"If only I had. We've been working on this for a year, we've put everything into it."

"Everything?"

"Heart and soul," Alison said, her soul clearly depleted by the experience.

"Still here, Flint?" Gavin came up from behind.

"I'm just reading up on the story of the decade."

"We're not going to be sunk by a junior lecturer from

an obscure provincial polytechnic." Gavin turned to the others to shrink Flint's stature. "He didn't want to believe Mother, he thought Excalibur was a fake, but nobody steals the replica of a fake sword. Now he knows the truth he's feeling foolish. He's wishing it was he who found it. My mother will be remembered for Excalibur, what will you be remembered for Flint?"

"Integrity."

A deep thrust wounded Gavin and he flinched. "If it were not for you, we'd still have both swords."

"I doubt it."

Gavin half turned to Alison. "He's part of a scheme. Once Mother was dead, they decided they would destroy her discovery."

"Who?" asked Flint.

"The establishment, the academics, everyone whose ideas she overturned."

"Well they moved bloody quickly! The replica was taken before the discovery was even announced."

A scowl greeted the retort. Gavin squared up to Flint in an ancient, almost Neanderthal threat-posture. An automatic response was buried in Flint's male genes. He straightened himself to his full five-feet-ten. Weight for weight, height for height, it was an even match. Flint was reassured to have the bulkier figure of Tyrone just behind his shoulder. "Could we have a word Gavin? Just you and I?"

In a Leeds pub, the response would have been "Outside".

"If you can say it to one, you can say it to all."

"I want to ask you about your mother."

A slow shake of the head greeted the request. Gavin still held his aggressive stance, his fists visibly clenching and unclenching beside his thighs.

110

"Gavin." The woman called Gwen now entered the room and it was as if a bubble had burst. Gavin relaxed and flicked his head in response to a bead of sweat trickling down from his hairline.

Gwen formed the fourth corner of a box around Flint and Tyrone. She said nothing more, but her presence acted like moderator rods in a reactor core. That she was Gavin's twin was in no doubt, she shared the way he hung his forehead in silent distrust.

"Shall we go?" Tyrone asked.

Here was a chance to escape before the fist-fight broke out.

"Well, thanks folks." Flint forced a cheery air into the chill which had fallen on the room. "That was very enlightening. Funeral when?"

"Thursday," Gwen said quietly.

"I wouldn't come, if I were you," Gavin said.

"I expect you'll be short on room, with all the cameras and press men, but your mother was a friend of mine – you won't object to flowers, will you? A little bunch, won't take up too much space. Flowers can't talk, flowers can't watch you."

He felt a tug at his sleeve.

Alison kept up her PR image to the end, red lips spread sweetly into the nest of wrinkles. "I'll show you out."

For some time, Tyrone and Flint sat in the Spitfire, fifty yards down the street from the school.

"They're cashing in," Tyrone said.

"Before the ashes are cold," Flint mused. "Do you believe the great international conspiracy of academics?"

"Nar, most academics couldn't conspire to make a cup of tea."

"Where are we staying?"

Tyrone showed him the page in the hotel guide, then the town map. Flint memorized both.

"I'll see you there." He got out of the car.

"Don't pick any fights."

"I'm a pacifist, right?"

"Yeah, but are the other side pacifists?" Grinning at his parting shot, Tyrone revved his Spitfire then screeched away down the quiet backstreet.

Flint walked back towards the school, then loitered beside black railings which led up to the stone gateway. Gavin came out shortly afterwards, climbing into the red Peugeot, then throwing it into a jerky two-point turn. He stopped sharply at the gate to watch for traffic, then burst onto the street in a cloud of blue diesel fumes.

Gwen owned the second Peugeot, a white limited edition. Flint was by her side before she'd unlocked.

"Hi, we didn't have a chance to talk."

Chapter Eleven

Gwen shared the bubbly brown hair, so rampant in her brother. Her soft jawline might be the same as his, with beard removed. Her cheeks were less ruddy than those of her mother, her voice abraded by fewer years, her west country vowels shortened by Oxbridge education.

She appeared shocked by Flint's sudden appearance in the school yard. Too shocked, perhaps, to oppose his appeal. A host of bridge-building platitudes had tumbled from his lips and she had been unable to find polite means to resist. Any resolution in her character had been clearly shaken by the loss of her mother. Gwen proved an easy victim to charm and sympathy.

"At least, could I beg a lift into town? I don't bite."

Flustered, she took her own seat and unlocked the passenger door. She drove more sedately than her brother and Flint found the motion mildly soporific. Only a few minute's drive lay ahead, so he plunged in with a question about the night Harry had died.

"I don't understand what business it is of yours," the driver said. Her tone was polite, offended rather than aggressive.

"One, I was an old friend of your mother's—"

"She never talked about you."

"Old, old friend."

Brown eyes shot across at him, then focused back on

113

the tailgate of a lorry. Contact lenses glinted as sunlight caught them edge-on.

"What's your genuine reason?"

"I'm doing my job: I'm a contract archaeologist, trowel for hire. You have a nervous insurance company; more so since the weekend."

"Whatever you think, we're not doing anything underhand."

"Someone is. I thought you might be able to guess who."

"If I did, I'd tell the police."

She turned into the Sainsbury's car park. "I need to do some shopping."

"Can I push your trolley?"

"I'd rather be alone." Gwen was spoiled for parking spaces, but dithered over which to choose. With a whirr of the wheel and a jerk of the handbrake, she brought the Peugeot to a halt.

"If it isn't too painful, could you tell me what happened on Saturday morning? I understand you were coming down to your mother's for the weekend."

"I've had a long day. First there was the inquest, then the meeting." Gwen continued to grip the steering wheel as she spoke.

"Look, Gwen, time is short. In a week, the inquest is going to resume and it will bring down a verdict of accidental death on your mother."

Gwen was watching the shoppers passing by; empty hands left to right, full trolleys right to left. She watched as if at a tennis match, not caring who won what point, not even caring who was playing. Her eyes shifted left-right-left and she was trying to ignore Flint's probing.

"It doesn't strike you as strange that we had not one, but two inexplicable events in twenty-four hours?"

The windows began to steam up, and still Gwen would not respond.

"Look, to shut me up, can you tell me what happened on Friday night and Saturday morning?"

Slowly, Gwen spoke, as if reciting a shopping list. "The police, the reporters, friends, neighbours, relatives. Everything falls to me, you see. I've my own house and husband to look after, and I work. We're expecting a hundred people for the funeral, at least."

"Please, five minutes and I'll vanish from your life." Flint used his hang-dog, forgive-me, expression. It had been his last-ditch college chat-up ruse, saved for 1.30a.m. when the lady in question was poised on the doorstep of her digs.

"It will make the insurance people a whole lot happier if I can convince them everything's above-board."

At last her eyes flicked his way. "You're a bully – I've heard about how you operate."

"Oh, who from?" He sensed that Gavin had already plugged into the archaeological grapevine in order to understand who his opponent was.

"It's a strange thing you do, poking into other people's lives."

"Investigating dead people is what I was trained for."

"Meaning Mother?"

"Suspicious deaths have a habit of occurring in groups. The quicker we sort this one out, the more people will be alive at the end."

"You really are a suspicious person. You're never insinuating that mother was murdered, are you?"

"It's not beyond the bounds of probability. If you know otherwise, please convince me."

"She wasn't murdered, it was an accident."

"Convince me. I'm a scientist, I'm a slave to evidence.

115

Now you came down to stay at the house, the three of you had supper, I presume?"

"Yes!"

"Then what? How did your mother end up in the lake?"

Gwen was still gripping the steering wheel as she sighed, haughtily, adding more mist to the windscreen. "We had supper and I went to bed early." She gave a strained smile. "That's a little treat of mine – Derek, my husband, is a real night-owl. When he's away travelling, I go to Mother's and enjoy early nights with a good book."

"And presumably it's a quiet corner of the country, so you would have heard any unusual sounds. Do you know when Gavin came to bed?"

"Gavin virtually followed me upstairs." The response came quickly, her expression impressing him with its sincerity. "I heard Gavin come upstairs, then I heard mother taking Rimmy for a walk."

Rimmy had to be another Arthurian name, Flint was sure. A dog named Rimmy must feature somewhere in the mass of tales and Harry had given its name to her brainless Alsatian . . .

"Time?"

"Oh grief! Half-past ten, a quarter to eleven."

"And then what did you hear?"

"Nothing."

"No mother coming back, no dog barking, no cars, no intruders, no Gavin brushing his teeth?"

"Nothing after Gavin left the bathroom. I put the book down after a few pages because I was so tired from the drive."

"So, you slept, you woke, you went down for breakfast?" His hand motion urged her to continue the tale.

116

Gwen's face was now a colourless oval, her mouth dry, her words unwanted.

"When I came down to breakfast, Gavin was outside. It was raining. He came running in – he looked so dreadful." Gwen paused for a very long time. To distract herself from tears, she searched her handbag for a shopping list. She found it and checked it with silent lips before she could continue.

"And?"

"Gavin told me what had happened."

"Tell me, as precisely as possible."

"You sound like that policewoman."

"Only the accent differs."

"Please don't joke."

In short sentences, Gwen told the story of the Saturday morning. It had been around half-past eight when Gavin had burst through the cottage door, covered with mud, soaked by rain and smeared with his own vomit. Grey-faced and shaking he had told Gwen of the body by the lakeside, face-up, clear of the water, long dead and cold as the ground where she lay.

This confirmed what the pathologist had let slip, but rather than admit his knowledge, Flint feigned ignorance. "Surely Gavin must have pulled your mother from the water?"

"No. That's what the police said, that's what they kept trying to make him say. They said he forgot what he really did. I mean, he could have done, I'd have been frantic, I was frantic!"

Wild, open eyes confirmed her fear. "Gavin told me he went down to the lakeside and found mother lying on the bank, on her back, with her arms crossed across her like so." She imitated an Egyptian mummy, exactly as the pathologist had done.

117

"And he tried to resuscitate her?"

"No. He said she looked too serene, as if she'd died in her sleep. Its strange, but I found that comforting."

"Could he have said that just to be kind?"

"He's not like that – as you know." Gwen attempted to smile.

Flint tried to remember how hard it had rained that night. Could Gavin have become soaked by the rain alone, without entering the lake himself? How muddy could he have become, kneeling on the turf, even attempting mouth-to-mouth on his long-dead mother?

"If your mother drowned, how did she get out of the water?"

"The police say that Gavin pulled her out and tried to revive her. Gavin said that he knew resuscitation would have been pointless."

"People's memories can go blank when they suffer severe shocks. It must have been a horrible experience, and perhaps he's simply blotted it out."

"Perhaps."

"When did the dog come home?"

"Rimmy died too. We found her the next day, beneath the jetty on the lake. I think she must have jumped in to save mother." Gwen gave a little sniff and even Flint felt wet-eyed as he imagined the pathetic scene.

"Did the police examine the dog?"

"No – we buried her, by the lakeside. We're going to spread mother's ashes on the water. I thought they should be together."

The dog that didn't bark puzzled Basil Rathbone in *The Hound of the Baskervilles*. Flint had never read the book, but in the film the dog failed to bark because the villain was a member of the household. Rimmy had been an excitable and barely controllable dog. At the very least, he reasoned, she would have jumped around barking before plunging into the water: surely someone in the house would have heard? Flint tried to remember everything about the lake, as it had been on that last morning with Harry, calculating whether the house was too distant for the noise to wake its slumbering occupants.

Gwen was muttering something to herself, something to do with bread rolls. "Did your mother say she intended meeting anyone that evening?"

"No."

"And why did Gavin go out the next morning?"

"He was worried; the door was unlocked, Rimmy and Mother were missing, Mother was due to be picked up at 8.30 to go to her conference."

"By?"

The sharp closure of her eyelids and the silent motion of her lips said 'oh God'. "Merlin – no, that's not his real name, he's called Colin. He's one of those Pendragons, but he's not normal. He scrounges off people, he's that kind of freeloading hippy we're always seeing on the news."

"A traveller? And did he turn up at the appointed time?"

"Yes, on the dot, in his horrid little van."

A new culprit had driven onto the scene, one far more credible than a matricide. "And what did this Merlin do when you told him what had happened?"

"I don't know, no, I don't remember and I don't care. All I know was that I went to see Gavin in the kitchen, and when I came back, he was driving away."

"Have you told the police about him?"

"No. Would I have your approval if I did my shopping now?" She gathered her handbag with intent to leave the car.

A raw nerve had finally been touched by his probing. For a second time within a minute, the polite and sensitive Gwen had dismissed Merlin on reflex.

"One more question."

Gwen pushed her door part-open and held it there. "The last one, I really must do the shopping."

"Why didn't your mother go to the opening session of the conference on Friday night? She was booked for dinner; all her friends were there, it was her annual get-together with like minds, yet she stayed at home and cooked supper for you and Gavin."

"Yes."

"Why?"

"She was free to do as she wished. Those Pendragon people aren't her friends, they bitch and back-bite and quarrel about this word in a poem or the name of this castle. Mother had found better things to do."

Gwen opened her door to its maximum extent and placed a foot on the tarmac. Flint took the hint and did the same.

"Thanks a lot Gwen – sorry about the way I intrude, I'm as sensitive as a herd of elephants when I get going."

"I know you only want to help, but it's hard for us all, especially Gavin. He's still shocked. Give him space, don't upset him."

"Does that mean I'm barred from the funeral?"

"No – it might be awkward if Gavin makes a scene – but do come."

"What about Merlin, or Colin, or whatever he's called? Will he be coming?"

"No," Gwen stated. She was out of the car now.

"Pity, I need to —"

"I wouldn't bother," she said. "He's not worth it, he'll waste your time and start begging money off you. He

120

won't be coming to the funeral, he's mad, just forget about him."

Forget about him? Hell no, thought Flint. Gwen locked her car, give a silent farewell with a blink of her wet eyes, then moved off in search of a trolley. A sense of elation crept over him. Matricide had always seemed implausible: now he had a real suspect.

Chapter Twelve

The average L.A. private eye would spend his nights in a seedy downtown hotel, with a bottle of Bourbon for comfort. As this was Bath, and Flint was an archaeologist, he'd booked himself into a Georgian pub offering seven Real Ales and full English breakfast. He was only a few blocks away from the Roman baths at the heart of *Aquae Sulis* and when the modern world allowed, he would find the excuse to drop in, and drop back into the past for an hour or so.

Tyrone had staked a claim in the twin room, lying on his chosen bed, half asleep, half watching the local television news. Several sheep in the Quantocks Hills had been mysteriously torn apart and an 'eye witness' reported seeing a cat-like shape bounding across a field at dusk. Every age spawned more myths and legends and the 'Beast of Exmoor' was a modern addition to the list.

"Don't touch the mutton pie," Tyrone said, then aimed the remote control at the set and killed the picture.

"Wouldn't dream of it."

Flint took up his case and unpacked, yawning heavily as he remembered that a long, long day had followed a long and sleepless night. Even the Real Ale bar might be forsaken for the lure of a freshly made-up bed.

Once they had bantered over the qualities of the

room, the choice of beds, the dinner menu and the state of the plumbing, Flint retold Gwen's version of events.

"So we have another suspect," Flint concluded, arms behind his head, talking to the ceiling.

"Do you know anything else about this jerk called Merlin?"

"He's called Colin."

"Would be."

"You're denigrating people again."

"No, no, there's an old West Country legend about Colin, king of the fairies."

"King of the fairies," Flint repeated.

Tyrone took up a ring-binder in which he'd filed the paper notes they had made so far. A few moments sifting the pages brought him to the lists of conference delegates.

"Colin T. Barker. He wasn't at dinner."

"Aha, was he booked for dinner?"

"No." Tyrone betrayed his disappointment. "Not for any of the meals. He was a non-resident."

"Of course – Gwen said he was a traveller; he was probably camping somewhere."

"Wait on, I met him," Tyrone said. "Do you remember the train-spotter? A weasely guy with a pathetic little beard and that kind of black roll-neck sweater that went out of style in 1975?"

"About your age?" Flint remembered the figure in black, lurking by the bar on the Friday night, looking out of place amongst the grey heads. Yes, he'd made an appearance on Saturday too, and had been at the press launch in London.

"Harry said she'd introduce me to Merlin; that must have been who she meant. She seemed to have a soft spot for him; he may have a story to tell, most people have if you allow them the chance."

"If we get the chance," Tyrone said. "So we've got two priorities: first, we eat something, or I'm gonna die. Then, we find the king of the fairies."

Mutton pie was on the menu, but ignored in favour of the lasagne: a disappointing pre-potted affair heated beyond boiling point in the microwave. The battle for Real Ale was won, but the Campaign for Real Food had a long way to go.

In a dark-panelled hallway between the lounge bar and gents' toilet, Flint made a phone call to the secretary of the Pendragon Society. Without reluctance, Hewitt revealed a few more fragments of information about Colin T. Barker, aka, Merlin. He was a standing joke, a misfit in the Society and only Harry took him at all seriously. He never took meals and never paid for accommodation; he would sleep in his van and eat sandwiches to save money. Merlin had, of course, no fixed abode, but gave a forwarding address at Southampton University.

"Southampton?" Tyrone was clearly thinking of the price of petrol.

"Department of Business Studies. And we all thought he was mad enough to be an archaeologist."

"We could drive down tomorrow."

"OK, but we'll ring them first thing and see if anyone's at home."

He slipped his phonecard back into the machine and reported to his paymaster in Leeds. As he spoke, Flint was ingenious and discreet, contracting some of Tyrone's unhealthy disrespect for other people's motives. Humphries was told nothing of Merlin, Flint choosing instead to waft an air of suspicion around MPP.

124

"We want to pop into your local office later in the week, that OK?"

"Yes, you should," Humphries said.

Flint wanted to enquire which fool had been suckered into insuring the sword, but asked, "Who do we want to see?"

"The manager, South-western region. He's called Euan Trepennick."

A noise of alarm must have escaped Flint's lips.

"Flint? Are you all right?"

"Yes, yes. I'll speak to you tomorrow."

Humphries never spent a moment longer on the phone than he had to: it was the mark of a man who knew that time was money.

"Euan Trepennick is the local office manager," Flint repeated as they went back into the bar. "There can't be two of them."

Tyrone wiped crisps off his file and hunted out the delegates list. "Missing from dinner on the Saturday and breakfast on Sunday."

"Well, well."

"He could have planned coming just to see the presentation on the sword."

"Then why didn't he? And why book extra meals? We'd better check." Flint went back to the pay-phone. A young, blue-suited salesman was explaining to some woman (possibly his wife) why his return home would be delayed. On his turn, Flint redialled Patrick Hewitt and begged information on a second of his society members. Now Hewitt spoke with greater consideration, as if he respected Trepennick's privacy more than that of the itinerant Merlin. Yes, Euan was a long-standing member, yes, he normally attended the conference and yes, he was often at Harry's side. Hewitt ventured no tacky details about a man who was clearly a close friend.

"He's Cornish," Flint explained, when back in the bar.

"I'd never have guessed – he sounds like a character from *Poldark*."

"His office is in Bristol, he sells insurance, but his real love is Welsh and Cornish folklore."

"Another amateur."

"Well, we're amateur detectives, so I guess we'll be evenly matched."

Tyrone's features drew themselves into a protracted yawn, which Flint immediately contracted.

"And so to bed," he said. "And tomorrow, we have four choices on the menu; what do you fancy?"

Tyrone's options ran to Bristol, Southampton, Bath or Frome. Gwen could not be convinced of their need to see her again, and Mr Trepennick's secretary rebuffed them with a plague of prior commitments. For good measure, Flint had begged Hewitt for the telephone number of Charles Evans in Frome, but Evans complained he was busy and put them off until Friday. Fate, or the lords of chaos, saw the Spitfire heading for the south coast on the next leg of their Arthurian Anabasis.

A late start was inevitable, real linen sheets proved seductive, as did the breakfast. History unfolds slowly and on the last day of his thirty-fifth year, Flint was in no mood to hurry it along. They chose a scenic route and took lunch in a Tudoresque Winchester coffee shop. Tyrone made an excuse to go shopping for half an hour, so Flint wandered into the cathedral. He bought a postcard and sat in a pew, writing a brief message to Tania; now presumably back in Vancouver. Dark and

126

cold, the cathedral promoted melancholia and for several minutes, Flint felt very alone and very aware of growing old; worse, growing old alone.

Hurriedly he wrote Tania's address and slipped the postcard into his jacket pocket, then left the gloom for a brisk walk uphill to King Arthur's Hall, where he was to meet Tyrone. On one wall of the Hall hung a huge round wooden table, painted dartboard fashion and weighing three tons. At each place-setting was written the name of a knight, and at the top, 'Arthur'.

"It's fourteenth-century," a voice whispered from behind.

He half turned to acknowledge Tyrone's return.

"Edward the First had it made as part of a propaganda campaign against Welsh nationalists. He promoted the image of Arthur as an English Medieval knight in order to kill off the legend that he was a Celtic hero who would one day return to sweep the English from Britain."

"We've always moulded legends to suit ourselves."

"If you think about it, that's what Museum Projects Plus are doing."

"With the Arthur legend, or with the facts of Harry's death?"

"Both. Their motive is clear, their backs are to the wall and they're fighting off insolvency."

"A bit like UNY-DIG?"

Tyrone contorted his face, as if to dismiss his own gloomy warnings of financial catastrophe. "We should pull through."

"Worth a prayer down the cathedral?"

"Better ask for a miracle, just to be sure."

*   *   *

127

Even in vacation, some of the administrative staff of Southampton University were still to be found at their posts. Flint could drop sufficient names in the Archaeology Department to enter Business Studies with established bona fides. He'd arranged to drop in during the afternoon, when 'someone' would briefly be 'around'.

"Oh yes, poor Colin," the businesslike woman said, meeting them outside her office. They talked in the corridor, then walked along to the departmental office, where filing cabinet drawers rumbled open and secrets of the past were pulled out one-by-one.

"Colin dropped out about three years ago. We keep mail for him and he collects it from time to time."

"How far did he drop?"

"He had a nervous breakdown at the end of his second year, during the examinations. He never came back, except, as I said, to collect his post."

"When did you see him last?"

"Me, oh I don't know; not this year, but then I'm not the only member of staff. He drifts in, then drifts out."

After a week in which people had spoken obliquely, with incomplete truths and concealed motives, it was gratifying to meet someone quick to co-operate. The woman checked a sheet of photographs dating to Colin's first year. Her finger came to rest below the face of a short-haired, beardless freshman with square metallic spectacles.

"Poor Colin."

The face bore little resemblance to the Rasputin-like figure who had slunk around the conference, but Flint asked the woman for a couple of good quality photocopies taken for reference. People with guilty secrets had been known to shave off their beards.

"He was really nice," she said. "Polite, always interested in what you had to say and very clever. He was on line for a First."

She found the address given when Colin joined the faculty.

"He lived in Hull!" Flint said.

"Someone's got to," Tyrone added.

"But this is a pretty ancient address – do you know where he goes between his visits here, or how he earns his keep?"

The woman's face twinged at the question. "I don't think he has a job as such, but I know he sometimes performs card tricks at fairs. He showed one to me once."

"A travelling conjuror? Did he ever call himself Merlin?"

She looked baffled, as she should. Baffled described Flint's state of mind succinctly.

In the lobby of the department, he located a pay-phone, telephoned a number in Hull and spoke briefly to Mrs Barker, Colin's stepmother. No, he didn't live at home any more. No, she had no idea where he was. No, she had no address, no telephone number, no form of contact.

It was a small country, in a shrinking world. Within a few hours, Flint could have driven to any part of it. He could have used phone, or fax, or computer to make contact with anyone who wanted to be part of modern society, but this excluded Merlin. Merlin followed a different set of rules: no house, no job, no ties. He could vanish without even needing to hide.

Flint was pessimistic as they drove back westwards. He admired people who followed alternative lifestyles, but they could be damned hard to find. Tyrone was more optimistic, even bullish, convinced he had identified

129

someone worthy of the title 'suspect'. Convinced too, that he would prove easy to find.

"I know that type," he said. "Always on the scrounge, anything for a free feed. I bet your life he'll come to the funeral."

Chapter Thirteen

"Happy Birthday!"

As Flint stretched himself from another glorious night's sleep, Tyrone tossed something from the other bed. Reflexes took over where the brain was still slumbering. The box was book-sized, but light, and rattled as Flint caught it. Silver paper was covered in bug-eyed aliens. The message card read:

> *'Old archaeologists never die,*
> *they simply become residual.'*

People who have birthdays on April the First tend to keep quiet to avoid the obvious jokes. Out of the parcel came a video of *Monty Python and the Holy Grail*.

"I thought you needed it to keep a sense of perspective on King Arthur." Tyrone was pleased with his own choice. "The Pythons were all scholars you know, there's more critical insight in that film than in half the serious essays about Arthur. It's an example of how myths can be reworked to suit any audience."

"Many thanks, Dr Drake, for the gift of this erudite and scholarly work. How shall we celebrate my thirtieth birthday?"

"Thirty-fifth."

"I was rounding off the fractions. So, shall we have

131

a lazy day? Hang around the pub, working our way along the guest beer list? Find a good restaurant for lunch? Browse the book shops, mooch around the Roman baths?"

"We could go to the funeral."

"Perfect idea!" Flint exclaimed. "Nothing could be nicer. Happy birthday, Jeffrey." At least his new suit was a sombre grey.

Tyrone had been wrong about Merlin. He did not come to the funeral, unless present in the form of a crow in the grounds of the crematorium. A fresh, bright April morning saw Lady Dunning sent to join her ancestors, with the two archaeologists lurking at the back of the congregation. Mourners lingered in the sunshine after the curtains had closed and people allowed their grief to slip away. The faces were becoming familiar: Patrick Hewitt, for one, was sniffing at the spring air. Gwen worked her way along the trail of flowers which had been laid on the grass beside the door. She read the cards one-by-one. Flint hovered, watching the woman in the plain black dress. She smiled one of those brave smiles of one whose world was in turmoil.

"Isn't it a shame they will all die? Your lilies are very beautiful, thank you. And Mother would have appreciated the message."

"I had to come."

"Yes, of course, thank you."

She stopped speaking. Gavin was heading their way, a pair of reporters at his side. The funeral was being milked until its udders squeaked. Flint found himself in shot as a photographer found an angle on the mass of flowers and the bereaved children. He stepped promptly back into the

132

crowd, but Gavin turned his way, narrowing his eyes, speaking below his breath.

"Do the decent thing. Don't come back to the house."

One could resent the tone, but only a cad would ignore such a request.

"Did you say the same to Merlin?" Flint asked, remaining cool.

"As a matter of fact, yes. But he had the decency to stay away."

"I was very sorry about your mother," Flint said.

Gavin swallowed something, a little ire perhaps. He glanced away, fighting his own façade. "Yes," he said.

A brave-face-smile broke through Gwen's anguish for one moment. It was directed at Flint and he translated it as 'thank you now go away'. He nodded politely then turned away, looking for Tyrone, but spotted the portly figure of Patrick Hewitt, standing on the grass, talking to a large-framed man in suitably subdued tones. Despite his broad chest and upright bearing, the man leaned on a walking stick with his left hand.

"Ah, Flint, I don't think you've met Euan Trepennick."

"Dr Flint." Euan held out his right hand, clad in thin brown leather gloves. Sad blue eyes looked straight through Flint to green fields beyond. Silver-grey, his hair was parted neatly, its fringe taken across the forehead in a flamboyant wave. His manner and his grim expression carried no flamboyance.

Flint shook the hand, shocked by the sudden, sharp grip Euan used for a handshake.

"I tried to find you at the conference, but you were missing."

"Yes." Euan looked towards the crematorium, leaning heavily on his stick. "Other things happened."

"You're in insurance?"

133

"All my life." He was a good decade older than Matt Humphries, probably two. With neat, traditional suit, watch-chain and firm chin, Euan had a style and solidity that the younger insurance executive lacked.

"Not all your life, Euan," Hewitt chided, as if selling insurance was a wasted existence.

Euan simply grunted, unable to be shaken out of his personal grief. Perhaps he was vulnerable and Flint could strike.

"Could we have a talk, sometime?"

"What about?"

"Insurance."

Euan inclined his head and took half a dozen awkward steps towards the gate before he stopped. "Is the rumour true?" Euan asked quietly, as Flint caught him up.

"Rumour?"

"You had another midnight visitor."

"Ah, that rumour. It wasn't midnight, but yes, it's true."

Euan cleared his throat, still not looking Flint in the eye.

"You wrote out the policies on the swords, didn't you?"

"I did."

"And on Harry's life?"

"Yes."

"Big losses?"

"Ha."

"And now it all looks a little fishy."

The insurance man now snorted. 'Ivor the ink', the graphic designer from MPP was making his way towards them.

"So who's next?" Flint asked hurriedly. "Two swords plus Harry, that's three insurance pay outs. Why not four?"

134

"What are you suggesting?"

Flint was watching Ivor approaching, so the voice from behind came as a shock. Gavin had detached himself from the reporters and marched up unnoticed. "Dr Flint is suggesting that we killed my mother for a few pounds. Isn't that right? Do you honestly think her life was so cheap?"

"Gavin, I—" Euan began.

"Of course, don't worry about it, Euan. Forgive and forget."

Forgive what? thought Flint, whilst squaring up for Gavin's next broadside.

"Mother would have liked to see you here. You're just the man to squelch Flint's great criminal conspiracy."

Flint said nothing. Ivor was now beside Euan, immediately recognizing he'd walked into conflict. Gavin continued his game of isolating Flint.

"Flint thinks, you see, that after we killed our own mother, we stole our own sword —"

"Swords," Flint said, with deliberate bluntness.

"Pardon?"

"Swords – both swords have been stolen."

If one had swept off Gavin's head with Excalibur he could not have looked more astounded. Flint would have loved to have that expression captured on film and framed for posterity. Whilst Gavin was reeling, he summarized the second theft in a dispassionate, matter-of-fact voice.

"A single, well-briefed, thoroughly professional thief broke into college on Monday. He waited all night, then at dawn on Tuesday he stole the sword."

"The genuine sword?" Gavin asked.

"The genuine fake sword, yes."

Gavin's left eye began to tick, his lips quivered.

"I imagine the police will be in touch."

135

Lips quivered a little more.

"Gavin!" Gwen's voice called from amongst the mourners. Again it was her role to diffuse a crisis. Gavin said nothing more, even when Gwen came up and took his arm, he did not protest. As he was led away, he simply stared at Flint, mouth agog, eyes bulging in disbelief.

Ivor was on the verge of chuckling.

"He took it badly," Flint said.

"Unlike yourself," said Euan. "You seem to be taking this very light-heartedly."

"A fault of mine."

"Is it true?" Ivor asked.

Ivor said "shit" when Euan nodded confirmation. "Humphries rang me this morning. He couldn't control his glee."

Had Flint heard right? "Humphries?"

"Like you, he takes little seriously."

Flint had noticed a transient discomfort in Euan's face as Gavin had blundered into their midst, then there had been that 'forgive and forget' nonsense.

"We must have a talk, privately."

Ivor caught the remark and Flint became even more aware of being in a nest of strangers, with interlocking loyalties and unpredictable friction. He wasn't sure how close Ivor was to Gavin, or to Alison, or had been to Harry. Now Patrick Hewitt was closing in again; the secretary, the linchpin of the Pendragons. Names and faces surrounded him and Flint was causing offence at every step. Again he addressed Euan.

"Why don't we have lunch sometime? How about tomorrow?"

"I have a prior engagement for lunch."

"OK, when do you knock off? I'm chasing up old

Charles Evans in the afternoon, but I could pop around afterwards."

"If I say no, you'll keep pestering me, won't you?"

"'Fraid so."

"Shall we say five o'clock?"

"Wonderful."

Euan found a business card and pressed it into Flint's hand. He described how his office could be found and Flint became more confident with every 'left', 'right' and 'roundabout'. He'd make a nuisance of himself at Harry's lawyer's office in the morning, then it would be Charles Evans after lunch, Euan at teatime and with luck, solution by suppertime.

Tyrone sought sweeter prey. The policewoman, Detective Sergeant Chaff had been amongst the congregation and he was quick to move to her side once they were under the perfect blue sky.

"Ah, Dr Drake."

"Hello Stephanie, you're looking very neat."

"You should be in black."

Tyrone was conscious for the first time of his plum jacket. "It's all I brought. What are you doing tonight?"

"You're trying to pick me up? At a funeral?"

He shrugged. "I'm acting under orders."

"From the hairy one?" She began to walk towards the line of cars parked in the road.

"The police come to funerals to see whether the crooks turn up," Tyrone stated.

"I've come to pay my respects. There are no crooks in this case."

"Someone nicked our swords."

"So you reported – that's being dealt with, but not by me. Leave it to the professionals." She stopped by the

Spitfire, cast an eye over the damaged wing, then knelt beside his rear tyre, digging a fingernail into the tread.

"It's on the legal limit," she stated.

"Is it?"

Chaff walked slowly around the car, tut-tutting at the other tyres, then stood, shaking her head like a schoolmistress.

"So what do I get? Ten years hard labour?"

She managed a smile. "Get some new tyres."

"How about dinner tonight?"

"No."

"We're making up a party – it's Jeff's birthday, we're going to an Indian."

"No. And if you're driving on the same road as me, keep your distance."

Flint came up as the policewoman escaped in her Vauxhall.

"How's it going, stud?"

"Oh she's warming. We've been discussing rubber."

"Gavin has barred us from the funeral feast, so we have to buy our own lunch. I vote we go back for a ploughman's at the pub, then invade the Roman baths and overdose on inscriptions. I'm a bit sick of the Dark Ages, I'm getting withdrawal symptoms, I need a bit of classical culture to restore my sanity levels. After that, we'll hunt out the best nightlife *Aquae Sulis* can offer. I need to party."

As his birthday parties went, Flint's thirty-fifth proved quite civilized. Three distant acquaintances were dredged up for a mini-banquet in a Tandoori house, and two of them actually turned up. Over the evening, it was clear time had passed more quickly than any of the four imagined, the good old times proved truly old and not so good, conversation remained polite and inconsequential.

138

It was a drab way to start a year. No hangover, no memories one would like to forget.

Friday continued the trend. A morning visit to Lady Dunning's lawyers proved futile. No details of her will would be released until after probate and the solicitor refused to discuss her libel action against Charles Evans. To hear his side of the story they drove through the Mendips towards Shepton Mallet, rolling green hills capped by rolling grey clouds. Charles Evans lived in one of a trio of retirement bungalows slotted into an agricultural village on the southern slopes of the Mendips. He was not at home. They hung on his doorbell, peered in through windows, even called on his neighbours but Evans failed to appear.

"Senile old git," Tyrone muttered, as they sat in the Spitfire. Thin rain spattered onto the hood and dripped through a slash above Flint's left arm. Tyrone was wearing a camouflage army surplus jacket as a waterproof. He'd taped the name 'Drake' over the breast pocket. Any minute now, if he became bored, Flint expected his assistant to start stripping down the Bren gun which lay amongst the luggage in the boot.

Two hours crawled by. If he was out, Charles Evans did not return. Tyrone wiped the windscreen repeatedly to clear the view.

"I'm hungry."

"You're always hungry."

"No, but I'm really hungry."

"You've got a tapeworm."

When Tyrone told him it was five o'clock, Flint scribbled a note on a sheaf of writing paper and posted it through the letterbox of the bungalow. Defeated and frustrated, they drove a few hundred yards to the village shop. Flint crossed the road and went into the telephone box beside the pub. He was already late for the rendezvous with Euan Trepennick and telephoned his apologies. A female receptionist was told that Flint would be delayed for another half-hour.

As Flint left the callbox, Tyrone emerged from the shop with a pair of Cadbury's cream eggs. Still at the far side of the road, he tossed one into the air and Flint caught it neatly in two hands.

"Owzat!"

Two old ladies frowned at their antics.

"He'll wait for us," Flint said.

Tyrone bit into the cream egg as he started the car.

"Do you want me to drive?" Flint offered.

"Not after last time." Tyrone engaged the gears and moved away, not bothering to check his mirror, paying no attention to the van which smoothly moved off in his wake. Tyrone swallowed another mouthful of sticky chocolate and fondant. "We want to get there, after all."

Bath lay some twenty miles away, across the Mendip Hills, now falling into a gloomy early twilight of a rainswept English spring. Tyrone turned on his side-lights, but not so someone else. The orange van was still following, its driver using no lights.

A road sign pointed the road to Bath.

"Bath," said Flint, with his short-voweled pronunciation.

"Barth," Tyrone corrected with his best BBC English. "*Mons Badonicus*, or so says Charles Evans. I read one of his papers, you know. He claims Bath is the site of the battle of Mount Baden, AD 518, but the earliest accounts of the battle don't mention Arthur at all: he was added by the Welsh."

A little sleepy, and more than a little irritated, Flint

allowed Tyrone to ramble on with his deconstruction of the Arthurian legend.

"Now Badon was supposed to be Arthur's twelfth and final battle, but then we have Camlann cropping up in the Annals of Wales for 539. It's anomalies like that which make the whole mythology just fall apart."

Flint thought he'd joint he debate, if only to keep himself awake. "But 'Camlann' simply means 'great slaughter' in Welsh, so Camlann and Mount Baden could be one and the same. Bath is just close enough to Glastonbury for the legend to have shifted that far. The wonderful thing about Arthur is he's all things to all men and in as many places as you want him to be."

As he spoke, Flint watched the rain-soaked hills rather than the twisting road. Ancient riddles took second place to modern riddles and Gavin still occupied the role of chief villain. He worried about Merlin, and would worry until he met him. He worried about Charles Evans' motives for avoiding the meeting. The past and the present were shot through with death and conspiracy, growing gloom and a watery end. Tyrone was rubbishing Valerie Chastel's idea of a Breton Arthur as the Spitfire neared an outside bend. He noticed motion in his mirror, the van without lights was moving to overtake.

"Prat!" Tyrone cursed, then ran out of road. The orange van was in the outside lane, swaying towards him. The lightweight car shuddered and slewed across the wet road. Tyrone braked, Flint gripped the dashboard, a fence rushed towards them, the car began to slide, then jerked back and hit the timbers head-on. Flint ducked as the windscreen shattered and the car lurched downwards. The next jarring impact brought Flint's jaw slamming into the dashboard, then threw him upright. Another impact came, this time solid, then an object the size

141

of a sack bounced up the bonnet and carried away the rest of the windscreen and hood. His head was thrown up and clouds spun dizzily by. With the final impact came darkness.

PART TWO

Chapter Fourteen

Being dead solved many problems, it opened many possibilities. Flint could invite Julius Caesar to lunch, or go on a pub-crawl with Atilla the Hun. He could ask Harry 'whodunnit' and why. He could even seek out the 'real' Arthur and sift out the facts from the rubbish of mythology. But dead people can't write papers, or deliver lectures or stand in the witness box. Why was his mind wandering like this? Why were messages of pain flooding every sensation? He must have been at the dentist, he always had peculiar dreams at the dentist.

After a few hours, or a few moments, he awoke. His face hurt, his shoulder hurt, he could smell something awful. He could hear running water, dripping water. He could hear the wind, see a stark tree, see a flock of sheep running up a slope. All down his arm was a warm, wet, stickiness.

The red ooze of death ran from his shoulder to his knee. It splashed across the handbrake, where Tyrone's hand still rested. It doused the dashboard and the shattered remains of the windscreen. Tyrone's hand moved. Blood-soaked, the hand lifted off the handbrake and touched his shoulder.

"Doc, Doc!"

"Tyrone?"

With his mask of blood and ripped combat jacket, Tyrone could have walked off the set of a Vietnam video.

"They crashed us off the road!"

"Are you all right?"

Tyrone unclipped his seatbelt and stretched back his neck.

"Petrol!" he mumbled, trying to unfasten the door. "Gotta get out."

Flint opened his own door and tumbled into water, banging his hand on a rock. The Spitfire was nose down in a stream, water bubbling through the wheel arches. Tyrone climbed over the seats and slid out of the passenger door to help Flint to his feet.

"OK?" he asked.

"Alive," Flint responded, still not quite certain of his facts.

In the movies, American cars crashed in a spectacular explosion of flame, but the Spitfire simply sat in the stream, its engine ticking as it cooled, petrol and oil being carried away as a rainbow on the surface of the water. The silence was beautiful in itself.

First Tyrone, then Flint was drawn towards a bloody ragged bundle that was caught up in a tangle of hood, fence posts and windshield in the void behind the seats. A very dead sheep had left a broad stripe of blood and offal across the camouflage.

"I thought all that was yours," Flint said.

"I thought it was yours. They tried to kill us!"

Flint looked back up the slope. The road wound around the head of a small valley and crossed a bridge over the stream. A gaping hole in the fence could clearly be seen, as could the tyre marks and trail of destruction running a hundred yards down towards the wrecked car.

Two figures were standing at the gap; men in jackets, broad-shouldered and young. They were coming down.

Still dizzy, Flint recognized that the crisis was far from over. "Time we got out of here."

"Bastards!" Tyrone cursed. He pulled up the boot lid, which was half hanging open.

The men were closer now. Flint could see their faces in the gloom: white men, young men. Tyrone pulled out the Bren gun.

"Tyrone, the toy gun trick doesn't work, I've tried it!"

"Right Bastards!" Tyrone spun around, a blond, blood-soaked incarnation of Arnold Schwarzeneggar. The men stopped, exchanged one look, then ran.

"Yeah run!" Tyrone yelled.

Flint slumped against the car, laughing weakly. Tyrone continued to yell B-movie threats and abuse.

"Hey, hey, Arnie. Much as you'd like to, you can't waste them. The gun doesn't work."

And it was heavy. It went limp in Tyrone's arms and he dropped it onto the wet turf.

"Your policewoman was right about your tyres."

"We're alive, and remember who was driving."

Yes, Flint could recall the way the car had slewed across the road, then corrected itself just before it hit the fence. Somehow, Tyrone had retained control of the bouncing car, parking it upright and front-first at the bottom of the valley. Rolling in a soft top would not have been funny. Wasn't there a saying amongst pilots that a good landing is one you can walk away from?

The thumping in Flint's head was growing worse, so he settled down onto the wet grass, rolling onto his back allowing the rain to splash his face, spreading his arms crucifix-form.

"What a way to spend Easter."

The blasphemy was wasted on Tyrone, now busy around the wreck. He jerked the slippery mass of sheep and hood onto the ground, then walked around his car. The bonnet had half risen, the front bumper had been left behind. One front wing had disintegrated in a cloud of rust, the other one, the grey undercoated one, was buckled. The radiator was pushed back and punctured and both headlights were eyeless. The damage caused by Flint's argument with the gatepost now looked insignificant.

"My car, just look at it! The bastards!"

Flint still gazed at the sky, enjoying the rain, enjoying being alive. "It's only a possession – that's what insurance companies are for."

Ow! Talking hurt. Flint touched a hand to the side of his face that had met the dashboard. He still spoke to the clouds. "Was it insured through Humphries's lot?"

"No."

"Pity."

Flint moved each of his limbs in turn. Nothing *seemed* broken. He rolled his head from side to side, trying to understand the damage to his shoulder. "Look on the bright side. Now you can buy your jeep."

Tyrone stooped down to the stream, scooping up freezing water to wash sheep from his face. Once the blood had gone, a smile crept in to take its place.

"Yeah."

An ambulance arrived with wailing sirens, but departed in more sedate manner, taking the casualties to Bristol General Hospital. Tyrone was released on the Saturday morning and collected by Detective Sergeant Chaff, which must have made the injury worthwhile. Flint remained 'for further tests', an ominous phrase which

148

can mean anything from 'we think you're dying' to 'we cocked up the X-rays'.

His head and jaw were swathed like a mummy. He shook it slowly when the nurse asked if he was in a private health scheme. If he was, presumably he could pay to make the pain go away. Her name was something enormous and Polish and she reminded him vaguely of Brezhnev. He mentioned that he'd once visited Warsaw, but she only raised her bushy eyebrows, before striking his name off the list she carried. Then he was alone, with his thoughts, with six other patients and with a long view of a grey movie on the ward television. It was an English Period melodrama; he spotted Margaret Lockwood, but soon gave up guessing the title.

Someone had tried to kill him: someone with little sense of poetry. To have died on his birthday would have given his tombstone a neat symmetry. He thought of the stonemason suddenly troubled by arithmetic, trying to work out whether the victim had been thirty-five or still thirty-four. Flint smiled, then the pain struck home once more.

Someone had tried to kill him. A long list of names dangled before his eyes and any of them could have been responsible. In the West Country amongst the Pendragons, the Dunnings and the MPP crew he was an alien, neither trusted nor wanted. He was out of touch and now he was out of action. With no chance of making a score he should retire hurt before he was bowled out.

Detective Sergeant Chaff and two uniformed men followed Tyrone down the slope in the Mendip Hills. The archaeologist had his right arm in a sling: it was a good fashion accessory and supported the elbow he'd cracked on the door handle. The black eye, and the large dressing

149

where the seatbelt had burnt his neck added to his piratical appearance. An ill-fitting set of casual clothes had been loaned by the hospital to replace his torn, sodden and blood-soaked army surplus gear.

Chaff paused momentarily beside the sheep. "Now we know the secret behind the Beast of Exmoor: it's you two killing off the sheep."

"Did you catch the two villains?" Tyrone asked. "Our descriptions must have been spot-on."

"If you mean two students from the Art College who witnessed the crash, they came in and reported it. They also reported that when they had tried to help, a madman threatened them with a gun."

She was looking over the camouflage finish on the car, now largely spoiled by mud, blood and scratches. "They said that a man in a combat jacket was going mad with a machine-gun. Does that ring any bells?"

One of the uniformed men opened the boot and passed out the luggage which had been abandoned overnight. Next he brought out the Bren gun. He spaced his words as he spoke. "What – is – this?"

"Bren gun, 1944 . . ."

"Yeah, yeah," Chaff said, being handed the gun, her arm sagging at the weight. "We know what it is, but why is it in your boot?"

"It's decommissioned."

"A bit like your car? Have you a firearms licence?"

"Not yet."

"Well, I think we'll keep this until you get one. The county will be an awful lot safer. Do you know that one of our local papers has printed a 'Mad gunman on the loose' story in its early edition?"

She was trying to make him feel small, but Tyrone refused to shrink. He stuck his free hand into a pocket and

150

watched passively whilst the policemen took photographs and made notes. Chaff leaned on his Bren gun, butt down, as she issued orders.

"It's a write-off," one of the men said. "I'd take all the valuables out of it, then arrange for a scrap dealer to tow it away."

Moisture formed in his eyes. Tyrone had bought that car in his undergraduate days. He'd painted it, cleaned it, loved it, won women and traffic offences with it. The loss was personal.

"It's only a car," Chaff said, giving him a slap on his fit shoulder. "I think we ought to go over your statement again now I've seen the state of things."

Tyrone snapped out of mourning. "Over lunch?"

"Coffee and sticky buns at the station is as far as I'll go."

"That's a start."

Tyrone was already at Bristol Templemeads railway station when Flint arrived later that afternoon. He was slouching on a bench, surrounded by their luggage. Flint sat down next to him.

"The Return of the Mummy," he mumbled through the bandage.

"Is your brain OK?"

"Yeah, still there. Nurse said mustn't use it for a week."

"Was she pretty?"

"No; yours?"

"No."

"Another modern myth dies."

They contemplated the departures monitor for a while before Tyrone spoke again. "I got her home phone number."

"Nurse?" Flint asked, pronouncing it 'nurfe'.

"No, Stephanie."

"And the thugs?"

"'fugf'?" Tyrone mimicked the pronunciation. "Those two were do-gooders, a couple of students. They saw a van crash into us and came to help."

"Damn good job that gun was a fake, then. Imagine the parable of the Good Samaritan if the injured traveller had pulled a gun. What sort of lesson would that teach us?"

"That the New Testament post-dates 1944." Tyrone's spirit, if not his car, was still intact.

"Did the Good Samaritans give a description of the van?"

"Box-back, red or orange, but I saw that much. It had been following us for miles, you know. I think I even saw it in the village, when we were buying the cream eggs."

Skin turned to goose flesh at the implications. "They certainly meant to get us. And they got us."

"It's time for some revenge."

"You mean time to give them a second chance to kill us? No, it's time to go home and have my mum say 'Ooh Jeffrey you could have been killed' and doss on her settee and watch the reruns of *Jesus of Nazareth* and *Ben Hur* and scoff the chocolate cake she made for my birthday. We're cutting our losses and crawling back north with tails between legs. 'Sorry Matt, old mate, we tried'."

Tyrone stood to his feet. A train was rumbling towards the platform.

"We'll be back. We need the work, we need the money."

"We need proper work and kosher money."

"But if they tried to kill us, it means we were close."

"Damn right. As close as I ever want to be."

Chapter Fifteen

Pain subsided, bruises faded and Easter passed by. Arthur, and Harry and the sword, and Flint's shaven chin receded into the past. The events of a tragic week in the West Country could be viewed with a historic perspective, like an ancient artifact in the conservation lab could be cleaned and preserved without needing to be understood.

It was the University vacation, but the dedicated academic is never truly on vacation. Archaeologists are supposed to dig, so the first-year students were given a five-day crash course in the rudiments of survey and excavation. For UNY-DIG it was an opportunity to train cheap labour for the summer digging season.

An injured arm gave Tyrone the perfect excuse to avoid any heavy work. He was never one to lead from the front, always happier behind a desk or a computer terminal where the past could be reduced to clean script and neat figures. For Flint, five days of organized mayhem in rainswept Ripon offered the perfect excuse to avoid thinking about the chaos he'd left far to the south: just what the nurse ordered.

Someone had attempted to kill him, or at least had been indifferent to whether he had survived the crash. The police were silent on possible suspects and Harry's inquest had closed with a verdict of accidental death. Soon the new term would be upon him. Keen and promising students would demand his time. Dull and protracted committee meetings would steal it. He returned from the field course determined to concentrate on being Flint the lecturer, not Flint the detective.

Back in the UNY-DIG office at the University, a fortnight's mail waited patiently for attention. Across the room, Tyrone was working through the accounts. He would sigh or snort at intervals. The way he ran his hand through his hairline, then pulled at his neatly-cropped crown betrayed his problems.

"How bad is it?" Flint asked, skimming a letter into the 'pending' pile.

"I'm going to have to make myself redundant."

"That bad?"

"We're still owed over eleven thousand pounds, not counting that invoice I sent off to the insurance crowd in Leeds. Is there anything in the post?"

"Three tenders turned down. One new one, the Doncaster Robin Hood centre."

"That's crazy, Doncaster must be fifty miles from Sherwood Forest."

"So was Robin Hood. He was born in Wakefield, just around the corner from my gran. The Merry Men hung around in Barnsdale, a few miles north of Doncaster and bushwhacked merchants using the A1. The real Robin Hood probably never went near Nottingham in his life."

"Shall we go for it?" Tyrone would pursue the scent of any potential contract.

"One English folk hero at a time, that's my rule."

"I thought you'd given up on Arthur?"

So he had, until that morning when a fax slithered from the machine and was stuffed into his pigeonhole. Squeaking around in his chair, Flint felt as if he occupied the 'siege perilous', the seat at the Round Table reserved for the perfect knight. Any other who dared to occupy it would be destroyed. Was he worthy, thought Flint, or if he ventured out again, would he be destroyed?

The fax lay at the bottom of the 'pending' tray, just below a copy of the previous day's *Daily Express* removed from the common room. It would only take a few minutes to leaf through the last minute travel bargains, then with just a couple of phone calls, the knights would be committed to the quest once more.

"It would help if there was a reward for Excalibur," Tyrone continued. "We only need ten K to square the books."

"You're our financial genius, tell me where we're going wrong."

"We're hamstrung by the college. If we didn't have to pay their overheads, we'd win more tenders."

"I sense a tug on the leash."

"If this was my company, I could run things the way I wanted to."

"Sack yourself and go freelance."

Tyrone grimaced, although he was already clearly assessing the possibilities. "We've got to sort this Arthur mess out first."

"Why?"

"Because we were made to look like idiots, we were set up. I want to get the bastard who smashed up my car and nearly got us killed."

"And Harry, don't forget Harry. And her dog."

"Let's avenge the sheep too, but let's not give up."

"I'm not giving up – we have a lead."

That fax was pulled from beneath an overburden of 'pending' mail. The Metropolitan Police had attempted to trace the stolen swords via Europol and had received a curious response from Italy.

"Know the Museum of Roman Culture?" Flint asked.

"Rome, yes. They've got that terrific model of the ancient city."

"Two years ago, a Byzantine cavalry sword was stolen from their reserve collection." Flint lifted the fax as written proof.

"Our sword?" Tyrone pounced on the idea.

"It could be; look at the description; the size and weight are about right."

He passed the fax across and Tyrone nodded gravely as he assessed the contents. "DEVS NOBISCVM." Tyrone read the motto said to have been inscribed on the stolen sword. "Stolen! So Lady Harry was a crook."

"Or very gullible."

"So what now?"

"We need to find out if we're talking about the same sword. Remember Julio Lippi at CCL?"

"Yeah, a real poseur." Tyrone almost snarled with scorn.

"Perhaps, but he's at the Museum in Rome now. I rang him earlier, he's going to sort you out at that end."

"Me?"

"For better or worse, I'm going to Newcastle on Friday. Get yourself a bucket shop flight – your Italian will get you by. Unless of course, you'd rather go to Newcastle."

"No, Rome's fine."

The gauntlet was down and Flint had picked it up. The *'Express'* travel section fluttered across the office and Tyrone snapped it between his hands.

"Off you go then."

Between Rome and the sea lies an epitaph to Fascism,

156

known as the EUR. Mussolini's grandiose suburb was never completed, overtaken by other, less aesthetic projects in 1940. The wide, empty streets hold none of the appeal of bustling central Rome. Tyrone was a true classicist and thought little of the brutal architecture of the monumental buildings, whilst the Museum of Roman Culture would have offended the eye of any cultured Roman. Once past the security desk, a forbidding exterior is replaced by a dark and gloomy interior, worst visited on an overcast day with drizzle falling from Italian skies.

"You brought the weather with you," Julio said as he shook Tyrone by the hand. Tyrone had discarded the sling and his face now carried only a hint that it had been badly bruised.

Julio had been at Central College London when Tyrone was an undergraduate. The disdain they felt was mutual, Julio had an impeccably polished chat-up technique but none of Tyrone's intellectual drive. Julio won the girls, Tyrone won the first Class Honours and the PhD. It was known that Julio's father had money and it was whispered he knew people in the Mafia, but then Tyrone's father had money and was something in the Freemasons. When Julio clapped Tyrone on the shoulder and promised to lead him to a good restaurant and on to a chic nightclub, Tyrone fell into an insincere old-chum-weren't-the-old-times-great routine.

The pair had more in common than either would admit.

The Byzantine sword had been stolen from a conservation laboratory, along with a dozen other finds of varying value and antiquity. The photographs Julio produced were poor: Italy has such an abundance of archaeology they can sometimes be careless. The British, with their

157

impoverished ancient history, pay almost extravagant attention to detail. Julio was plainly embarrassed when Tyrone laid out sheaf after sheaf of detailed photographs, drawings and X-rays.

"The sword was Byzantine, it was brought back from Albania during the 1930s."

By 'brought back', Julio was disguising the word 'looted'. He brought in the conservator who had cleaned the sword. She was in no doubt about the blade.

"It read *Deus Nobiscum* along here, but this here, I don't know the English words . . ."

Tyrone shifted to Italian. "The guard?"

"Guard, yes. Is different."

On the Italian photographs, the guard was a bronze disc, the grip did not survive and the pommel was a plain sphere, also of bronze.

"These pieces are north European, not Roman," Julio said, pointing to the cross-guard and pommel on Tyrone's pictures.

Immediately, Tyrone visualized an expedition to Denmark, then to Norway, Sweden, the possibilities were enticing. Julio read too much into his gleeful expression.

"So you might be able to get our sword back?"

Tyrone could not be as positive as he'd like to be. In a casual tone he asked the all-important question "Is there a reward?"

"No, it's worth little – three, five million Lire."

"What, ten pence?"

"No, no, one maybe two thousand pounds."

Tyrone was fully aware of the conversion rate and Julio was slow to raise a smile at the joke.

"No reward," Julio repeated.

His brow crumpled by deep thought, Tyrone rested on his elbow and studied the two scale drawings laid

158

side by side. Both swords shared the same inscription, both had low intrinsic values and both were now missing. An idea began to form in Tyrone's mind, what he called a Flintish idea, offbeat and perpendicular to the normal line of thought. Julio was shaking his head.

"It's not the same sword," he said.

"No," added the conservator.

Deep in thought, Tyrone repeated, "No."

Tyrone stood up, pulling himself away from his Flintish ideas. He began to put his material into order so he could pack it back into its carrying case.

"I'm afraid you've wasted your journey," Julio said.

Tyrone ceased frowning and began to beam. "Oh, I wouldn't say that. Where's this restaurant you were telling me about?"

At least two archaeological congresses take place on each of the weekends leading up to the Easter break and those following on. After a short break, conference season would continue through the early summer. It was a central plank of Flint's academic life that he wangled at least one expenses-paid trip per term and had to fight against inconvenient clashes.

EMADARG could have been a Celtic chieftain, or perhaps a New Age synthesizer group, but the small print of the poster on the University notice-board proclaimed this was the Early Mediaeval and Dark Age Research Group. Their annual meeting would be in Newcastle that weekend. Whilst Tyrone was sipping cappucinos and rehearsing the Italian version of 'do you come here often?', Flint was drinking Newcastle Brown and trading gossip.

Mussolini would have liked the conference venue,

159

a student hall of residence designed as a forbidding concrete fortress, intruder-proof and escape-proof. It was more modern than Edgar Jenkins Hall, but the rooms were equally bleak, the corridors equally labyrinthine and the radiators served more to trap dust than circulate heat.

EMADARG proved to be the kind of conference Flint could warm to: plenty of fresh postgraduates, digging archaeologists and active academics. Lectures probed the real Dark Ages, not the romantic fantasy of the Pendragon Society. Yes, some of the slides were upside-down, but they showed actual sites and genuine artifacts, which were discussed in wholly scientific debate.

Around the bleak and functional bar that Saturday night were a number of familiar faces Flint had encountered in Bath a fortnight before: Pendragons in different guise. The conference organizer was an acquaintance and had sent Flint a provisional list of delegates by electronic mail. It was what had drawn him north at a day's notice.

"Mr Evans?"

Charles Evans had been sitting in one of the low-backed soft orange chairs, lips tickled by the froth of a half of Guinness. Across a low circular table sat Pauline Cook, another Pendragon who had missed her prepaid dinner at Edgar Jenkins Hall.

"Dr Flint. How are you? I heard —"

"I'm fine, my assistant is OK, but his car was a write-off." A stiff and troublesome neck and shoulder came back to give lie to what Flint had just said.

"Oh, the car crash!" Pauline Cook said. "How awful."

"Dreadful," Evans echoed.

Flint slid himself onto the yielding orange seat beside

Pauline Cook, who was bright-eyed but dressed in a shambles of old green cardigan and kilt, not unlike a fifty-year-old schoolgirl. Flint had been hoping for some instant apology from Evans. None was offered unprompted.

"We came down that Friday."

"And I was out, so sorry, the date simply slipped my mind. I haven't been well, you see, I had written you down as coming on Saturday."

"Yes, well, I've got you now." Flint winked at Pauline Cook. "He can't escape, can he?"

"He can't," Pauline confirmed. "You stay put Charles and be interrogated." She half whispered an aside to Flint, "I'm correct in saying you're the detective one?" Her accent indicated that Newcastle was home territory.

Charles Evans took in rather too much of his Guinness and his old school tie recorded another stain.

"I was intending asking you of your opinion of the Arthur Roadshow," Flint said. "I've spoken to a number of people about it; most people are rubbishing Harry's ideas about a Roman Arthur."

"Quite right. Arthur was a Welsh hero, he defeated the Romans, read your texts, my boy."

"That's tripe!" Pauline said. "Don't listen to this old fool."

Evans first flashed his eyes at the rebuke, then snarled with better humour. "This is an academic conference, what are the likes of you doing here?"

The white-haired man squinted at Flint and gave a self-indulgent cackle. "Further Education teachers think they know everything. Take it from me, Arthur was Welsh."

Pauline came back instantly. "The Welsh don't have any history, so they stole ours."

161

"Ah, get away!" Evans argued. "I have to listen to this woman every year."

"If you're looking for the true Arthur, he's right here," Pauline said. "His Battle of the Caledonian Forest is the only one we can truly place. You see, Arthur operated in northern England, fighting the Picts. All the legends originated on the Scots borders and were adopted by the Welsh bards at a later date . . ."

So around and around the argument went: Arthur was Welsh, Scots, British, Breton, Roman. The mists of time wrapped him firmly about and would never be parted, no matter how hard scholars would try.

"And Excalibur?" Flint blurted into the cut-and-parry of debate. "Who believes that Harry had found the real Excalibur?"

"Nobody," said Pauline. "Excalibur was an invention of Geoffrey of Monmouth."

"Caliburn goes back into Welsh myth!" Evans objected.

"But who did Harry tell that she'd found it?" Flint brought the discussion to its point.

Neither said anything immediately. Both looked guilty.

"Well, you knew," Pauline accused Evans.

"I know, I know, and he knows that, he's asked me before."

"But who told you?" Flint asked.

"Well, Euan Trepennick told me," Pauline said, "he was drumming up support for Harry, so she could read her paper at the conference. I told him not to be silly, Excalibur never existed."

Flint turned to Evans. "But you just said that you believe in Excalibur – so did you believe in Harry's find?"

"No." Evans glanced towards the far end of the room, squinting at something. He looked back, deep into Flint's eyes, as if imparting the wisdom of age. "Some people think that dear departed Lady Dunning was the leading expert on Arthurian Britain. Others think she was a stuffy, obstinate old woman without an ounce of scholastic ability. I'm in the latter category. Excuse me, I must . . ."

The tiny sign on the door at the end of the room read 'GENTS' and Evans lumbered towards it. Flint knew of so many talented archaeologists and ancient historians named Evans, but this, he was sure, was not one of them.

"He didn't like Harry, did he?"

"That can't be surprising, can it?" Pauline replied.

"Why did she sue him?"

"She brought out a book – *A Guide to Arthur's Britain*. Her son published it, did the marketing and all that. Well, Charles reviewed it in a magazine – which was it now? Well, he wrote something to the effect that the only accurate pieces of information were culled from other people's books. In short, he accused her of plagiarism, which is possibly true, but one shouldn't put such things in print."

Flint had to agree. Academic egos were touchy at the best of times. "We missed you at dinner, at Edgar Jenkins, on the Saturday night."

"Did you?"

"We took a kind of roll-call."

"I was . . . no, I couldn't face the conference, not after hearing about poor Harriet."

"But if I understand the politics of the Pendragons, you were not one of her confederates?"

"We are rather more subtle than you think. I was very fond of Harriet, even though I disagreed with her. Charles is in fact very close to her in terms of their

163

historical viewpoint, but, as you can see, there was no love lost."

Flint had seen this so many times in so many clique-ridden learned societies. "Oh God, save us from society politics!"

"But the Pendragons can be wonderfully enervating," Pauline said. "We're like a big happy family. Harry was like a sister to me, and Charles and Euan and Patrick are like cousins who one only sees at family reunions."

"What about Merlin?" Flint asked. "Not the wizard, the young chap who lurked around at the beginning of the conference. Where does he fit in the family tree?"

"Black sheep?" Pauline smiled. "Poor, poor Colin. He can be endearing, but . . . an embarrassment to the Society."

"I'd like to meet him, I was hoping he might turn up here."

"No, he'll be at a funfair somewhere. He drives around the country in one of those *deux chevaux* vans."

"Harry seemed taken by him."

"Well, he could be charming, when he washed, which wasn't always. He's very witty and of course we don't have many young members. I think Harry took him under her wing in order to indoctrinate the Pendragons of the future. In ten years time, we'll all be losing our marbles and dear Colin will most likely be president."

A loud cheer came from the younger end of the room. A student bounced across one of the soft seat settings and landed in a spare place amongst old friends. Flint knew the lure of the annual conference, a once-a-year chance to meet a particular set of people. It was an excuse to let down the hair and counterbalance the intense tedium of historical research.

"I imagine your annual family reunion must be a lot of fun."

"It is," she said. "It's not quite . . ." She jabbed her finger towards where the students were still playing fools, "but I'd never miss it."

"But families bicker, there are skeletons in the cupboard?"

"A few, just enough to keep tongues gossiping."

"Pack a hundred people of mixed sex off for the weekend and things are bound to happen. Last night, for example, whoever was in the room above mine spent an entertaining night."

Pauline Cook actually blushed. Perhaps she'd missed the sexual revolution. "Our conferences are not like *that*."

"No hanky panky? No juicy scandals? What were people saying about Harry, the night she didn't turn up for the opening session? People always talk about the one who isn't there."

For some reason, Pauline's eyes strayed towards the Gents' toilet.

"I'm very worried about your friend Charles," said Flint. "Someone arranged a crash the day I was supposed to meet him. I don't know who, but my suspect list is pretty short." He lied a little here; it was growing longer by the day. "I'm looking for someone who didn't like Harry. I'm looking for someone with a motive to kill her."

"It can't have been Charles," Pauline said, all the good humour now gone.

"He knew precisely where we would be that afternoon and he had a good reason for wanting us out of the way."

"But Charles is so frail, he suffers from high blood

pressure! That libel writ from Harry was taking its toll."

"So he had a good motive to kill her – you can't libel the dead."

Chapter Sixteen

The cottage at the edge of the moors was one Flint could grow quite attached to, were he given the chance. He enjoyed being there, when not at College, or at a conference, or excavating, or staying over with friends. Some day, he would make time to make himself a home, although he suspected that day might not come until he retired.

After driving down from Newcastle in the UNY-DIG van, he turned on his gas fire and popped a video into the machine, before settling down with beans on toast in lieu of Sunday dinner. The time seemed apt to watch the rest of John Boorman's *Excalibur*; myth and gore, Carmina Burana and Wagner, Cheri Lunghi and Helen Mirren with her kit off.

By now he'd brushed up on his Arthurian lore and could spot the joins where Mallory was added to a bit of Geoffrey of Monmouth, or where the director threw in new ideas of his own devising. That was the way that legends grew and became indistinct. As Arthur lies dying, Sir Percival lobs the sword into the lake of Camlann to see a hand rise from the water and catch it (but surely it should have been Bedivere – he'd have to read Mallory again). It was the fourth or fifth time he'd seen the film and the end still stirred him. The romance of Arthur was irresistible.

*   *   *

Tyrone returned to the office next morning, equipped with
a sprinkling of amusing stories, but no solid results from
his Italian jaunt other than one slightly offbeat theory
concerning the dragons on the sword hilt.

"Don't rehearse theories before Humphries," Flint
warned.

"Sure, but I'm going to have to look into it. I'm going
to fax everyone we can think of in Scandinavia and
north Germany, museums, weapons specialists, private
collectors."

"We've talked to so many already – we have parallels
for the dragons on the sword hilt."

"Published parallels," Tyrone said. "Now I'm looking
for unpublished sword-hilts. We know for a fact that
most stuff is never published and just lies around gath-
ering dust."

He was right. "Do it, we've nothing to lose, but tell
everyone its urgent, write the faxes in German to give
them no excuse not to reply. We can't afford to wait
six months whilst museum curators excavate the backs
of their storage cabinets."

"Will do. How was Newcastle?"

"Fun, but I'm not sure the investigation got value for
money."

He described what he'd learned of the internal politics
of the Pendragons, revealed to be complex and full of
petty feuds. Flint had drawn a chart, laying out the
relationships of the key players, with details of which
branch of the Arthurian story-tree they clung to. Tyrone
ran over the diagram, adding a few details, picking holes
in the characters one by one, directing grievous slander
at each in turn. Any motive for murder was obscured
by the web of enmity and loyalty, personal grudge

168

and academic respect which enveloped the Pendragon Society.

Tyrone sank deep in his chair. "We need more data. When are you meeting Humphries?"

"At one. I'm treating him to an executive lunch in Val's Diner."

"Spam, Spam, eggs and Spam?"

"That's the idea. Coming?"

Matt Humphries found the egalitarian college canteen unsettling. Staff and students ate together in the upstart University. The only discrimination was between smokers and non-smokers and Humphries found himself pitched on the wrong side of the Green Line.

"Do you eat here every day?" he asked, his voice tinged with disrespect for the cuisine.

"Only when forced," said Flint. "I'm up to my armpits in work, otherwise I'd have suggested a cozy pub. There's a good one near Towton."

A University sausage was jabbed with suspicion. It quivered and refused to yield. Flint was tucking into the vegetable curry, scooping it up with the extra poppadom. Tyrone faced a microwaved cheeseburger: tasteless, but probably harmless.

"You had a rough time, down south," Humphries said. "It was worse than I expected."

Flint raised an eye over his poppadom. "What did you expect?"

"Trouble, but only academic trouble. I thought you'd stir up a few crusty professors, but they're more desperate than I guessed they'd be."

"I wish you'd told us things were so serious."

"It wasn't necessary."

"And the villains of the piece are who?"

169

Humphries shook his head vigorously. "If we knew that, we'd be out of the woods."

"Have you looked deeply at that company, MPP? They've laid off three-quarters of their staff, which suggests declining fortunes."

"They sent me their portfolio; it looks impressive," Humphries said.

"But can they do sums?" Tyrone asked.

"What do you mean?"

Flint stopped eating so he could explain. "About five years ago, people who thought they'd never make a bean from archaeology suddenly thought they saw a chance to turn a profit. A new museum was opened every fortnight and existing attractions had to upgrade, modernize and pull in the crowd to escape cuts in funding. Organizations like MPP jumped on the bandwaggon, but it was a short ride and it ended in tears."

"Why did they fail?"

Tyrone cut in with the answer. "Putting on a suit and calling yourself a cultural heritage consultant doesn't turn a soft arts graduate into a businessman."

"Cue recession," Flint said, "and companies like MPP went to the wall one by one."

Humphries asked what they had discovered before the car crash, Flint responding with an edited version of the facts. The insurance man lost interest in fighting his food as the story unfolded.

"At the moment, we can't prove any of our suspicions about MPP, they're just theories, they won't stand up in court."

"We're in for a lot of money if that sword doesn't come back," Humphries said. "A lot of money – unless you can prove that Lady Dunning was trying to pull a fast one."

"No, I think Harry believed the sword to be genuine,

she was still on cloud nine the day before she died, telling me how fortunate she was to have found it. Harry didn't want to make millions out of the find, she was a victim as much as your company was a victim. Perhaps more."

"You mean?" Humphries dragged a University knife across his throat.

"Adds up, doesn't it?" Tyrone said.

"But the inquest verdict was accidental death."

Flint demurred and Humphries tried to draw him on the point. "You keep hinting, but you have to tell me what you think happened. I'm paying the bills."

"Look, archaeology is not a precise science. I dug a villa a year or two back and every now and again a reporter would wander up and ask me a question such as 'what date is it?' I'd say 'third century' and that's what he'd print. What I actually wanted to say was 'third century at the moment, based on one dodgy coin that we haven't had cleaned and may turn out to be later'."

"Sorry, I missed the point of that."

"Half-completed research is as useful as half a bicycle. Let's look at what we know: Lady Dunning is dead, I don't believe by accident. It may have been suicide, but there are too many people with an interest in seeing her dead. You could hold a whole party on her grave – a crowd would turn up to dance."

"So she was murdered?"

"Someone whipped both Excaliburs and someone tried to kill Tyrone and I when we got too close to the truth. Now what I want to know is, are all these events connected?"

Humphries sucked in his cheeks, momentarily out of his depth. "They must be."

"Are you sure? Do we have a linear plot, where motivation A leads to crime B? Is there a single mastermind

171

behind the whole thing or are several strands of conflict intertwined?"

This was Flint's theory, born of many hours gazing at the charts he'd prepared. Humphries gave up on the meal and pushed it away, squeaking back into the green plastic chair.

"I can hire private detectives."

"We're cheaper," Tyrone said.

". . . and we've felt our way into the case. We've got a few ideas and a couple of leads. We were on our way to talk to Euan Trepennick when we had our little scenic detour in the Mendips. He's presumably the man who brought the business your way; he's the best person to advise you on how to unwind it."

The put-down was instant. "Trepennick's a waste of time, they should show him the door and put someone with a bit of spark in his place."

"It must be a tough old world in insurance."

"You're bloody right, you don't know the half of it."

"We still need to see him. He's in the Pendragon Society, he was an old friend of Harry's and he works for you. In a sense, he's at the hub of things."

"He's not at the hub of anything, believe me, he's washed up. This sword business is going to finish him."

Just a hint of satisfaction tainted Humphries' words, giving Flint another factor to ponder: the internal politics of Northern Consolidated Assurance could prove to be as Byzantine as those of the Pendragons.

"I suppose you would save a few quid if one of the beneficiaries turned out to be the murderer. In fact, you'd save a few more if you could contest the claim for the loss of the swords, that is, if you've not already paid out."

"We're stalling at the moment," Humphries said. "But we can't stall forever. That woman who runs the show down there, Alison wotsit, she was in advertising once, she knows how to play the media. We don't want her bringing a legal action for breach of contract until our case is watertight."

"So you need more evidence," Tyrone said.

"And you want more money?"

"More time," Flint said.

"Time costs money."

"A hundred pounds a day, plus expenses, as Bogart would put it."

Humphries had already heard the tale of the trip to Newcastle and the weekend in Rome. "Yes, it was the expenses I was worried about."

To obtain a sense of perspective, Flint spent that evening alone in his cottage, guffawing his way through *Monty Python and the Holy Grail*. It proved a good antidote to *Excalibur*. The case had its ridiculous aspects and Flint took his usual oblique approach to the problem. The character known as Merlin had no obvious motives to link him to Harry's death, or to the theft of the swords, or to any scam being engineered by MPP. Nevertheless, he had a role. Everyone dismissed him, yet he had been special to Harry. Perhaps he was the one who would know whether she truly believed in Excalibur, or more importantly, when she ceased believing.

As he watched the Python team lampoon the myth scene-by-scene, Flint sensed that he needed to eliminate the most ludicrous elements of the plot in order to arrive at a logical conclusion. From a whole cast of jobbing academics, Merlin stood out as the eccentric exception.

The following afternoon, Flint braved the A1079 in the green Vauxhall van owned by UNY-DIG. He was bound for Kingston-Upon-Hull, once famous for fishing fleets, now famous for not having fishing fleets; people blamed the EC, or Iceland, or North Sea pollution, or the Government, depending on their personal bias.

As he drove, a map of England drifted through his mind, with little red dots scattered across it: one for each place he'd visited on this wild chase. The distribution of the dots began to resemble the map of Arthurian Britain. He'd not yet been forced to go to Wales and had barely touched the Scottish borders, but there was time. At the very least, he would have to revisit the South West again. He had hatched a plan at college to double-up his lectures so he might be able to escape for another week without disrupting his students' preparations for exams.

The Barker house was in the midst of a turn-of-century railway company terrace amongst the grimmer outskirts of Hull. When a heavy-faced man came to the door, it was as though he was expecting someone else.

"I'm Dr Flint – we spoke on the phone."

"Right, come in, come in."

Carpet slippers shuffled on the hall rug. Mr Barker called into the kitchen, announcing the arrival. Flint was led into the lounge and took his seat on the mustard sofa. The room had been wall-papered in blown anaglypta, painted magnolia and scented with pipe-smoke, cat, and just a hint of fried supper. Italian football was being shown on satellite television. A bald crown in a circle of black bobbed like a target before the TV screen, as Mr Barker hunted for the remote control. Regaining his seat, he turned down the sound, but the picture remained. The mustard armchair lurched as he sat back into it.

"So you're a friend of our Colin?" Mr Barker had very

bushy eyebrows, which would wobble as he talked. The manner in which his body strained the waistband of his trousers and the buttons of the white shirt spoke of a lifetime's diet of chips and duty-free allowances.

"Friend? Not quite. I'm a university lecturer."

The woman who came into the lounge was as wiry as her husband was rounded.

"This is Dr Flint; he's from the university."

Mrs Barker offered tea. Flint requested milk and one sugar.

"Our Colin went to University."

"Yes, Southampton. But not any more, do you see him often these days?"

"No, he writes sometimes."

"Ah, you wouldn't have an address?"

Mr Barker's chest heaved, and all else heaved with it as he sat with hands firmly gripping his armchair. "We don't know where he is, we never do. He travels a lot, you see."

"I need to see him, urgently. One of his friends is dead."

"Oh. Who?"

"Lady Harriet Dunning."

A wheeze accompanied the news. "Lady Harry? That's sad, he'd be cut up about that. By, she was getting on a bit though, I'm not surprised."

"Presumably he's told you all about her?"

Mr Barker was uncomfortable. "Why?" he began. "Why are you asking? I'm sorry, but, you know . . ."

"It's all to do with insurance."

"Ah, so our Colin might get a bob or two?"

"Possibly." Yes, thought Flint, it was possible that Harry would leave a small legacy to her protégé. It might explain Gavin's hostility towards him.

"In a way, I'm glad, you know. Don't get me wrong, but Lady Harry weren't good for our Colin. He hasn't been very well and he does some daft things. Lady Harry only encouraged him to be strange."

"Was he interested in King Arthur before his breakdown?"

"No, he was going to be one of them stockbrokers, he was set on it. His girl was studying to be an accountant, they were going to get married when they both finished college and move to London. By, they'd have made some money those two. Big house, sports cars . . . he told me how much he was going to be paid, it was like winning the lottery every month."

Flint looked along the obligatory row of family photographs. He counted five Colins in various stages of growth; the final picture was one of a spotty, clean-shirted undergraduate bound for the fast lane of finance. By his side in the latest, dreamy print was a fresh-cheeked young woman, with Roman nose and dark and bubbly perm. Her dreams had been whisked away together with Colin's sanity.

"I understand he had a breakdown before his finals."

"Aye, and he was never the same. His girl waited for him to get better. She was a grand lass, they called her Isabel. She waited for him to get better but he didn't want to know her. She still sends us Christmas cards, for a bit she were like our daughter."

"Do you have a daughter?"

"No, Colin's our only one. Maggi's got two kids from her other marriage but they're out of the nest now."

"So did you bring Colin home after his breakdown?"

"I wanted to, but his mum was dead you see. She had a tumour when he was little." Mr Barker touched his

176

side. "He liked my second wife, but he didn't get on with Maggi. That's her in the kitchen."

Not quite a wife in every port, but one per decade, thought Flint. "What do you do for a living?"

"I just retired early." Mr Barker gave a grin. "I was a steward on the North Sea ferries."

And a bit of a lad in his day, no doubt. Colin had clearly inherited his father's wanderlust, if satisfying it on land and in the mythological past, rather than at sea and in the real world. Flint had known students on the edge of breakdowns. Those who fell into the abyss sometimes left something behind when they crawled out the far side: their ambitions, their talent, their confidence. From what Mr Barker said about his son as a child, and as a young man, Colin seemed to have lost every vestige of ambition during the breakdown and had emerged from the darkness with a new persona.

"Has he contacted you in the past month?"

"No."

"Has he ever mentioned Excalibur?"

"Who? I can check his letters?"

He was on his feet and out of the room in a few moments. A cup of tea arrived. The latest Mrs Barker made a few polite comments about the weather and the state of the roads, before a shout from the back of the house summoned her to help in the hunt for the letters.

Mr Barker returned with a plastic wallet stuffed with postcards and letters written on cheap exercise paper.

"He writes a lot of rubbish most of the time. I can't even read what he says sometimes. He tells me where he's been: he's been most places and meets all kind of folk. It's a life, that's what I think. It's his life, he's doing what he wants."

Flint was given the wallet.

"There's nowt personal – have a look at them."

He found the last five letters, spaced over a year and a half. The handwriting was eccentric and left-handed, the style hurried for one without house, or career or family to demand his time. Colin made Harry the centrepiece of every letter, as if he only wrote when he had something to say about her. He always called her 'Lady Harry'. The letter of January the Fifth was long and rambling. One paragraph only hinted at what was to come:

'Lady Harry has made a fantastic discovery which will make us all famous (well, it will make her famous, but there will be enough reflected glory to go around). It might just make us all rich too – watch out for me on TV around the middle of March.'

The letter rambled on to say he'd had a terrific idea for a TV show where he would cast fortunes for guest celebrities. Such eccentric dreams told Flint nothing, but that one paragraph indicated that Colin/Merlin thought he would be actively involved in the Arthur Roadshow – something the others at MPP had denied. He was also under the delusion he was going to grow rich.

"Money!" Mr Barker said. "He'd have done all right if he'd just finished what he first set out to do."

"Yes, but we're not all made to be office workers, are we? How exactly does he earn his living now?"

"He's on the dole, though I expect he does things on the side."

"Like casting fortunes?"

"As I said, it's his life."

It was his life, and Mr Barker knew little about it. All which was going to be learned was learned in twenty minutes and Mr Barker's eyes kept straying towards the

178

silent Italian footballers. As Flint was shown to the door, Mr Barker reached into the back pocket of his trousers. He pulled out thirty pounds in creased ten pound notes.

"If you find Colin, give him this, he were always short. Tell him we love him."

The affection from the gruff, ex-seaman was touching without being embarrassing. Flint felt his throat dry as he took the money.

"I'll find him."

Chapter Seventeen

Colin (and Merlin) were no longer strangers. Flint was beginning to know the lad, as if he was one of his own tortured students pouring out his worries in a counselling session. Like many bright young northerners, Colin had been embarrassed by his roots. As soon as he'd torn himself away from the plebeian backstreets of Hull, he'd begun to rebuild himself. He dropped his accent, he met a polite ex-public schoolgirl from Sussex, he learned a new political creed from the *Telegraph* and the *FT*. The new Colin T. Barker was almost complete, almost ready to slide into that city suit when the image had collapsed.

A friend in the local branch of the Richard III Society had obtained a listing of medieval fairs scheduled for the year. Several were held each weekend during the spring and summer months as owners of castles and stately homes vied to remain solvent.

Nottinghamshire is well off King Arthur's track and having hijacked Robin Hood, has sufficient legends to keep the tourists happy. Behind some Earl's country retreat, an arena had been marked out by a rope cordon. Around it was a circle of tents and marquees, most in modern canvas, a few gaily striped in medieval fashion. The paying public milled around, hands in pockets, vaguely amused and vaguely curious. Falconers, jugglers, coppersmiths, armourers, weavers and craft potters kept the ancient arts alive. Children pointed and asked questions. Trying to remain reserved, their fathers touched chainmail suits which dangled from wooden frames, taking themselves back for a moment to the age of chivalry. The fantasy was broken by their womenfolk, pulling them away to the stalls and justifying the need to buy a hand-embroidered cushion or pot-pourri basket.

Flint strolled slowly through the throng. History was alive, or at least, had been resurrected for the day. Some of the exhibits were phoney, some were cheap profiteering, but the fair carried the essence of Middle England – the England that never was.

Crouched beside a smoking fire, cutting into a circular pie was a young woman swathed in an apple-green kirtle, with a plain sackcloth apron tied around her waist. Blonde, wavy hair escaped from her cap and partly masked her face, but as a hand wiped back the hair, Flint stopped. He'd seen this woman before, although usually garbed as a Civil War musketeer.

"Ruth?"

She turned her wide face to meet his, and smudged soot onto one cheek. "Dr Flint!"

Two years before, he'd known Ruth in different, painful circumstances. Since then, she had left Yorkshire and vanished from his circle.

"Aren't you out of period? I thought you were strictly seventeenth-century?"

"No, I'm fourteenth-century today."

"What's that?"

"Humble pie, like a slice?"

"What's in it? No genuine 'umble I hope?"

"No, I used sausage."

Even in the course of an investigation, eating innards

181

would be beyond the call of duty. Flint the sometime vegetarian squatted beside her (the grass was still damp) and took a small slice of the pie as Ruth described both original and modern recipes. He shuddered slightly at the dry, lardy taste.

"Good," he mumbled. "Do you come here often?"

"Not here specifically, but the troop tours the country."

"You've defected from the English Civil War mob?"

"Yes, I wanted a change."

As she said this, her eyes moved towards a knightly figure, standing with his shining back towards them.

"New friends?"

"That's Roger."

"Hope he's good to you."

She gave a smile, which confessed a host of pleasures. "Are you still investigating people, or have you settled back into ordinary college life now?"

"I'm investigating, I'm afraid. It seems to be my lot."

Ruth fluttered her eyelids and drew herself back. With a touch of amateur dramatics she asked, "And what is your quest, good sir?"

Flint played along, bowing his head slightly. "Fair maid, I seek one called Merlin."

"Merlin? That prat?" The play-acting ceased. Ruth had always been one of the boys and had always spoken her mind.

"You know him? Is he here?"

"Yes, in the black tent near the toilets. You can't miss it, he's got a great big sign which says 'Merlin' outside. He tells fortunes, but I don't believe all that stuff, do you?"

"No."

"He's completely mad, he takes all this so seriously. You can't have a sensible conversation with him."

With a clank and rattle, the tall young man with the

mane of black hair, fiery eyes and distinctive bright steel breastplate turned their way and came towards the fire. Flint was introduced to Roger, shaking the metal gauntlet he offered. As they talked, Ruth put an arm around the metal-clad back, and Roger rested an armoured forearm on her shoulder. One may have to seek it in strange corners, but one could find romance in the world.

A black cylindrical tent, with traditional conical roof, had been pitched at the bottom of the site, at the end of the row of commercial marquees and just before the refreshment tent. Perhaps Merlin had put his half-completed Business Studies degree to good use.

MERLIN the all-seeing
Your Once and Future Self Explained

Within the half-open doorway, Flint could see an empty chair, small circular table, a crystal ball and a pair of sandal-clad feet. He stooped and entered the gloomy interior.

"What truth do you seek?" intoned a dramatic voice from the corner. The figure leaned forward in his own chair. He was a young man, cultivating a forked beard which would be brown for many disappointing decades. His dark eyes were set into deeply depressed hollows. A cloth cap had been chosen in favour of an archetypal pointy wizard's hat (he wouldn't want to look silly, after all).

"Do I close the curtains, or what?" Flint asked.

Merlin used a disposable lighter and brought a candle to life. Flint loosened a rope and the tent door fell closed. Immediately he realized he could *smell* Merlin.

"Runes, cards or the ball? It's three quid, or a fiver for the full forecast."

183

"Better make it a fiver," Flint said, putting the money into a hand which trembled ever so slightly. "Are you doing a good trade?"

Merlin ignored the question and took out a bag of wooden chips and cast them onto the table top. Quickly he turned them over to conceal the engraved side, then shuffled them.

"Pick twelve," he said.

"Look, I'm a friend of Lady Harriet Dunning. You were too."

"Pick twelve," Merlin repeated, taking only a brief moment to react.

Flint picked twelve chips and Merlin laid them in a circle.

"I was at Edgar Jenkins Hall. I remember seeing you in the bar." He left no room for Merlin to doubt his sincerity.

"Dr Flint," Merlin said.

"I'll take it that you knew my name already; you didn't divine it."

"No."

"I'm concerned about the circumstances of Harry's death. It was very inopportune. I thought you might be able to enlighten me."

"I loved Harry dearly," the magician responded. He turned a rune face-up. "Discovery," he said, then turned over more runes, pronouncing the name of each. "Danger . . . death."

"Egg-plant," said Flint, pointing at the fourth. "Slow Train Coming . . . you can make the runes say anything you want them to say."

"You'll meet a woman from your past."

"I just did, five minutes ago. We ate humble pie."

"Oh, you mean Ruth."

"She a friend?"

"Oh yeah, we have great times together."

This did not quite accord with what Ruth had said, so perhaps Merlin was less perceptive than he believed. Someone so far out of the mainstream must at times feel the need for friends wherever he could find them.

"Do you enjoy this life? Wouldn't you rather be an executive with Unilever or ICI, out in the real world?"

"This is the real world, this is life. Being chained in an office is slow death. Money is an illusion."

This was the kind of philosophy you could find on old Pink Floyd albums. "So that's why you dropped out? That's why you blew your future?"

"This is my future," he said, then blew out the candle.

Alarmed and alert, Flint tensed on his stool, but Merlin made no move, making his hollow voice dominate the tent. "Imagine darkness and cold, forever and ever. You're alone on the edge of nothingness then suddenly . . ."

Flame flickered from his lighter and Merlin's features took on a skeletal aspect. The light vanished.

". . . then darkness, forever and ever. That moment was your life. Insignificant, tiny and transitory."

"You've been reading too much Nietze."

"I have to be what I have to be."

"But I met your dad. He showed me pictures of Isabel, your fiancée, your ex-fiancée. She's lovely; whatever happened?"

Merlin relit the candle. "I would become a name on a credit card, the man who owned the latest sports car, the man who always paid his taxes, the man on the 8.15 from Bromley to Victoria. The man the company dump when they have a bad year."

"OK, I get your point, capitalist materialism has never

done anything for me, either. How you live your life is your affair, but I want to understand some contradictions. You were very close to Harry, but her family —"

"Hate me," Merlin said. "Gwen deserted her. Gavin uses her. They're not interested in what she found or what she achieved."

"So how were you going to become rich and famous on the back of Excalibur?"

Merlin gave a careless shrug, as if making a million were the easiest thing in the world. "I was part of her team – the team that found the sword, not those who are exploiting it for money."

Flint detected some doublespeak here, but allowed it to pass. "And Harry swore you to secrecy?"

"Yes."

"OK, let's think about the night Harry died. Did you see her that day? Was she with you?"

"No."

"And you were going to pick her up on Saturday morning, at what time?"

"Eight-thirty."

"You vanished pretty soon after you learned the news."

Merlin said nothing.

"Was it a shock, or did you already know she was dead?"

"Don't be ridiculous."

"I'm not the one with the black cloak and crystal ball!"

"We are living in great times, but there are many who will not believe in the Once and Future King!"

"None. Nobody believes it. Harry didn't and neither do you."

"Don't I?"

Flint had to change tack, to move back to co-operation and away from confrontation.

"OK, so you do. I assume you believe that Harry found the true Excalibur and I assume she believed it too."

"Yes."

"When did she stop believing?"

"She always believed."

"Right up to the end? She never had doubts?"

"It is Arthur's sword," Merlin stated. "Harry knew that."

Flint knew that arguing against conviction was futile. He may as well debate Easter with a mullah, or vegetarianism with a lion. Merlin had devised himself a very particular niche and wasn't going to budge. It was time to go. He placed thirty pounds on the table.

"Your dad wanted you to have this."

Merlin shuffled the runes again. "Take one more, this will be your watchword for the year."

Flint looked at the thirty or forty wooden counters and picked one at random. It was one he'd picked before.

"Discovery," said Merlin.

Glittering in the sun, a sword blade crashed downwards, halted by the armoured shoulder of a knight. The figure groaned and recoiled a yard, before swinging his own, blunted weapon at his attacker's shield. Another well-rehearsed crunch of metal-on-metal was followed by another and another. Flint stood, hands-in-pockets, watching the spectacle. Say 'King Arthur' to anyone in the crowd and nine-tenths of them would expect him to have fought in armour like this. Reality was always duller than fantasy. With a clatter, the knight called Roger collapsed onto the turf in bloodless death.

Tyrone came up from behind, munching a hot dog. "Brilliant, isn't it?"

"Not enough gore."

"I bumped into old Ruth, she said she'd seen you. That's her bloke who's just been given the headache."

"I found Merlin."

"And?"

"He's just one knight short of a round table. He believes in the sword and so did Harry, apparently. Of course, he denies being anywhere near her when she died. Any ideas what we do next?"

"I found his van," Tyrone said. "If you can call it a van."

"Well done." Flints thoughts coalesced around a fleeting glimpse of a van aiming to run the Spitfire from the road. "Was it orange?"

Tyrone was shaking his head with a snarl of disappointment. "If it was, I'd have slashed his tyres."

"Let's have a look – lead on, MacDuff."

Beyond the tents was a carefully screened field reserved for the modern-day transport of the exhibitors. It was the work of a few moments to locate the old yellow Citröen 2CV, spray-painted with black-edged mystical symbols, its van-back resembling half an old dustbin.

Flint walked around the vehicle much as he would walk around any of the exhibits at the show; without suspicion and without great interest. Even the encounter with Merlin seemed little more than part of the pageant; his was a mind out of time. Neither Merlin, nor his van could be taken seriously. This was Californiology: investigating for the experience, not in the hope of discovering anything of substance.

Circling the van, kicking its balding tyres, Tyrone derided French craftsmanship and Merlin's artistic talent. Flint stuck his forehead against the glass window of the dustbin-back. If Merlin was a nomad, all his life should be here.

He shielded his eyes and stared hard into the gloomy interior. An assortment of carrier bags and bedding was piled on the floor and a green parka had been thrown carelessly on top. Half concealed behind the driver's seat was a rucksack – last seen vanishing through a fire door.

Chapter Eighteen

"Crafty bastard." Flint recalled the humiliation of the débâcle at the London college. "We have our thief, old son."

It took only a few moments to fit together the clues. Merlin had been at Edgar Jenkins Hall, he could easily have discovered the number of Tyrone's room, waited until both archaeologists were firmly entrenched in the bar, then taken the replica.

"Harry must have told him that we had it," Flint said, leaning against the back of the van.

"S.A.T," said Tyrone. "He's our Stupid Art Thief."

"Not so stupid – he came to the press conference and worked out who was escorting the real sword . . ."

". . . the real fake."

". . . so he popped across to CCL, wandered into the library or the common room in broad daylight, then hid in the loo whilst Gerald locked up. He'd been for an interview there a few years ago, and he could have wangled an external reader's ticket for the library. If he's as bright as people say he is, Merlin could have known the building inside-out."

"Shall we shop him?"

"Not yet." Flint looked around for witnesses. Being an anarchist was a positive benefit at times like this. "Merlin has rejected all the norms of orthodox society, you know."

"So he'd understand this?" Tyrone drew out his Swiss Army knife and chose a slender blade.

"Go on, nobody's looking."

Flint had hardly finished speaking before Tyrone had prized open the flap-window on the nearside door. In went his arm and the door came open. With Flint watching for trouble, Tyrone rummaged through the bedding.

"Hurry up."

"There's nothing here."

An odour of unwashed linen flooded out of the car.

"What's in the bag?"

The rucksack was pushed in his direction. It still contained a collection of tools, crude door wedges and nails. Merlin had stolen the sword, but where was it now?

"Nothing," Tyrone said.

"Scoot!" Flint hissed, ducking behind the car. "He's coming!"

Tyrone wriggled backwards through the door as Flint scurried away, bent double. A heart-pumping few seconds elapsed before the pair were behind a box-back Luton, waiting for the inevitable cry of alarm. When it came, Tyrone raised his eyebrows.

"Fight or flee?"

"Think. Ask yourself: is Merlin behind all this mayhem, or is someone pulling his strings?"

"What if MPP paid him to nick the swords?" Tyrone suggested.

"It would prevent them being examined too carefully, which would prolong the credibility of the scam. He's probably destroyed them by now."

"How do you destroy three pounds of iron?"

"OK, he's thrown them away, or buried them."

"Do you think he would?"

"If he was paid."

"But money doesn't matter to our Merlin. Think about it: he's the one fool in a million who still believes in the real Excalibur. Imagine you're an Arthurian loony and the mythical blade falls into your hands. What would you do with it?"

Tyrone ventured to look around the Luton van before replying. Merlin was still prowling around his own van in an agitated state.

"I'd toss it back into the lake."

Yes, that would be plausible, and damned inconvenient. If the delightful Tania were still around, Flint could drag her down with her diving gear and go fish for the sword. It was with a sense of double regret he recalled the postcard saying she was back in Vancouver.

"You would really throw away this sacred historical artifact?"

"Maybe I'd bury it. It's quick and easy. It would allow me to change my mind."

"So where do you bury it? In a field? In someone's allotment?"

"If I was really crackers I'd pick one of the top Arthurian sites: South Cadbury or Glastonbury Tor . . ."

"Tintagel, Slaughter Bridge, Arthur's Tomb, Badbury Rings, Stonehenge, Amesbury . . . Read Harry's guide-book, you've 350 sites to choose from and most, if not all, are scheduled. We need to become Merlin's friends."

Tyrone's eyes and cheeks bulged. From his throat came a choking noise, as if he was about to regurgitate his hot dog. "What?"

Flint breezed around the van. "Come on."

A pair of sandals and the rump of a ragged pair of jeans projected from the back of the Citröen van. Merlin

192

was checking whether any of his possessions had been appropriated.

"Sorry about the window," Flint said.

If he'd thrust a burning brand against the enticing target, Merlin could scarcely have yelped with more conviction. As he turned, his black cloak fell back to conceal the jeans. He pulled a strand of hair back into place.

"Coming for a drink, Colin? We ought to talk."

Tyrone sat beside Merlin as they drove away from the fair in convoy. His presence would guard against the conjuror attempting a vanishing trick. The 2CV rattled across the field, then strained to accelerate once on the road. The fuel gauge showed empty.

"You're out of gas," Tyrone commented.

Merlin banged the gauge. The needle didn't move. "It's broken," he said.

"That could be embarrassing."

"I calculate my mileage." Merlin creased one cheek in a lopsided show of pride. "I fill up once every two hundred miles."

"And how do you pay the bill? American Express Gold Card?"

"I pay my way."

It was so convenient to have a pub around the corner whenever Flint hit a crisis. One or two drinks and life looked a lot smoother. Not that he was an alcoholic, he just liked the atmosphere, the conviviality, the crisps and the odd pint of Real Ale. The cottage pies were good, even if 'home baked' meant 'home microwaved'.

Merlin ate as if it were his first meal of the day – which it was. He'd changed out of his soothsaying costume and donned a black 'Megadeath' T-shirt. With its skulls and

193

rock-gothic motifs, his outfit was a change of century but not of theme.

"Be nice," Flint had hissed to Tyrone, so Tyrone sat quietly, saying nothing, a look of sublime passivity on his face. As he sipped his pint of beer, Tyrone crooked his little finger. His false smile would have been in place at any cocktail party.

"Do pass the crisps," Tyrone said, his voice sweet and theatrical.

Flint narrowed his eyes, but fought hard against a bubble of mirth that ached to surface. Not only was Tyrone acting the fool, but Merlin-Colin made quips at every excuse. He was ripe to befriend.

"You may as well help now, Colin. Gavin will probably sue you for nicking his swords and spoiling his show. The insurance company will press theft charges and my old college ain't too happy about their knackered doors."

Merlin-Colin tucked into his cottage pie with gusto, nodding between mouthfuls.

"Even if the police don't try to break you, there's someone else who will. Someone killed Harry, someone tried to kill us and it wasn't the Beast of Exmoor."

Colin-Merlin finished his plateful and dabbed his whiskered lips with a napkin. His fingernails were long, but not dirty. His clients would never cross a dirty palm with silver. The Merlin persona seemed to be slipping away. His expression was now thoughtful, his words considered. "I knew something was going wrong before it all happened. I always go down a few weeks before the conference, so I can sign on at the local dole office and get to know the area. I've got a copy of Harry's book, I'm trying to visit all the sites."

"The Arthurian sites?" Flint had only eaten half his pile

of chips and few of his cannonball peas. He offered the plate and it was accepted with an apology.

"Soothsaying is not the world's most lucrative trade," Merlin confessed. He raised his bushy eyebrows. "One cannot always predict when one might eat again."

"Is that why you nicked the swords?" Tyrone now intervened.

"I'm not interested in money," Merlin snapped back.

"So why?" Flint asked, with more concern and less aggression. He frowned at Tyrone and his assistant rose to refill the beer glasses.

"Where does one start with a tale so complex?"

"At the beginning?"

The second-hand chips and peas had to be consumed before Merlin would begin, and then he made a few false starts. Flint called him 'Colin' whenever he could to encourage the personality shift.

"Harry and I went to Tintagel on a day trip, the week before she died. That's when she told me how desperately worried she was over what Gavin was planning for the sword."

"She never gave you any hint that the sword wasn't genuine?"

"Of course it's genuine – even your own tests show you that it's genuine."

Flint wasn't going to argue. Knowledge is power.

"So Harry was worried, and you were at the conference the night she died. Did you stay all evening, or just long enough to establish an alibi?"

"I didn't kill her – that was Gavin, Gavin killed her."

The strength of conviction was so persuasive, it had to be based on substantial evidence. "And how do you know? Prescience?"

195

"He suffered from the Oedipus complex, mother-loves-son-hates-mother. Gavin was using her, and at last she found the will to say no."

A kind of logic was being formed, not stable logic supported by facts, but a working hypothesis that was better than nothing.

"So why did you steal the swords?"

"To thwart Gavin. Harry was a strong woman, but he's weak, intellectually weak. He was going to use the sword to make money: books, television and then he'd sell it to an American museum."

"So you stole it and returned it to its rightful place."

Colin-Merlin smiled. "You'd like to know, wouldn't you?"

"It would be easier to bugger Gavin's plans if we had the swords."

"Mmm."

Tyrone was back, sliding foaming glasses of beer across the table. "Why did you nick the replica?" Tyrone asked.

"I wasn't sure which one you had – I thought it was the original in the box. By the time I knew, it was too late."

"S.A.T," Tyrone said.

"What?" Merlin missed the joke.

"And I suppose it wasn't you who charged me off the road."

"That was Gavin."

"Does he own a van?"

"No," Merlin faltered in his divination.

"That was a guess, wasn't it? You should try the runes on that one. Try Charles Evans too: he had a motive."

The sage looked uncertain for a few moments. "Gavin," Merlin said firmly, with a nod. "It has to be."

"Have you told the police?" Flint asked.

"I haven't told them anything."

No, thought Flint. No one had told the police anything. All joined an unspoken conspiracy of silence; the frightened, the incompetent, the eccentric and the guilty were all protecting each other.

"OK, what say you tell us what you've done with the replica."

The suggestion was greeted with wariness.

"Call it a start, a statement of faith. You lead us to it, we'll keep it to ourselves, not say a word for the time being. It belongs to MPP and they're about to go bust, so even if we do return it, the thing will be worthless. It will be sold off as a curiosity at a fraction of what it cost to make."

Colin Barker nodded. This was the original Colin now, the level-headed business student who could recognize a hopeless situation and knew a deal when one was offered.

"Yes, perhaps, but you're not having the true Excalibur." The statement was made with gravity and came as a warning note that Merlin could easily regain control. Flint immediately shifted ground. "Take us back to the week before Harry died; did you see her on the Friday?"

Colin answered immediately. "No – I was going to, but she was busy. She'd been talking to you and it upset her. She was worried about the court case, you know, over her book. She was on edge because of the conference, and Gavin was giving her trouble about the press launch, then of course she was ill."

"Ill, how ill?"

"She had cancer, didn't you know?"

Chapter Nineteen

The logo on the door of the green Vauxhall van was a white trowel raised in a clenched fist. Above it ran the motto *'ubi sterans ibi aes'* : where there's muck, there's brass. Below it was stencilled the acronym UNY-DIG. The logo had been Flint's idea, Tyrone devised the acronym and the Latin motto began as a joke cracked by the unit's first client.

Flint was driving north in the slow lane of the M1. With care he fell back from the coach, leaving a hundred and fifty metres of space between himself and danger. Immediately, a car transporter spotted the gap and moved into it. Its brake lights glowed and Flint pressed his foot on the brake, empathizing with Merlin's rejection of the modern world.

The young soothsayer had been left in Nottinghamshire, with the promise that he would meet them at dusk on the coming Tuesday. Flint toyed with the name of the rendezvous.

"South Cadbury."

"Camelot!" said Tyrone.

"Camelot!" echoed Flint.

"It's only a model!" They both knew the Monty Python film backwards, yet both laughed.

"Do you think there's something puerile about people who recite film clips to each other?" Tyrone asked.

"Undoubtably."

"But it's not as puerile as dressing up as Merlin and pretending to tell fortunes. Do you trust that creep? I bet he's lying about Harry being terminally ill."

"Could be." Flint was concentrating hard on that car transporter, weaving about in front of him, a whole pile of red Fords ready to come bouncing off the top deck and into his path. Tyrone continued to denigrate Merlin, whose history, appearance, manner, outlook and way of life epitomized everything Tyrone hated most.

"I bet she wasn't ill, I bet that was one of his crackpot predictions. The runes probably told him she had cancer."

Eminently plausible, Flint thought. There had to be more to the Harry-Merlin relationship than met the eye.

"He's just the type to spook old ladies with phoney soothsaying," Tyrone said. "I bet he made up everything he said today. He told us what we wanted to hear, in return for a free lunch."

"Could be."

Colin (or Merlin) had been talked into revealing where he'd hidden the replica sword. When Tyrone had begun to name Arthurian sites he struck lucky on the third guess: South Cadbury Castle, close to the Somerset-Dorset border.

"What do we do if he doesn't turn up as planned?"

A giant lorry full of cornflakes ground past in the middle lane. Flint winced, and swerved, and braked, before replying. The seatbelt had begun to irritate the shoulder he'd injured in the crash. It was still painful to twist his neck to watch for danger approaching in the fast lane.

"If Merlin doesn't show, then it's time for you to chat up your friend, Detective Sergeant Chaff, she of the irrepressible sense of humour. If we give her the S.P.

on Merlin, she'll make mincemeat of him. Meanwhile, we have to assume he's telling the truth, if not the whole truth. We'll go home, pack enough socks for a week, cancel a few lectures then head south."

"Is that safe?"

"Only if we blunder around like idiots. This time we're going to find ourselves allies. Patrick Hewitt's been useful so far. Ivor seemed a decent chap, then there's Gwen —"

"Who is the twin sister of the prime suspect. She's hardly going to shop Gavin is she? What about having another crack at the insurance man? Euan Tweedledum."

"Yes – I'll ask him to give me a quote for life cover. Methinks I need it."

The cornflakes lorry had squeezed itself into the gap between Flint and the car transporter. Flint eased off the accelerator and fell back once more.

"Humphries offered me a good rate to take over the UNY-DIG policies," Tyrone added. "Shall we take him up?"

"Anything to save money. I had a memo from the prof. Apparently, the next Faculty meeting will discuss the UNY-DIG deficit."

"Oops."

"Keep scanning the job adverts."

Within twenty-four hours, suitable apologies had been made for lectures and seminars cancelled. Professor Vine, the head of department was a laid-back, understanding woman who felt in debt to Flint's extracurricular detective work. The professor was fighting the corner for UNY-DIG, telling the doubters that the archaeologists would run into profit one day, if given time.

Never wholly reliable, the green van carried Flint and

Tyrone back to Bath safely, without incident. With more than an eye to security, they checked into a bed and breakfast rather than one of the obvious public houses. It was a postwar semi-detatched house in a tree-lined back street of Bath, a late addition to the sheet of lodgings handed out by the local tourist office.

Divorced, with a teenage daughter at the University of London, Mrs Bates proved happy to enter into minor conspiracies. Flint negotiated his way around her house with a wink and a joke.

"And no lady visitors." Mrs Bates brought down her forehead, her blue-green eyes glinting through her fringe of dyed sienna curls.

For a moment Flint was reminded of Tania – an older Tania, Tania at forty-something.

"Perish the thought," he said.

Mrs Bates was instantly enthralled by her guests. Dr Drake and Dr Flint brought luggage which included a computer and printer. She was not, under any circumstances, to accept telephone calls from anyone other than 'Debs', who she was told was their secretary. She was not to tell anyone who her guests were, what they did or where they were going. Consuming the cakes and scones she produced for afternoon tea, they blew air into her constricted suburban life.

"Archaeologists?" she responded. "Wonderful."

Scores of diggers' tales were trotted out for her amusement, minus the squalor, the sex and the bad language. She was easily convinced that the pair led exciting, hectic lives. She'd seen the 'Indiana Jones' cycle and she knew, as a fact, that secrecy and guile were part of the game. Flint paid the bill in advance then set about using her telephone.

*　　*　　*

201

Breakfast proved an indulgent treat. Mrs Bates had proved quick to buy in vegetarian sausages, which made Flint happier to tuck into the 'full English' plate. They could afford a slow start to the new campaign; there would be no grand assault on the enemy shieldwall this time, rather they would probe gently forward until an opening could be seen. Allies would be sought one by one, in the lunch hour.

The chosen pub was crowded and central. Tyrone had been out of sorts all morning, keen to begin staking out hill-forts in the chance that Merlin turned up to retrieve the swords before the appointed time.

"What's Ivor going to tell us? I mean, he's in on it, isn't he?"

"We need a Trojan horse, if I can mix my myths for a moment. Ivor looks like your standard ex-art school illustrator. He's not a second-hand book dealer like Gavin, or a failed advertising executive like Alison. If we can win Ivor onto our side, we might just crack this."

Ivor the ink walked straight past the pair as they waited in the dark recesses behind the door.

"Ivor!"

"Hi." His round, cherubic face lit up.

"What's yours?"

"Lager top."

With a nod, Flint propelled Tyrone in the direction of the bar.

"This is very mysterious," Ivor said, taking a stool opposite Flint's corner bench. His jeans were slashed at the knees and thigh and he wore a zip-neck sweater in maroon. "I heard you do this kind of thing all the time."

"We're archaeologists, we dig, we probe the past."

"So what are you probing?"

"God knows, thought you could help."

Ivor raised his eyebrows. "I have to know what I'm helping with."

"Two missing swords and a lady in the lake."

"Do you mean poor Harry? I thought you were just interested in Excalibur."

"Swords lost, Harry lost, it starts to look suspicious."

"What, you mean murdered?"

"Possibly. There's certainly something underhand going on: two counts of theft for starters. Add possible fraud and you may as well throw in a murder."

The open-eyed jollity of Ivor's entrance had now become clouded. "I can't help you. I was here, in Bath the night Harry died."

"We don't suspect you!" Flint said.

"I should hope not!" The clouds shifted away from Ivor's expression. "I don't know why you're worried about Harry. I went to the inquest, the police said her death was an accident."

"Yes, there have been a spate of accidents."

"Oh! The car crash." Ivor touched Flint's hand in sympathy. "Were you all OK? You look fine."

Flint automatically lifted a hand to the left side of his neck and rubbed down onto his collar bone. "We survived, but the car is a bit sick and there's one sheep who's chewed its last blade of grass."

Tyrone also wore jeans: well pressed and certainly not ripped. He placed the drinks on the table, then immediately took over Flint's description of the accident. Ivor winced at the description of the wreck smeared in sheep gore.

"And did you see who was driving the other car?"

"It was a van," Tyrone said.

"It wasn't that kid, Merlin, was it?"

"No, his crummy heap of French rubbish would never have caught me on that hill. It was a Ford, an orange one, the model that replaced the Transit."

Ivor raised his lager top. "I'll drink to your escape."

Flint acknowledged the toast, warming to the young man's gentle smile. "I know our approach seems a bit Fascist, but better we ask the questions than the police; that way we can keep it in-house. Basically we're all on the same side: we all liked Harry, we all have an interest in the swords, so we're all in the same mire."

"What do you want to know?"

"The history of MPP, for a start."

"Did you see our Bog Lady exhibition?" Ivor asked.

"I did, it was excellent."

"That was the jewel in our crown. We had seven or eight staff when we did that."

"But along came the recession?"

"Right on – now there are two of us."

"Then Arthur rose out of the mists to save the company? I presume you're a director."

"Director sounds very pretentious. I like to think of MPP as a co-operative. We share the profits, if we make any profits."

"Which you don't," Tyrone stated.

Ivor raised no argument.

"So the surviving members of the co-operative now are yourself, Alison, Gwen and Gavin?" Flint asked.

"No, Gwen is standing in for Harry as she's an executor."

"I see." What Flint saw was another chink in the MPP armour.

Ivor rolled himself a thin cigarette with practised panache. "So what are you two planning to do?" he asked.

"Dig."

"Literally?"

Immediately, Flint spotted he'd made an involuntary slip.

"Metaphorically. At the moment, the police have closed the book on Harry's death and can't get anywhere on the stolen swords. To bring the police back into the case, we need to define a nice clean crime, an identifiable victim and a clear suspect. What we're doing is sifting the ground in advance of their big hobnail boots. If we can tidy things up so every-one is satisfied, perhaps the police can stay out of things."

"This sounds like some kind of deal."

"It could be, we never know," Tyrone said. "That's up to you."

Flint caught Tyrone's eye and frowned. There was no need to play the heavy. He turned back to Ivor. "You presumably did all the graphics on the Excalibur original?"

"Yeah, and I designed the replica."

"Did you ever doubt its authenticity?"

"No."

The disbelief on Tyrone's face could be read as 'he would say that wouldn't he?'.

"We brought in experts, we had carbon-14 dating done at Harwell. It's all in my text – you read it."

"And the story on the art-boards is the true story as you heard it?"

"Yes – there's no point making things up. So many of Harry's people were waiting for us to screw up and make a mistake, so they could jump in and make names for themselves."

"People like Charles Evans?"

"Yeah right, all those wrinkly academics."

"And us."

A puff of blue smoke and a blink of the eyelids acknowledged that Flint was marked as an enemy. "And you."

"It's obviously a scam," Tyrone said bluntly. "Admit it, it's all an insurance fiddle. Make up some stupid story about finding Excalibur, get some gullible idiot to insure it, then arrange the theft."

"Tyrone!"

"Harry gets cold feet, so someone in the gang bumps her off." Tyrone leaned in close now, pressing the knuckle of his hand against the bar-room table.

"Tyrone!"

"They're all in on it, Doc."

"Go buy us some crisps."

Tyrone looked startled, but Flint pushed a pound coin towards him. "Go on, three bags, any flavour except prawn."

Reluctantly, Tyrone rose to his feet and pushed his way into the crowd.

"Sorry about Tyrone – he's seen too many gangster movies."

"The enthusiasm of youth," Ivor said, with a hint of whimsy. "He's way off the mark, you know. There's no great plot, you'll see. All the drama is coincidental."

"OK, the project was born out of a billion-to-one find, and since then has been dogged by a string of unlikely coincidences. In a way they have all been convenient, even Harry's death. The insurance money would have saved MPP from going to the wall."

"You're wrong. We needed Harry to make the Road-show work. Even after she died, the show could have gone on and we'd have made enough money to keep solvent. Without the swords, it's nothing. The show was wrecked, deliberately."

If Ivor's claim was correct, then it was possible that no one at MPP knew Merlin had been involved with stealing the original sword, but Ivor would never admit it in any case. The artist leaned back on his stool, adopting a considered pose.

"So who hates the project enough to wreck it?" Flint asked. "Charles Evans?"

"If I was a detective, I'd investigate you two, I would. You might be the crooked ones out to make money. It makes sense – you were sent here with the intention of destroying the project." Ivor said this with a twinkle of amusement, as if he was making a parody of Gavin's posturing.

"You don't believe that: Gavin might pretend to, Alison might protest for the cameras, but you know where we're coming from."

Ivor strained at his cigarette and said, "Mmm," as if he enjoyed the interrogation. "Yes – I'm afraid MPP can be a very melodramatic place to work. Harry was theatrical too, you know. They made a great act, the three of them. Gavin sulks, Alison has a habit of shrieking and throwing pencils when she's mad at someone and Harry, well, Harry could be a right old battle-axe when she got going."

"I can imagine. And what did you do in the war, Ivor?"

"I kept out of it, I'm not the business end of the operation, I'm just the ink."

His talent was what had kept MPP displays away from mediocrity. Flint recognized this, and said so.

207

"You're too kind," Ivor said, scrunching his cigarette into an ashtray. "And now I'm suitably flattered, what else do you want me to tell you?"

"OK." Flint leafed through his mental list of blank areas of the case. "Where does Merlin fit into all this?"

"Nowhere: well, he's nothing to do with us."

"Was he ever anything to do with you? Was he an employee, or anything?"

"No, he was one of Harry's hangers-on. Gavin hates him and Alison wouldn't even let him in the office without Harry. Merlin thought we were committing some form of heresy by putting the Roadshow together, and Alison was afraid he'd smash up the equipment given a chance. Now he'd be a good suspect if you're looking for the one who stole your swords."

Flint may have changed colour, or flinched at the accuracy of Ivor's observation. It was an obvious intellectual leap once one knew Merlin's views.

"There you are," Ivor said. "I should be a detective too."

"Join the team."

"I'm happy as I am. All you have to do is find our swords, then the insurance company is off our backs, you get paid, we get on with our work. Everyone will be happy."

"Except Harry: she'll still be dead."

"Harry is dead, whatever happens. If you want to get suspicious about Harry, ask yourself who gains the most from her dying. Who gets the house, who gets all the dosh she's got stashed in the bank? The sword was insured for half a million – who owns that?"

So it was half a million, Flint had never been sure.

"Presumably Gavin and Gwen share it all? But isn't Gavin a good mate of yours?"

Ivor gave languid smile. "He's sort of a mate of Alison's."

"Mate?"

"As in mate." Ivor stuck his finger through the handle of his beermug, then withdrew it. "But not any more."

Chapter Twenty

Tyrone had not returned with the crisps. Instead he'd taken them out to the benches and had worked his way through the bags one by one, watching the traffic churn by. He barely raised an eyebrow when Ivor walked past him, with a cheery farewell.

"What the hell are you playing at?" Flint demanded.

Tyrone simply gave a shrug.

"He's on our side, for God's sake. For the first time, we've made contact with someone with a vested interest in helping us and you behave like you were in the Gestapo."

"He's gay," Tyrone said, as substitute for defence.

"What?"

"See the earring?" Tyrone touched his earlobe. "It's a sure-fire marker. He's gay, I'm telling you."

"So what? You say that about half the people we meet. It's not a criminal offence, he can't be hung for it, so what difference does it make?"

"I wouldn't like to get too friendly with him, that's all."

Bigot, thought Flint. Anyone who wasn't a white middle-class heterosexual English male fell short of God's great aim, in Tyrone's opinion. Even amongst this master race the possession of a beard, bicycle, vegetarian cookbook or union card marked the owner as suspect.

Flint only tolerated it, because Tyrone veered towards self-parody rather than labour the point in company.

Tyrone popped open the third bag of crisps and offered one. Flint glared for a moment, then took the peace offering. He lowered himself onto the bench opposite Tyrone, back to the traffic.

"Sexual orientation notwithstanding, Ivor made some good points, when you allowed him to."

"He could have been lying." Tyrone destroyed more crisps in a single, crunching mouthful.

Flint's temper and tolerance were exhausted. "He's an artist, not a gangster! And, as I said, he made some good points, if you'll listen to me."

"I listen to you," Tyrone said, sitting upright and folding his arms. "Ready when you are, Dr Flint."

"Thank you, Dr Drake." Calm down, Flint told himself. Don't rise to the bait. He had to turn the personality clash into more constructive debate. Tyrone still carried a look of insolence on his face; it had to be ignored.

"Now, Ivor set me thinking. First he told me that Gavin and Alison are ex-lovers."

"That would liven up the office. Has Gavin left Alison for Ivor?"

"Don't be daft. I only mention it because it gives the case an extra dimension we have to be aware of."

It was useless trying to talk to Tyrone in this mood. "When are you meeting the policewoman of your dreams?"

"Half an hour."

"Mind if I play gooseberry?"

"No."

"I'll see you there."

Flint walked off alone, vowing to cool his head by strolling along the riverbank, taking in the Georgian architecture, playing the Renaissance man for half an hour. In

211

fact, Bath has little by way of a scenic riverside walk. He reached Pultney Bridge, then almost immediately turned back and frittered his time gazing through windows of souvenir shops.

A little late, he managed to find a certain fast food restaurant. The UNY college magazine had once been threatened with a writ for organizing a petition criticizing its products, so it was now referred to as 'a certain fast food chain', or simply, 'Certains'. Tyrone was hovering beside the entrance, when Flint came up from behind. Just visible through the plate-glass windows was a pair of crossed legs in tights, one shin swinging free as Chaff waited.

"Of all the burger bars in all the world she has to come into mine," Flint drawled. "Why here for God's sake?"

"It's the only place she'd meet us." Tyrone maintained his surveillance on the legs. "I suggested a quiet bistro, but she thinks I'm trying to chat her up."

"The very idea."

All the aggression had gone from Tyrone's manner, having been replaced by a perceptible nervousness. Flint entered the restaurant first. In navy blazer and skirt Detective Sergeant Chaff had chosen a table by the window and was lingering over a cardboard carton of coffee.

"Hello," she said. "I've not told anyone I'm here; does that make you happy?"

"As birds," Flint said. Below the blazer she wore an ivory jumper, stretched taut by her broad shoulders. Flint could have pinched himself – why was his mind always drawn to memories of Tania?

"It doesn't make me happy, but I can live with it," Chaff said. "Now what's going on? There are channels —"

"You're our channel," Tyrone said gravely. "We need someone we can trust."

"Oh yeah?"

212

"We need information that only you can give us."

His eyes, and Chaff's eyes both fell on the briefcase by her ankle.

"And I need a cheeseburger, fries and rootbeer."

Sophisticated, thought Flint. He'd avoided fast food outlets of all description since the outcry at college over the environmental petition. Today he made an exception and brought a loaded tray of 'Certainburgers' up to the window seat.

"Stephanie's traced the van that rammed us," Tyrone said when he returned.

"It was a Ford," Chaff repeated for Flint's benefit. "It was stolen from a rental depot in Bristol that morning. That garage usually leaves its vehicles on the forecourt with the keys on top of the sun visor. If you know they do that, then its easy to steal one."

"It shows you someone planned to do us in," Tyrone said.

"No, it shows that it was a stolen van," Chaff corrected. She was always matter-of-fact and showed little interest in speculation. "Teenage joyriders do this sort of thing all the time. You may have just been unlucky."

Flint worked his unlucky collarbone as she said this. "Where was the van found?" he asked.

"Bristol, again."

"That's where we were headed."

"Coincidence."

"I hate putting things down to coincidence," Flint said. "It's a way of saying we don't have enough data to connect two events."

"We don't," she said.

Flint tasted his burger and remembered the second reason for his boycott – he hated the things. "Were you at the inquest when it resumed?"

"Yes – I brought the papers along." She tapped her briefcase with the toe of her flat-heeled shoes.

"You couldn't give us a resumé could you? We were seriously incapacitated at the time."

"Walking wounded," Tyrone added.

Chaff raised her eyebrows and adjusted her short skirt before she told them.

Attending inquests was a routine Chaff took for granted. The Coroner's Court differed, the players changed, but the corpse was equally dead. In the case of Lady Harriet Dunning, no suicide note had been found and no other persons were suspected of being involved. The cause of death was drowning, the verdict was accidental death.

The only curious incident had occurred when the Coroner asked Lady Dunning's son Gavin about the discovery of the body.

"And when you found your mother's body, you pulled her clear of the water?"

"No, she was on the bank already."

"Are you sure?"

"Yes."

Gavin Dunning had seemed as far from sure as anyone could be. He had no colour to his face, he was trembling and carried deep purple bags beneath his eyes.

"So you tried artificial respiration?"

"No."

"Why not?"

"She was dead, she was . . ." he stopped.

"Yes?"

"Cold."

"Let me paraphrase, if I may, the pathologist's report. In this, our expert witness says your mother died of

214

drowning. She could not have been on the bank, she must have been in the water."

"I can hardly remember."

"And the pathologist also said there had been an attempt at artificial resuscitation."

"Well, I would have tried, but then . . ."

"So you did try?"

"Not properly, there was no point. I may have started."

"You may have? Is your memory at fault Mr Dunning?"

"It's a bit of a blur, it was so much of a shock."

Gavin Dunning stood down and Chaff's superior, Inspector Roper had taken the stand, offering no evidence of foul play. The Coroner had quizzed him on one major point.

"Inspector Roper, how do you reconcile the discrepancy between the statements given by Mr Dunning and the pathologist's report?"

"Mr Dunning was understandably very distressed when he called us. I've read that when people suffer a shock, they can lose their memories for up to twenty minutes."

"So you are saying that Mr Dunning cannot remember dragging his mother from the lake and attempting to revive her?"

"That is what I believe, sir, yes."

"When you interviewed Mr Dunning, were his clothes wet?"

"Yes sir. He had changed his trousers by the time I arrived, but we took away his coat, trousers and boots for examination and all were wet and covered with mud."

"Was it possible for him to have become so wet and grimy without entering the lake?"

"It had been raining quite heavily and the ground was muddy where the victim lay."

"Could you answer yes or no to this question?"

Roper had paused before replying. "I'm afraid I don't know."

The Coroner was barely satisfied, but returned the verdict of accidental death in the absence of any evidence of violence or suicide. Harriet Dunning's extraordinary luck had turned overnight into extraordinary ill-luck. It had been just an accident.

Chaff retold as much as her notes enabled her to recall, speaking the parts verbatim. Flint asked to see the scene-of-death photographs and she brought them from her briefcase with some reluctance.

"This is a little irregular, but they were available at the inquest, they're not secret documents."

Amid the carnage of burger wrappings, torn ketchup sachets and half-finished cartons of fries, photographs of a pale Lady Dunning passed from hand-to-hand. As testified, she lay in the mud on her back, arms across her chest.

"What about rigor mortis?" Tyrone asked.

"Yuk," said Chaff. "Not at lunchtime."

"Surely she'd have been stiff by the morning. Gavin couldn't have just laid her out like this."

"I think rigor had set in by the time we arrived, certainly by the time the pathologist came onto the scene."

"We'll have to hunt out a textbook and read up on pathology," Flint said. "Still, I imagine the pathologist knew what he was doing."

"He's very good," Chaff added.

Flint drew attention to two circular marks visible in the muddy shoreline beside Harry's knees. "What are these?"

"Bootmarks."

"Too small, much too small."

"Stones?"

"No, they're holes."

"They look like stake-holes," Tyrone said.

Chaff questioned him. Tyrone explained, with great authority, how an ancient wooden hut would decay, leaving only holes where its supporting frame once stood.

"We did put a tent over the body to keep the rain off. It's probably where we put the poles."

"Wouldn't allow it on my site," Flint grumbled.

"Yes, but we don't have all the time in the world," Chaff said. "The job needed to be done there and then, we can't wait a thousand years before we investigate a body."

Such jibes were commonplace, Flint had heard them all before. Archaeologists have all the time in the world, it seemed, but not today. "Did anyone mention the dog?" Flint asked.

"What could we say about the dog except that it was dead? My boss, Inspector Roper, made the suggestion that the dog had gone into the water and that Lady Dunning had waded into the lake to rescue it. That was the story the local paper carried; it seems likely things like that happen all the time."

Chaff could not be persuaded to stay longer and left the two archaeologists sifting through the rubbish of late twentieth-century popular cuisine. Flint found a stray french fry and nibbled at it.

"Can you go to Cadbury on your own?"

"Sure – Merlin won't be there," Tyrone said, his eyes following Chaff down the street.

"O ye of little faith."

"I bet he did it you know. Gavin's a bit of a prick, but nobody kills their own mother. That leaves Harry and Merlin to set up the original scam, or even Merlin on his own, trying to bring his prophesies to life. When things went wrong, he killed Harry and stole the swords to cover up."

"Plausible, but he didn't strike me as being potentially violent."

"You should read the tabloids more often. You'd say he's the quiet type, a loner with no friends who lives in a fantasy world with a mother-surrogate fixation on an old lady? Hand his character profile to a police psychologist and they'd list him as a potential serial killer."

Yes, Tyrone was right, as usual.

"And if you were, your next victim would be?"

Tyrone lifted his hand, and aimed his index finger at the polystyrene burger carton. He jabbed it viciously, puncturing the box with a crack. "Us."

"Someone's tried that."

"They might try again. That's why I don't want to get friendly with any of them. And I don't trust Merlin."

"We have to trust someone."

Tyrone drove Flint out to the western suburbs, then set off alone for the Dorset border and the rendezvous with Merlin. He was still predicting failure as he drove away.

When Gwen Calman came out of school that evening, checking her handbag for car keys, she was aware of a figure leaning on her white Peugeot, arms folded, apparently fascinated by a set of newly-returned martins diving amongst the eaves of the old wing of the school.

"You're sitting on my car," she said.

Flint broke from his trance. "Sorry: I was deep in thought."

"Yes, I suppose that's what you do best – think."

He inclined his head in false modesty.

"So why are you sitting on my car?"

"I need a lift back into town – Tyrone dropped me off, he's gone elsewhere."

"If I give you another lift, you're going to ask me questions again."

"It's the nature of the beast."

"'If once you pay him the Danegeld, you never get rid of the Dane'." Gwen quoted.

"Hillaire Belloc?" Flint guessed.

"Kipling," Gwen said. "It was one of Mother's favourite quotations." Her eyes made one circuit of the car park, confirmed that no pupils were watching, then told him to get in.

She drove for a few minutes, then as the suburbs opened up into parkland, Flint asked her to find somewhere to stop. Gwen turned the car into Victoria Park, her expression oozing distrust. She was frightened of him.

"I don't bite," he said, as the handbrake creaked on.

"You do all manner of things," she stated. "Your friends and colleagues in London don't hide your secrets, do they?"

"Ah, someone has been snooping on my private life."

"We can all do it; it's not your exclusive preserve. I don't understand why an archaeologist gets involved in this kind of underhand work."

"Call me a stickler for truth and justice."

"You have the morals of an alley cat – everyone says so. You have no respect for law and order, or religion or anything decent."

"That's going a little far; I pursue an alternative lifestyle. Dull-minded people think that's immoral; now you're not dull-minded, are you?"

"Yes, very."

Gwen gave him a stone-faced, indignant, disapproving confirmation that she would not be charmed onto his side.

219

"Would dull-minded people disapprove of what went on between Gavin and Alison Wright?"

"That's their business; and it's all in the past, so you needn't intrude on Gavin's privacy."

"Who's idea was the Excalibur scam? Was it your mother's, or Gavin's, or was it Alison's? I'm trying to grapple with a whole web of relationships. All my suspects are bound up with ties of affection, or family, or business."

"Suspects? There are no suspects."

"And of course we have the Pendragon Society, absolutely riddled with rivalry and petty intrigues. There is something going on, Gwen. Now are you going to tell me what it is, or do I have to prove it?"

"Prove it."

"I can't."

A look of disbelief crossed her face. "You admit your own impotence? You? The great Dr Flint?"

He nodded, grinning.

"What the hell do you want?"

"If I can't prove any of our theories, I want to start disproving them, one by one, reduce the options, remove suspects from our list."

"Well you can remove Gavin and myself."

"OK, shall do. What's Gavin doing tomorrow morning?"

"He'll be at his shop, I imagine."

"Can you meet me at your mother's house?"

"I have to work."

"Call in sick."

"No."

"You see, it looks to me as if Gavin is lying, and the police know it, but have been willing to assume he was suffering from some sort of post-traumatic stress. Your mother drowned; she was dead before she left the water.

Someone therefore pulled her out and laid her on the bank. Gavin denies it was him, but if the death was an accident no one else could have pulled your mother from the water. See my problem? See why I need to perform a straightforward scientific test?"

Gwen was almost trembling, whether with fear, or anger, or indecision.

"To show you Gavin did nothing wrong," she stated.

"Yes, to rule Gavin out of the equation."

She weighed up her moral duties and her loyalties. "If I were to report myself sick, I could be at Mother's house by ten."

"Brilliant. Are there any spades at the house? We've brought one, but ideally we need two – and a pick."

"What on earth are you going to do?"

"We're going to exhume the dog."

Chapter Twenty-One

Repeat a piece of fiction often enough and it becomes fact. Everyone knows that Arthur lived at Camelot – everyone except those who know that Camelot was invented by Chretien de Troyes and embellished by Mallory. For those who shrug off such inconvenient facts, South Cadbury Castle holds the strongest claim to be the 'real' Camelot.

Tyrone had driven down in the UNY-DIG van immediately after dropping Flint at the school. He parked in the village then walked across farmland to the hill whose wooded slopes were encircled by the ditches and ramparts of an Iron Age fort. Cadbury is no fairy-tale castle. At its apex, the hill is bald with no glittering towers to hold captive maidens, no dungeons and definitely no dragons.

He sat at the very summit of the hill, at the point called Arthur's Palace, aware of the supreme, frustrating irony of the Arthurian stories. Camelot was a myth and Cadbury is a myth-within-a-myth. It is a fact that Camelot was a twelfth-century invention. It is a fact that the association between Camelot and Cadbury was a fifteenth-century invention. Infuriating for those who would kill the legend of Camelot, it is also a fact that modern archaeologists have discovered a grand hall and massive wall dating to the age of Arthur. The remains lay buried beneath where

Tyrone now sat. He hated that kind of synchronicity; archaeology should encourage feeble legends to wither, not provide them with new and substantial roots.

Where was Merlin? The sun was already edging towards the horizon, and there was no sign of the eccentric in black. In a more charitable moment, Tyrone suspected the clapped-out 2CV had let down the would-be enchanter. Over to the west he could make out the dim outline of Glastonbury Tor. The area was crowded with Arthurian sites and Merlin could have picked any one of them.

Tyrone had arrived two hours early and spent the time pacing around the perimeter, looking for the elusive scars which would betray a hastily dug hole. With eighteen acres to search, he knew that a proper search would take several days, even if he dared take the metal detector from the van. But searching would be fruitless, he knew. If Merlin had lied about his intention to come to Cadbury, he had probably lied about the sword being buried there.

A deep bank of cloud on the horizon swallowed the sun and immediately, the air fell cold. No Merlin, but Tyrone was not surprised, not even disappointed. This was what he'd expected; he'd told Flint that this is what would happen.

Allowing gravity to lead the way, Tyrone half ran down the slope to the castle entrance at the innermost rampart. He trudged down the track between the trees without meeting a soul. Only a gentle breeze ruffled the young wheat beside the track to the village church where the UNY-DIG van was parked. In the gloom of dusk, Tyrone pulled himself up onto the graveyard wall and took out his mobile phone. The landlady answered and brought Flint out of the shower.

Mobile phone calls are expensive and economy was so easy. A few words said it all. "Strike one, boss," said Tyrone. "You know you wanted allies, people we can trust? Well, scrub Merlin off your list."

Strike one, as Tyrone had said. Flint's second gamble came next morning. More miles were added to the expenses bill as Tyrone drove from Bath to Glastonbury and beyond. Both were in digging gear: Flint in jeans and careworn purple arran, Tyrone dressed for combat in camouflaged trousers and khaki pullover with reinforced elbows. Gwen met them in the courtyard of the Dunning house.

"I don't like this," she said. "I've had to lie to be here this morning. I'd had to tell school I was sick. Must you dig up poor Rimmy? It doesn't seem right."

"Better us than the police," Flint said. "Has Gavin gone?"

"He was out when I arrived."

Tyrone was unloading tools from the rear of the van.

"You said we could borrow another spade," Flint said.

"Oh God, in the shed – the door on the end."

Flint selected a spade and Tyrone collected a bucket and mattock from within the outhouse, then they followed Gwen towards the mere. Over his shoulder was Flint's army surplus satchel.

"Where did you bury Rimmy?" he asked.

He had been right about the name 'Rhymhi', a bitch with a walk-on part in the far-fetched Arthurian yarn entitled 'The tale of Culwech and Olwen'. Gwen and Gavin had buried her close to the mere, in soft earth below a break of slope, a few yards higher that where their mother had been found.

The tools hit the ground with a clatter and Flint unslung his satchel. He would habitually stuff this with useful items when travelling. Useful items always included his trowel.

"You brought a trowel?" Gwen asked as he took it out.

"Have trowel will travel."

Gwen stood for a long time, looking out over the waters where she had scattered her mother's ashes only the evening before.

"You're tenacious," she said.

"We are, I'm afraid. It's for the best, Gwen."

"But digging —"

"We're archaeologists, it's our way to understand the past. Your mother would heartily approve."

Wet eyes and a nod made a pretence of agreement, then Gwen wandered away. Flint checked that his camera was working, then checked the overcast sky. A cold, damp wind was blowing in from the Bristol Channel and rain could not be far away.

"Let's get this over with."

Tyrone pulled away the loose turf and then both set to with the spades, digging away the sticky brown loam. The grave was less than a metre deep and the diggers soon saw the flash of fading golden yellow hair. Trowels were needed only to expose her rump and her legs, then the dog could be pulled free of the ground.

Rimmy had grown bloated with gasses as she decomposed from the inside. Laid out on a black plastic dustbin liner, her lifeless white eyes lolled skyward. Tyrone brought up a bucket of water and began to splash the carcass clean.

"Don't it half pong?" he said.

Suddenly, Mrs Bates, 'Full English Breakfast' seemed

225

a mistake. Flint paused in his work, but black-brown crystals in the mouth drew his attention.

"Is that blood?" Tyrone asked a rhetorical question.

Flint waggled the jaw, then tested three loose teeth. One fell half-way from its socket. "She's had a tremendous smack on the jaw."

"Kicked in the teeth?"

"Possibly." He gingerly lifted the limbs, one by one. "Look at this."

When he pulled up the left foreleg, he was easily able to bring it to meet the body with a right angle.

"This should still be fully articulated," Flint said. "I don't know much about dogs' anatomies, but that leg looks broken to me."

"That's how commando's used to kill guard dogs."

"Like how?"

Tyrone adopted a commando pose. "Right; you face the dog, and when it leaps on you, you grab both its legs and rip them apart. It causes a heart attack."

"To you, or to the dog?"

"The dog. I bet if we cut it open, there won't be water in its lungs."

"Rather not." Flint stood up, and moved a pace away from the smell.

"I bet it didn't drown."

"And she didn't bark. Question is, did she die before Harry, or afterwards?"

"Before, I'll bet. And if someone killed the dog . . ."

"Same someone killed Harry."

Of course he'd suspected this much, but now he had the proof before him, the horror of the idea swamped the thrill of discovery.

"Have you finished?" Gwen called from higher up the hill.

Tyrone looked at Flint. "Take it away in a doggie bag?"

Flint winced at the pun. "That would be showing our hand."

Gwen had come as close as she would. "Finished?"

"As I said, negative evidence," Flint called back. "We'll just tidy up."

"Be quick," she ventured no explanation, but stood watching at a distance.

A half-dozen rapid photographs were taken of the scene, but would show little of the key evidence. The rotting body was pulled back to the hole on its dustbin liner. A second bin bag was laid over the top. Flint would have wrapped up the body, but feared it might disintegrate, or at least, that the distended organs would burst. Earth soon concealed the plastic, then the turf was replaced and pressed down. Gwen called down the hill again, her face contorted by worry.

"You'd better hurry, I saw Gavin drive past. He's probably going to the shop."

Four minutes later, the green van was speeding out of the village and finding the road to Bridgwater. D.S. Chaff was ready to believe anything of the eccentric pair. Once she had been located and brought to the police station, she took much convincing to act on the suggestion she exhume a dog to turn a closed case of accidental death into an open murder file.

Several other officers had to be consulted, in person and by phone. At the point where Flint despaired and Tyrone was moaning about missing lunch, Chaff breezed out of her office and issued a tired, "Come on, then". Almost three hours had elapsed and it was well into the afternoon. Rain had already fallen and more threatened as Tyrone parked in the yard beside two Peugeots.

Smoke billowed from behind the outbuildings. Gavin came to meet them, his face blackened with soot.

"You're too late," he said.

"You dug her up," Flint stated.

"I'm not having you nosing around on my land, understand?"

D.S. Chaff's car pulled into the yard. Gavin went straight up to her door and was pleading his case before she had a chance to step out. "I want to report trespassers."

"If you wouldn't mind, sir, I'd like to see your dog." Chaff pressed past Gavin, to where Flint and Tyrone stood in a state of agitation.

"He's burnt it," Flint said.

Gavin grinned.

"Did you use plenty of petrol?"

"Oh, gallons."

"Would you show me, please, sir?" Chaff flashed irritation towards the two archaeologists. Both dug their hands deep into their pockets, anticipating anticlimax.

With a cocky self-confident air, Gavin led them around the outbuilding to where the smoke arose from a mound of hot ash. A pile of kindling for the range had been added to a pyre made of packing cases and supermarket boxes. Vents in the ash glowed red as the wind swirled around the building. The smell of burnt meat carried on each gust, but the bones projecting from the embers were disarticulated and charred to ashy waste. Stray raindrops hissed into the fire, spitting derision on their efforts.

"He's destroyed the evidence!" Tyrone protested.

Chaff gave a deep sigh. The downturned corners of her mouth conveyed disgust: it was as if he'd cracked a

228

smutty joke in front of her mother. She turned about and walked back towards her car without saying a word.

Gwen now ventured from the house, a look of absolute panic on her face. Gavin went to her side and slipped a protecting arm around her shoulders. His smile of wicked satisfaction said 'Victory is mine'.

As he looked from brother to sister, Flint recalled Tyrone's bold assertion that nobody kills their own mother. The twins retreated back into their house, Gwen shaking her head, Gavin making loud and obvious comforting noises.

Chaff was leaning against the wing of her car. As Flint caught her eye, she actually smiled.

"You two are either the world's most brilliant detectives, or the two most flat-footed, I don't know which."

"Plump for brilliant."

"You know things, and you're not telling me."

"A lot of what we know is rather far-fetched. It wouldn't satisfy your standards of evidence."

"Like a dog that's no longer here?"

"Why did he burn it, if he had nothing to hide?" Tyrone said.

"To annoy you?" Chaff said. "To stop you digging up his poor dead dog a second time? People grow attached to their pets."

"The dog was killed," Flint said. "This is a murder and you should start taking it seriously."

"King Arthur? Excalibur? Batty old women digging swords out of ponds, and you want me to take it seriously?"

"Deny the obvious, think laterally."

She nodded, sensing that Flint was somehow putting her down. "OK, so here's something to baffle your university brains. Try laterally thinking about this one.

Last night, there was a break-in at Glastonbury Abbey. Nothing was taken, the intruder was seen, but got away. This sounds kinky enough to be right up your street. Any ideas?"

Tyrone looked at Flint. Flint looked at Tyrone. Both spoke the name at the same time.

"Merlin!"

"Who?"

An unseen message passed from one archaeologist to the other and both began moving towards the van.

"Where are you off to now?" Chaff asked.

"The Abbey," Flint replied, pulling open the driver's door. "We have to get there before he tries again."

Chapter Twenty-Two

At the centre of Glastonbury stands the Abbey, a ruined skeleton, beautiful in its desolation. The policewoman, the two archaeologists and a warden walked beneath soaring arches and between the towering, roofless walls. The gloom, solitude and the cold echoing floors experienced by medieval monks had given way to light, and air, and freshly mown grass. As a blue-bowler, with a reverence for nature and a suspicion of institutions, an Abbey in ruins brought Flint closer to God than an Abbey complete.

"This was Avalon," Tyrone explained to Chaff, moving his hands in rhythm to his words. "It's the oldest extant Christian site in England, reputed to be the last resting place of Arthur and Guinevere."

Chaff nodded, faintly amused by this variation on the chat-up technique. One of the Abbey wardens led them directly to the Choir, where a small plot of wet grass marked the spot where Arthur's tomb once stood. Like the presenter of a BBC documentary, Tyrone posed beside the grass and described the scene.

"In the twelfth century, three metres below my feet, a bunch of monks claimed to have found Arthur's coffin."

"So they dug him up and reburied him," Flint interrupted.

Tyrone frowned; this was his scene. "Of course, the body has disappeared, along with a bronze cross —"

"Lead," Flint corrected.

"Yeah, lead, but still conveniently lost."

"So?" Chaff asked.

Flint knelt by the turf, pointing out the fine lines which ran across it. In places, the grass was yellowing. He asked the warden if the plot had been disturbed: the answer was no. Out came a pair of trowels.

"You're not going to dig another hole?" Chaff asked. "Is there a dog here too?"

Tyrone went back to the van to fetch the metal detector, whilst Flint negotiated with the warden and with Chaff. Given cautious permission, Flint began experimentally lifting at the turf. Without effort he turned back an area over a metre long. The soil below was clearly disturbed. Tyrone returned with the metal detector, passed it over the ground and the machine immediately growled recognition. Next the trowels came into play. Merlin would have had little time on his first clandestine visit to the Abbey: the hole need not be too deep. They dug for ten minutes, the sun emerging from cloud, Chaff and the warden saying little, the two archaeologists intent on their art.

Tyrone ceased digging as his trowel clinked against metal. Fingers then played the part reserved for brushes on proper excavations. Sunlight caught bright steel as soil was wiped away from the blade.

"What is it?" Chaff fell to her knees beside them.

"Our replica."

"You don't sound very thrilled."

"We want the real one," Tyrone said.

Flint stood up and raised a muddy hand to his stiff shoulder, working the joints around, silently cursing

Merlin. Without any reverence, the replica Excalibur was drawn from Arthur's grave plot, carried to a nearby water tap and the dirt washed away.

"He was coming back for it," Flint explained to Chaff as he wiped his trowel clean on the turf.

"Who?"

"Merlin."

"Who?"

"Do you have half an hour and a great deal of patience? If so, I'll explain."

"I want to know what you're talking about."

"He was going to retrieve this sword, but must have been scared off. It's the one he stole from us at Edgar Jenkins Hall."

"Why? Why would anyone steal a sword and bury it, and why here?"

"This is Arthur's tomb," Tyrone said, "Well, one of them. It's a logical place to bury Excalibur."

Chaff was shaking her head. "King Arthur . . . Merlin . . . I'm sorry but this is getting just a little out of hand. Who is Merlin, what's his real name? Where does he live?"

Flint gave her a brief description of Colin T. Barker and his alias; Tyrone threw in a few lines to undermine his character and amplify his role as villain.

"He's crackers, and dangerous."

"Crackers? Dangerous?" She may have been making a point about eccentrics.

Flint went on to describe Merlin's multicoloured 2CV van. "It shouldn't be hard for you to find."

"Why would I want to find him?"

"Suspicion of theft, fraud, reckless driving and murder."

Chaff shook her head.

"OK, breaking into an Abbey and disturbing hallowed

ground. Scepticism notwithstanding, we need to find Merlin and you need to find Merlin. I'm not suggesting you arrest him, but we need to find out where he's hidden the real sword."

She held up a hand to halt him, traffic cop style. "I think it's you who need to do the finding out. Show me a crime – a proper crime – and I'll take action."

"But this is it; this is the tip of the iceberg, there is a crime, several crimes."

"I'll see you boys around," Chaff said, turning on her heel.

"I'll call you," Tyrone called after the vanishing figure.

"She doesn't believe us," Flint said.

"No, but you only told her a fraction of what we know." Tyrone kicked at the soil. "This means I was right about him burying the swords."

"Yes, but where's the other one? How many more candidates do you think there are round here?"

"About fifty," Tyrone said. "But anyone in their right mind wouldn't bother with forty of them."

"Who says he's in his right mind?"

"But he's operating in a rational way."

"Maybe, but we're not," Flint said, his mind now drifting beyond the Abbey, trying to decide what he must do next.

"No?"

"No – you run after Chaff, try and raise her interest in the case. I have to corner Alison before Gavin gets to her."

Sergeant Chaff drove Tyrone to Glastonbury Tor in her car. Perhaps romance would blossom as they searched the hilltop for signs of furtive scrapings. An unlikely feature in the flat Somerset farmland, the Tor resembles an enormous heap of dung dumped by a giant primordial beast striding through the wetlands. A church tower on its summit only emphasizes the dramatic romance that has inspired the inventing of so many tales.

Walking around the summit of Glastonbury Tor in ever-increasing circles revealed no signs of recent excavation.

"So why should he come up here?" Chaff asked, her eyes down on the ground, hunting for clues as she had been taught, and as Tyrone had been taught.

"It's feasible that this was the original Isle of Avalon; see how high we are?" Tyrone now stopped and rested a grimy hand on mud-smeared combat trousers. "This was probably an island in the sixth century and there is in fact a sub-Roman settlement up here, excavated in the Sixties. Spooky that, isn't it? Even the name Glastonbury means Isle of Glass, which has magical connotations in Celtic myth. It's jolly difficult squashing all these stories; there's a sort of historical conspiracy to keep Arthur alive."

"History was never my strongpoint at school."

"No? Well, the various assorted legends have this as the place Excalibur was forged, as where Arthur was buried —"

"Not at the Abbey?" She looked back to the south, to Glastonbury and beyond to the Quantock hills and the glitter of the Bristol Channel.

"Legends are elastic; you can stretch them any way you choose. Imagine the Arthur story was written by tabloid journalists two hundred years after the event."

He walked right up to the tower, found his bearings and pointed off to the west, beyond the town. "Over there is Wearyall Hill – some people confuse that with the Tor. That's where Joseph of Aramathea is said to have landed with the Holy Grail."

"I've got a tea towel with that on," Chaff said idly.

"Well there's no evidence the Grail ever existed, either. It's all medieval fantasy."

"Aw, you're spoiling it. Next you'll be telling me there's no Santa Claus."

"That's our business, finding the truth about the past."

"But why are you grubbing around like private detectives? Shouldn't you be giving lectures, or be digging in Egypt?"

"We're consultants," Tyrone said. "Or at least, I am. Jeff does the lecturing, I negotiate the contracts."

"Wheeler-dealing in archaeology? I don't believe it."

"It's true, that's what all this mystery is about, people trying to make the business pay."

"Oh is it?"

Tyrone was trying so hard to impress that he failed to notice her change of tone.

"And what is it about?" She leaned back against the stonework of the tower, one foot resting against the wall, hands in the pockets of her charcoal grey anorak, trying ever so slightly to appear demure.

"I'll explain."

Without considering his words, he began his BBC-style presentation once again. Some of the mannerisms had been copied from Flint, others from David Attenborough. He told her of their fears about Harry's death, about the theft of the swords and how Merlin was involved. He told her of the hype which would save an ailing company, and of convenient insurance policies which would serve as a safety net if the Excalibur launch failed. He told her his wildest theories born in Rome and of how Harry had somehow balked at the last moment and been eliminated by her confederates. He reviewed the methods, and motives for slaying young

236

Alsatian dogs and the significance of the dog that did not bark.

Chaff watched him carefully as he spoke, questioning every now and again. Her head was inclined to the right, her chin held high, her lips formed into a pout as she listened and considered his words. If she was impressed, she showed none of it. As he spoke, Tyrone began to feel fraudulent, as if he was boasting of improbable sexual prowess, or exaggerating the speed of his sports car. His narrative began to falter on matters of fact. Like the Arthurian epics, the plot lacked central form, characters came in and out at random, there was no continuity, no clear line between where truth ended and myth began.

The policewoman may have been taking mental notes, or merely humouring him. Tyrone begun to backtrack, inventing new plot lines and new suspects for new crimes. Then Chaff reached out and laid a gentle hand on his arm.

"Stop," she said, with more traffic cop overtones. "Let's look for this hole that's supposed to be up here. If we find the second sword, I'll start believing you. If we find this Merlin character, I'll start believing you."

"Promise?"

"But I have to tell you that I live with a copper named Dave who's six-foot-two and a damn good laugh, so you can forget the chat-up routine."

Feeling fifteen years of age, Tyrone said nothing immediately after the put-down. His hands found the pocket of the camouflaged trousers, then he shrugged his shoulders.

"Sure thing."

No appointments was now the rule. Nobody would know he was coming. Flint stalked the corridors of the redundant schoolhouse now used for Further Education classes and Mums and Toddler meetings and a regional drama group. He paused by one pale blue door. Through its panes, Ivor's ponytail could just be seen bobbing up and down beyond a surveyor's table. Through the next door, Alison Wright was seated before a computer monitor, her right hand moving a mouse around a cheese-shaped mouse-mat. The screen showed a colour picture of a cathedral, a cursor darted about its façade then with a click of the finger, the MPP logo appeared in the corner of the screen.

Trapped, he thought. Enslaved by her work, waiting to be caught. With as much care as he could manage, Flint eased open the door.

Alison turned sharply. "You!"

"Hi."

"Don't they knock up in Yorkshire?"

"No, we all keep our doors open; trusting sorts we northerners."

The wrinkles redistributed themselves. Surprise passed through annoyance into acceptance.

"Sit down – move that."

Flint removed two rolls of drawings from a swivel chair and sat with his back to a second computer monitor. Alison flicked her red fingernails towards the image of the cathedral.

"I'm writing a tender."

"I seem to spend half my life writing tenders and the other half reading the rejection letters," Flint said. "Times are tough in our business."

"Oh, we can't complain."

"Where is the Arthur Roadshow going first?"

"Nowhere without the sword."

She was expecting him to say something. Alison sat

with her red lips set in a straight line until Flint decided to let her enjoy his news.

"We found the replica."

"Did you?" She almost bounded into his lap. "Where, I mean, how . . . ?"

"We do know what we're doing."

"Well that's super news, I'll tell Gavin . . ."

"Do so, but it won't endear me to him, I'm sure. This morning we proved the inquest verdict was wrong. Harry's dog was killed, not drowned, killed."

"Oh God."

The implication sank home immediately. Flint was watching for a reaction – fear perhaps. "You understand . . ."

"Of course I understand! You seem to think you're dealing with simpletons. You seem to think we just sit around waiting for you to walk in and unveil your next outrageous accusation, but we don't. We meet, we telephone each other, we warn each other what you're up to."

When Alison smiled, it was less evil than patronizing. "We're not simpletons," she repeated.

A major problem in investigating the intelligentsia was that Flint's suspects were always intelligent, articulate and unlikely to make a step without calculating its consequences. They were unlikely to make slips of the tongue or be cornered into confessing.

"I need help, Alison, I really do."

"See a doctor."

"There's a conspiracy blocking my progress towards a solution; nobody will tell me what's going on."

"Because there is nothing going on."

"People don't give that impression. They don't give me straight answers."

"Ask straight questions."

Alison was back to being ice-cool once more, an excess of mascara spoiling attempts to read her eyes. Flint was distinctly unnerved. Ivor was amiable, Gavin bombastic, but Alison struck him as being the truly clever one. Advertising was a hard world and she must have learned a trick or two before falling into MPP.

Flint continued with care. "OK, so tell me why your little cabal hates Merlin so much?"

"Because he's a sick child who also needs help. He wants to join us, he wants to move into our office and help us on the Arthur project, but what can he do? Can he use one of these?" She indicated the CD-ROM machine. "Or the graphics plotter? Can he draw? Can he compose text? No, he's useless, he'd drag us down if we let him anywhere near the project."

"And let me guess why Gavin hates him; could it be because his mother used Merlin as a kind of personal guru?"

"Pet would be more accurate."

Everyone had it in for poor Merlin, thought Flint. Everyone except Harry. Perhaps that was the key.

"Was there ever any connection between Merlin and Charles Evans? I'm wandering here, I know, but if you and Gavin and Gwen and Ivor are all utterly innocent of anything remotely suspicious —"

"Which we are."

"If you are, I need another suspect. Evans was sued by Harry, so he'd have a good motive to push her into the lake."

Alison's computer chose this moment to bleep at her and she turned on her screen-saver of butterflies fluttering into infinity.

"We kept away from the feud with Charles Evans; that was strictly Harry's business."

"But MPP was Harry's business," Flint objected.

"No, we're a co-operative."

"But Harry was an old-fashioned matriarch. She regarded this project as her personal fief and her enemies would think the same. They could destroy her by destroying you."

"Or they could destroy us by destroying her," Alison said. "Is that what you're thinking?"

"On alternate days."

"And on the other days?"

"Someone close to Gavin might want him out of the influence of his mother."

Alison sounded sobered rather than angry. "Meaning me? I suppose you have worked out that Gavin and I once had a brief thing going, but I can tell you that's all over. It may amuse your tidy little mind to know that I have an alibi for the night Harry died. It is alibis you grub around for, isn't it? I can give you the name and address of my friend and the tacky details if that turns you on."

All this was said so nicely, so offhand, so sugar-sweet that the underlying antagonism was almost buried.

"I mean, what the hell, we may as well help you on your way."

"Please," Flint said.

"I went to London to prepare the press launch." Now she sounded irritable. "I had dinner with a reporter, I had breakfast with same reporter." Red lips smiled, satisfied. "Get the picture?"

The telephone rang and she reached over her monitor to collect it.

"Yes?" she said, sweeping back her hair. "Yes, he's here now." She gave Flint a wink. "All the usual things," she told the distant voice. "What story should we sell him?"

241

Flint felt his neck prickling. He hated being teased.

"He's found the replica, at least," Alison said.

The voice at the far end of the phone sounded male.

"He was asking about Merlin," Alison continued. "I know – and about old Mr Evans. Oh, is that true?" There was a long burst of monologue from the crackling receiver. "Sad though? OK, it's not sad. Shall I tell Inspector Flint about it? OK, bye."

"Gavin?" Flint asked.

"Yes, your good friend Gavin. He told me about your fetish for digging up dead animals. It must be horrid being an archaeologist, I couldn't stand the squalor."

"It must be horrid being in PR, I couldn't stand the squalor."

Alison stopped smiling, or pretending to smile. "I'm trying to be polite. I'm trying not to tell you to piss off and leave us alone."

"What was that about Charles Evans?"

"Charles Evans?" She said. "Yes, you and him should get together for a long talk sometime."

"Why?"

"He's dead."

Chapter Twenty-Three

Who better to ask about a sudden death than an insurance man? Euan Trepennick was the head of the South-Western region of Northern Consolidated Assurance, based in Bristol. Flint remembered the directions he'd been given: roads, roundabouts and where to park the green van. He arrived without appointment, conscious that his last unhappy attempt to visit Trepennick had been terminated in a stream bed in the Mendips.

It was a grey, clouded morning, but warmer than the day before. The Bristol office had none of the sleek modernism of the Leeds headquarters. It was Victorian, and listed, which gave the owners an excuse to keep it dowdy. Flint and the receptionist skirmished briefly before a voice echoed from an open office door.

"Show Dr Flint in, Susan."

Euan rose to his feet and shook Flint's hand, asking Susan to close the door behind her. "Dr Flint. I feared we might never get a chance to meet again. I heard about your accident – I trust you're none the worse for wear."

Flint touched the shoulder, today only slightly tender. Immediately he was conscious of developing a habit and pulled his hand away from the injury. "It made me think seriously about buying some insurance."

"Wise." Euan gestured towards a chair, palm upper-most. "As a rule, people don't buy insurance; insurance has to be sold."

"Whether people need it or not?"

"Oh, we all need it."

The silver hair had strayed a little since last combed, but his bow tie was neatly tied and the three-piece suit lent Euan a dapper, dignified trademark. Above his head yawned a watercolour of the Clifton suspension bridge. Euan sat back, fidgeting slightly to relieve pressure on his left leg. He was familiar with old injuries.

"How about Lady Dunning?" Flint asked. "Did she need insurance? I have the go-ahead from Matt Humphries, so you don't need to worry about confidentiality."

"Matt Humphries doesn't work in this office," Euan said.

"No, but what I'm saying is, I'm on your side."

"I see. You're the one who lost our swords?"

"They were stolen from us."

"The net effect on my balance sheet is the same."

"Sorry."

Trepennick cast back his head, obviously doubting the sincerity of Flint's contrition. "Did Matt Humphries send you with a specific brief to scuttle this office?"

"No."

"Well he wouldn't be straight with you, that's not his way. Forgive me if I sound a little tetchy, but my career is in your hands."

"My hands?"

"Oh yes. So convince me that we're on the same side."

So the hunch about office politics was true; Humphries and Trepennick were engaged in their own private war, with Flint playing the mercenary. Humphries gave the impression of being that hard-nosed new breed of executive, tough and ambitious that arose from the Thatcher years, whereas Trepennick was an Old School manager, content with what he had achieved and looking forward to a decent pension. At that moment, Flint decided to wave a flag of neutrality.

"I'm working towards a solution whereby you can avoid paying out on the stolen swords."

"So Humphries tells me; could you tell me how?"

No, was the answer, but Flint was gambling now. "If the whole affair with the stolen swords were a fraud —"

"Which it is not. I set up the policy; I have every confidence in the people I've dealt with. There's no fraud."

"But you said you have to sell insurance; whose idea was it for Museum Projects Plus to insure Harry's life?"

"It came about in discussion. First we insured the sword, then the replica, then the key personnel."

"Discussion with whom? Harry, Gavin, Alison?"

"Harry – we were old friends you know."

"Yes, you're a Pendragon. Presumably you follow Harry's strand of argument about the sub-Roman Arthur."

"Yes – I'm no academic, you understand, I simply dabble. I've always been interested in West Country Folklore."

"So why go into insurance?"

"You can't eat folklore. You're very fortunate in being able to make a living in a field you love."

Flint's 'love' of archaeology was sometimes as tenuous as the 'living' he was purported to make. He frowned for effect.

"I'm very curious, Dr Flint, as to what your own objective is. At what point do you go back to Yorkshire? What happens at the end of all this?"

"Harry's death is cleared up and the swords are returned

to their rightful owners, so your company doesn't have to pay out a bean."

"And in the course of your crusade, I lose my job, MPP goes bankrupt, a learned society is wracked by scandal and a family is torn apart by accusations of murder. Your principles carry a high price."

"So help me, and perhaps none of that will happen. I still don't know which villain is at the centre of all this skulduggery. Everyone is behaving so oddly, I don't know who to place at the top of my hit parade. Take Alison Wright, for example —"

"A very pleasant woman. Very above board."

"Then there's Gavin —"

"Devoted to his mother. He's more charming than he first appears."

"And Merlin —"

"Ah yes, Merlin. Very sad. I haven't seen him since before Harry died. Was he at the funeral? I can't remember."

"No."

Euan had a range of inscrutable expressions, each inexplicable. "Strange boy," he responded.

"Euan, you were one of Harry's oldest friends in the Pendragons, everyone says so. You're a cornerstone of the group, the power behind the throne."

"No, really. I'm just an amateur."

"They're all amateurs, it's just that some are more amateur than others. I have dealings with scores of societies like yours and they're all run by half a dozen stalwarts."

"I'm on the committee," he admitted, with a degree of modesty.

"So you fought Harry's corner when she wanted to give her Excalibur paper?"

"I smoothed ruffled feathers."

"You mean Charles Evans?"

"Poor Charles – you heard the news, I presume?"

Each day, a dozen personal tragedies crossed Euan Trepennick's desk for signature and compensation. He might have become used to it, but his expression had fallen to one of stone.

"I've lost two dear friends in the space of a month."

When asked what had happened, Euan gave an unemotional account of a sudden stroke, followed by three days in intensive care.

"They turned off his machine on Monday." Euan clicked his fingers. "Gone. I'd known him, what, thirty years, ever since this brought me back onto civvy street."

He slapped his left leg, stuck out stiffly before him.

"I'm very sorry."

"Are you? You're not disappointed that there were no suspicious circumstances behind his death?"

"I'm being seriously misunderstood down here."

"Oh, I'm sorry if that sounded peevish, but when an outsider comes down and is seen to be interfering —"

"In what?"

"In everything."

Flint could talk around the subject for hours, but he was getting nowhere. Nobody he spoke to admitted knowing, or suspecting anything underhand was taking place and he even began to doubt his own convictions. He'd go back to Bath, meet up with Tyrone and have an all-night brainstorming session to clear his thoughts.

"The funeral is tomorrow, at his village chapel," Trepennick said. "Charles was a Methodist; are you a religious man?"

247

"No – I've studied religion too deeply to believe in God."

Trepennick mumbled agreement. "There are professions which make one sceptical, even callous."

The pathologist had voiced similar sentiments on the morning after Harry died. An affinity with death brought about professional detachment from the whole idea of mortality, even one's own mortality. Idly Flint asked, "How much would the premiums be to insure my life, say for fifty thousand pounds?"

Euan leaned forward, adopting a critical, professional eye to the figure in old tweed and jeans. "Single life? No profits? Mid-thirties, non-smoker, average weight: then I'd say it would cost you twenty-five pounds a month, but I don't think I'd accept your policy proposal."

"Why not?"

Euan sat back in his chair, hands clasped across his belly. "You're a bad risk."

Flint was unsure if this was a threat, a warning or a Merlin-like prediction. His uncertainty showed.

"Don't take me wrong," Euan said. "But if you make a habit of pursuing people and accusing them of murder . . ." He opened his hands to a million gruesome possibilities.

"Are you staying in Bath?" he asked.

"I'm in hiding," Flint said. "False name, obscure address. I feel I owe it to my insurance company."

This amused Euan. "I wish you well, young man, but take some advice from an old hand. I've been on and off the Pendragon's committee for the past decade and I've learned that academics, and people who aspire to be academics need to be handled with great subtlety. It's not your finest art."

*   *   *

248

Tyrone spent the morning in the Bath central library and Flint joined him at lunchtime.

"How are you?"

"Bored stupid."

"We better hurry and find what we're looking for, because we're taking so long, the suspects are dying on us."

"Who?"

"Charles Evans – stroke on Friday." Flint rubbed a tired eye and thought of his last sight of Charlie Evans, hobbling towards the Gents' toilet in Newcastle. Perhaps the solution to the riddle had hobbled off with him.

"No foul play, of course. That would be too neat, too predictable, too easy for us. Scratch one more source of information. How far have you got?"

"About as far as thinking I deserved some lunch."

After lunch they returned to the library and ran through local newspapers of the previous year, hunting for any reference to MPP, or the Pendragons or the Dunning family or Northern Consolidated Assurance. The page-and-a-half of notes by four o'clock spoke of a fruitless day. Flint drove back to the lodgings, whilst Tyrone opted to walk back via the fax bureau to stretch his legs and clear a headache.

Parking space was at a premium in the leafy side-street and Flint had to park the van a good fifty yards beyond Mrs Bates' front gate. He was only just closing the house door when the landlady sprang to issue her warning, eyes wide and hands wringing.

"Someone phoned for you," she said.

"When?"

"About one o'clock."

"Man, woman?"

"Man – he asked if Dr Flint or Dr Drake was staying here."

Flint became tense. "And?"

"I said no, of course – he put the phone down straight away."

He could only smile.

"That was what you wanted?" she asked.

"Yes – excellent." He was regretting the rather obvious UNY-DIG van standing out in the road, but its distance from the lodging house might prove to be sufficiently distracting. All those he could trust had been asked to phone his college number and leave messages with Debs the secretary. Someone else was obviously ringing around the guesthouses and hotels trying to locate him. A hand groping in darkness had briefly been within inches of touching its prey.

"Was it them?" Mrs Bates lowered her forehead a trifle to show she was uneasy. "What would they do if they found out where you are staying?"

Burn the house down, thought Flint. Sabotage the car, murder us all in our beds. "Oh nothing," he said.

Mrs Bates offered tea and scones in the lounge and Flint welcomed the chance to unwind for twenty minutes. He heard about Mrs Bates' daughter, the architecture student, about her holiday in Tenerife and the trouble she'd had with the drains packing up. Somehow he found himself in the back yard of the house, lifting the inspection hatch and using his sacred trowel to scrape wads of mushy toilet paper into a bucket.

"I'm sorry about this," Mrs Bates said. "You are good."

Another wad of pastel-brown sludge went into the bucket.

"I've dug out worse than this."

At that moment he was recalling the dog he'd exhumed the day before. Now he had his arm fully extended into liquid ordure. Next incarnation, he'd choose a nice, clean, well-paid office job like Trepennick's. He pulled out a near-whole roll of toilet paper and sticky cotton wool he hardly dare think about. The liquid began to flow. The last black, greasy item felt like human hair.

Oh God, he thought. She's murdered her husband and flushed his body parts down the toilet.

The item may have been someone's toupee, but Flint now had a larger audience.

"Doc!" Tyrone rushed into the yard. "See this!" He began to open his briefcase amid the digging implements and spatters of grey slime which soiled the yard.

"Must I? I'm up to my armpits."

Tyrone at last realized what had been happening. "Shit!"

"Spot on."

Flint suggested Mrs Bate's flush the system a few times. Water began to gurgle in the pipe as he stuck his bare arm under the garden tap and rinsed it back to its normal pink. Tyrone could hardly restrain his excitement; he'd obviously jogged much of the distance from the centre of town.

"We've got what we were looking for," Tyrone said. "You know, my long shot about those Scandinavian museums?"

"Would you like tea, Dr Drake?" Mrs Bates called from the kitchen doorway.

"Yeah, great."

Tyrone took a long roll of fax printout from his briefcase and Flint hurriedly dried his hands on the back of his jeans in order to read it.

"And Dr Flint," Mrs Bates called again. "I forgot to

251

ask you about supper. I usually cook liver on Thursdays, but . . ."

"Fine," said Flint, drifting towards the fax which dangled from Tyrone's arm as tantalizing as Mata-Hari's seventh veil.

". . . so I bought pizzas."

"You're an angel." Flint had the fax in hand. It was from Copenhagen and it was over a metre long. It took only moments to assimilate the text and understand the diagram. Tyrone was justly pleased with himself.

"This must be worth a raise, boss."

Mrs Bates allowed the investigators to take over her dining-room table and they ate pizza as they worked. The laptop computer sat on the let-down front of her drinks cabinet and charts were scattered across the floor. As the evening wore on, she ferried in coffees and biscuits and cheese rolls and home-baked scones and anything else she could find to allow herself to pause and gaze at the sprawling mass of paperwork. A replica sword was propped up against her russet velvet curtains.

"Are you any nearer to finding the other one?" she asked, tray in hand.

Tyrone flared his nostrils at Flint. Flint shook his head and posted a pencil behind his ear. He accepted the fourth cup of coffee and chose a Maryland cookie from the biscuit tin.

"You don't have to stay up," he hinted.

The carriage clock had chimed midnight some while before.

"Oh don't worry about me."

"As you see, Mrs Bates, we have a room full of information. One bit of it is wrong. We have dozens of statements; one of them must be wrong too. We have

252

about ten possible suspects and they all seem to be guilty
– all of them. Not one, all."

"They could have formed a little gang," she suggested.

"It's called MPP," Tyrone grumbled.

"There's nothing more we can ask, there's nobody else
to talk to. The two people who might have helped most
are dead."

Flint took another cookie and bit it in half. Mrs Bates
inclined the tin towards Tyrone. He accepted the tin.

"Perhaps you've got it all," the landlady suggested.
"Your answer could be here," she pointed to a roll of computer paper. "Or here . . . if you've asked everyone."

"We've tried thinking laterally, testing the evidence
against all kinds of silly motives, but they are all
possible. No one will admit anything and the police
won't move until we can prove some kind of just
cause."

"What about that?" Mrs Bates kicked the toe of her
slippers at the Copenhagen fax which curled over the
edge of her fireplace. "After tea, you told me it was the
key to everything."

"Yes, but without the real sword, it's a worthless piece
of information. It's a clue, but it's not what the police
would call proof."

"You ought to set some kind of trap," said Mrs
Bates.

"We don't have any bait, Mrs Bates," Tyrone said.

It was twenty past twelve and she was still smiling.
"More coffee?" asked Mrs Bates.

"No thanks," said Flint.

Hurriedly Tyrone interrupted him, "Yes please. No –
make it cocoa."

"Milky?"

253

"Very."

She smiled, as if to say 'pleased to be of service', then went about her task.

"Christ!" said Tyrone, "She's worse than my mother."

Flint spotted that Tyrone had come awake. He was sitting erect once more, anxious to speak. "OK, three minutes to boil milk, what's your game?"

"She's right, we need to outsmart them; beat someone into confessing."

"You're suggesting physical violence?"

"No – intellectually beat them, get them on the run, make them panic, divide and conquer, go for the chink in their armour."

"Nice clichés for twelve twenty-nine." For a moment, Flint had been expecting Tyrone to make some brilliant logical deduction.

Tyrone held up a finger. "If we knew where Merlin was . . ."

"Which we don't."

"And if we now had the real sword . . ."

"Which we haven't."

"We could use this," he kicked the fax. "Either Harry knew the truth, or she was fooled by someone close to her."

"Gavin?" queried Flint. "Or Gwen, or Merlin, or Alison in league with Gavin, God this is hopeless! Just admit that this sort of speculation is futile, then we can drink our cocoa and go to bed."

Tyrone would not be put down, he was full of hope and energy. "We know the dog was killed, so we know Harry was killed. Thanks to the fax, we now know what MPP were up to, but we can't prove it unless we have the sword back. The events are obviously linked, so all we need to do to bring the police back into the case is to give them the fax and give them the sword."

Flint felt himself speaking through clenched teeth. "But we don't have the sword."

"Who's to know?" Tyrone said. "Ring Gwen. Tell her about the fax and tell her we've found the sword, see what she says."

"How many sugars?" came the voice from the kitchen.

"Sixteen," said Tyrone, without taking the look of challenge off his face.

"You're a tease, Dr Drake," Mrs Bates chided him from around the door.

"Go on, Jeff, do it. I dare you."

"One," called Flint, nodding as he replied.

Half-past midnight was an apt time for shocking schoolmistresses. The darkness hid the lies, the anonymity of the telephone allowed Flint to bluff without his face giving away the truth. Gwen protested at first, then moved the call to another room in her house and listened to the facts as embellished by wishes.

"So you have a fax," she said.

"And the sword," he lied, crossing his fingers deliberately to quench his own nerves.

"Well, you'd better bring it round tomorrow —"

"No," said Flint.

"You want something."

"I want to show you the fax. It will change the way you look at things. It will change the way you look at Gavin and at MPP and at your mother's death. It's the icing on the cake, the last piece of the puzzle. It proves that either your mother, or Gavin, or both of them were engaged in a gigantic hoax. Excalibur never spent more than a few days in the ground before your mother made her great discovery."

"You can't prove that."

"I can prove more than that. I can prove that Excalibur was stolen."

A very long silence followed. "Have you told the police?" asked a small, hesitant voice.

"No," said Flint. Such a statement carried risks, it made him vulnerable to those keen to extinguish the facts, but whilst he withheld information from the police, he retained the power it conferred.

Sounds of uneven breathing came over the phone. "Whatever you do, don't involve the police any more. We have to talk, you and I. Come to dinner, at my house, tomorrow night."

"Alone?"

"Yes – alone."

Chapter Twenty-Four

Come alone, Gwen had said. According to the police, Harry had died alone, which was a sobering thought for the morning of another funeral.

Charles Evans had been far from alone when the stroke felled him in Frome High Street and he had died in hospital at the centre of a small crowd of relatives and medical staff. In the small Methodist chapel in his adopted village, relatives from Welsh and English branches of his family mixed with former colleagues from his school. Representing the Pendragons were Patrick Hewitt and Euan Trepennick, but the Dunnings and the staff of MPP were absent, of course. Charles had been at the centre of the row over *A Guide to Arthur's Britain*; he had been *persona non grata* at Lady Harry's court.

Tyrone would be invited to a wedding every other month as his school and college friends gradually became hitched. Flint attended a depressing number of divorce parties as the thirtysomethings became unhitched. At their age, Hewitt and Trepennick must become used to funerals, seeing lifelong friends slip underground one by one. They stood in line by the graveside, waiting for their turn, watching Death working his way towards them.

When the words had been spoken and the preacher had closed his book and retreated back towards his chapel,

Euan Trepennick moved across the funeral throng at his usual, laboured, pace.

"This is very good of you," he said to Flint. "Charles would have been flattered."

"I gained the impression he thought us an impolite pair of ruffians," Flint said.

"Charlie was old school. He thought a great deal of fair play and proper conduct – a splendid wicket-keeper in his day, he could swing a bat too. I once saw him knock up a splendid fifty playing for the village here."

Hence the red leather ball dropped into the grave after the coffin. It wouldn't have been cricket to push Harry into that lake, and the old man probably lacked the strength. Patrick Hewitt had also now joined them, shaking hands and forcing a smile onto his Neronian features.

"Poor Charles," he said. "I suppose you never had a chance to get to know him properly."

"No. How did he cope with the libel writ?"

Euan shook his head slowly. "It wouldn't have come to court, it was a silly argument."

"It had been boiling up for years," Patrick Hewitt added. "They were cat and dog at committee meetings. We tried to talk them out of it, didn't we, Euan, but they wouldn't hear of it. It might have been easier if it were not for Gavin Dunning playing the Machiavelli behind the scenes."

"Stirring it?" Flint asked.

"Harry should have taken him in hand before he grew too big for his boots, eh, Euan?"

"Indeed."

Euan inclined his head down towards Flint, looking past him at the rolling green of the Mendips in spring. "By the way, you were very candid yesterday. I now

258

hear we have some news to celebrate. You found our swords."

Swords? Flint had to think rapidly. "Who told you that?"

"The police – they said you found our swords at Glastonbury Abbey last night."

"Sword singular," Flint said.

"Oh."

"The replica."

"And I suppose you've no idea . . ."

"No."

Euan straightened up.

"Sorry – would that have saved your bacon?"

"Bacon? No, I'm being fried and served up for breakfast."

"I'll have a word with Humphries."

"You overestimate your powers of persuasion."

A sharp nudge from Tyrone brought Flint out of the conversation. A dark-clothed figure was leaning over the graveyard wall.

"It's, ah, Colin Barker," Hewitt said aloud.

"Merlin," Tyrone said.

As one, the four men began to move towards where Merlin stood. He recognized each face in turn, hesitated, then turned and ran. Before Tyrone led the way from the gate, the star-spangled 2CV was pulling away from the roadside.

"What strange behaviour," Hewitt said.

"It's what we've all come to expect," Euan added.

"Follow him?" Tyrone asked.

"No." Flint dreaded the idea of a van chase. He'd seen enough tight bends in the Mendips to last a lifetime – hopefully a long lifetime. "Get on your mobile, find Chaff, let the police chase him."

259

"Police?" asked Euan.

"We all should have guessed," Hewitt said to Euan, then turned to Flint. "I wouldn't be surprised if he's the one who took your swords."

Merlin was arrested later that afternoon. After Chaff had telephoned Tyrone with the news, he declared that it could only be a matter of time before Merlin confessed to the whereabouts of the original sword. Flint was far from sure. Neither was he sure that dinner alone with Gwen was his brightest move. He was unconvinced that Tyrone would be of any help, parked half a block away in the green van.

No more appointments, he'd vowed, yet here he was, briefcase in hand, walking through the dusk along a street lined by spacious postwar houses. Uncomfortable in his suit, he could have been a commuter late home from a hard week in the office.

Number 37 was called Kintyre, detached and surrounded by lawn and leylandii hedges. It had a single garage, with no car visible, so the husband was presumably peddling conservatories in some other street not so different to this.

Flint waited at the wrought iron gate, weighing up the risks of entering the house. Only if Gwen were insane was he in danger. Moments later, he was ringing the doorbell and presenting a bunch of carnations.

"That's . . ." she looked him in the eye. "Very nice, thank you."

Her husband was often away lavishing praise on other people's houses, so had little time to devote to his own. It had been left to Gwen to plan the interior decoration: co-ordinated wallpaper and curtains with co-ordinated knick-knacks from Laura Ashley or some other middle-class style guru. In all his life, Flint had never lived anywhere so neat and clean and ordered and so obviously planned to please.

Leading the way into the dining-room was a pair of black shoes, surmounted by black tights and black dress which began just below the knees. Its midriff bulged, its back swept down between the broad shoulder blades. Gwen had washed her hair and pinned it back behind her ears which dangled with lapis lazuli earrings. Flint was still in his funeral suit, dressed for the occasion.

She spun around. "It's ready now, if you're hungry."

A duck had died for his benefit. Even if free-range, duck was a little too exotic and a little too like real animal for his taste. He'd not stayed vegetarian for long, but liked his meat well disguised to keep the concepts of death and dinner as far apart as possible.

Over the dinner table, Gwen could have been a different woman. She had made up her eyes with mascara to rival that of Alison. A necklace matched the lapis lazuli earrings and dangled over a wide and deep neckline. Her dress was almost off-shoulder, leaving her upper arms white and somewhat flabby, and giving a suggestion of allure. The schoolmistress had been replaced by something else.

None of the ambience could be taken for granted. If Gwen was no killer, she was very close to someone who was. Flint ensured that it was he who poured the Bordeaux demi-sec, swapping the glasses around when Gwen was busy fighting the duck in the kitchen. He took very small bites of everything, waiting for his hostess to be the first to tuck in, alert for alien tastes at every mouthful. He'd had a quick peek through the velvet curtains to check for intruders in the garden. He'd visited the toilet to wash his hands, but more to verify that no third person lurked beneath the stairs. Paranoia is excusable when you are convinced that someone is out to get you.

Small talk came first, and Flint told a few of his stories to break the ice. It showed he travelled often, met many people and he hoped it showed he cared.

"I'm surprised to find you're interested in the Arthurian lark," he said, when conversation drifted towards his current travels and his entanglement with the Pendragons.

"Why?"

"Children usually rebel against their parents' interests."

"I did, for a while," Gwen said. "I teach English now, I'm not a historian and I've never pretended to be one."

"So your input into the Arthur Roadshow was literary?"

"None, I only became involved when mother died."

"Ah, so you and Arthur have kept your distance?"

"In a way. I know all the Arthurian romances well, but I don't believe a word of them. If I did I'd have to believe Beowulf and the Odyssey and goodness knows how many other folk tales. Do you know what the Renaissance scholars thought of Mallory's *Morte d'Arthur*?"

"Tell me."

"They condemned it as containing too much sex and violence." Her eyes grew wider as she explained. "Women play little part except as objects of lust and victims of rape, incest and adultery. The heroes kill people at the drop of a hat, with rarely a speck of remorse. In some scenes, they are positively wading through mounds of hacked-off limbs."

The hacked-off limb of a duck could be seen through the corner of his eye and vegetarianism started to take on an appeal once more.

"Arthur is not a wholesome story," Gwen said.

"The code of chivalry was a licence to murder," Flint added, making one more bold foray into the pile of duck meat. "I saw *Excalibur* the other day. It's very gory in places, but for gratuitous violence, the original story wins hands down."

She gave a nervous smile.

"The police have arrested Merlin, you know." It was time to stop eating and drop the bombshell.

"What are they charging him with?"

"Oh – traffic offences to start with. It's a good way of keeping hold of him until they learn the truth about your mother."

"Her death was an accident," Gwen stated.

"And you're still convinced? Even now you know that Rimmy was killed?"

"I only have your word on that."

"Which brings me to this." He opened up Tyrone's briefcase and withdrew a photograph of a familiar sword.

"Recognize it?"

Gwen nodded, trying to see what else was lying in the case.

"This is a Byzantine cavalry sword stolen from Italy about two years ago."

He showed her the second picture, which showed the 'DEVS NOBISCVM' blade.

"Spot the similarity," Flint said.

"They're completely different."

"No they're not. They're not completely different, and they're not complete. Look at this."

With a sigh and look of tired disgust she was given a sheaf of the fax from Copenhagen. It included a line drawing of a sword hilt.

"This hilt is from the private collection of a Danish antiquarian, built up during the last century. He had his daughters illustrate a catalogue of his goodies, but the catalogue was unfinished at his death and only one copy exists." He allowed her to compare pictures, dragon-for-dragon. "It's a Migration Period Saxon sword-hilt, seventh or eighth-century. It was lost during the war: the Nazis plundered the estate."

Gwen pressed her lips together, seeking to bring moisture into her mouth.

"Add stolen Italian blade to stolen Danish hilt, add a Roman pommel from somewhere in the Empire, find a bit of walrus ivory of the right date and bingo, identikit Excalibur. Impossible to fault on date or style, it would pass all the physical tests and it would be very difficult to trace the individual parts because none have been published."

"Oh," said Gwen.

"Both our police and the Italian police were only thinking in terms of complete swords, so it's unlikely they would have spotted the hoax. It all boils down to Tyrone's lateral thinking; we stopped asking experts whether they had seen a sword like this, and we limited ourselves to specific components."

Gwen's expression suggested immense loss.

"Ten out of ten? Gold star?"

She poured herself a glass of wine, but paused before drinking it.

"I should have spotted this a long time ago," Flint said. "I asked a lady friend of mine to look at the sword."

"Lady friend? I expect she was pretty."

"As it happens, but she's also an expert on antiques. She said the balance of the replica was wrong; it was a clue that the sword was a kit, but I missed it at the time."

"She was pretty," Gwen said.

Flint pressed home his argument. "Excalibur was assembled with the specific intention of creating a sensation, which could be milked for profit. Now to my mind, there are only three possible culprits: Gavin, Alison and your mother."

He would have added Merlin to the list, but wanted to maintain the pressure on Gwen, not giving her an excuse to deflect the blame elsewhere.

"We could play combinations: Gavin and Alison perhaps, feathering their nest. Mother and son increasing the family fame and fortune. If it were all three, that poses a nasty scenario. Have you seen one of those caper movies, where the crooks stage a heist then start to bump each other off? *Reservoir Dogs*, now there's a cracking example. Fewer people, more shares."

"Mother would never do something underhand," Gwen stated.

"Perhaps that's why she was murdered."

"She wasn't murdered!"

"Perhaps your mother discovered she had been duped, that someone had planted the sword for her to find. She had fulfilled her lifelong quest, and it turned out to be a fraud. Your mother could be formidable when her back was up."

"Yes she could." Gwen looked around the table, as if she might clear the dishes as a substitute for listening to what she hated to hear.

"Everything points to Gavin," Flint said.

Now he held her attention. Gwen's brown eyes met his and refused to budge.

"Gavin's bookshop business can't be so profitable can it? And MPP is also going down the tubes —"

She interrupted sharply. "Gavin wouldn't hurt mother."

"He was in the perfect position to fool your mother into falling for the trick with the fake sword, just as he talked her into suing poor old Charles Evans. As far as we know, the only people at the house the night she died were you and he. You went to bed, he was still up."

"Gavin followed me straight away."

"So you say."

"What do you want?"

"The truth."

"Rubbish, you want something, everyone wants something."

"And what do you want?"

"You to go back to Yorkshire and leave us all alone."

"Believe it or not, I'm doing my job."

"So you're in it for the money," she sneered. "How much do we have to pay you to go away?"

Flint tried to appear relaxed, cool and laid back. "I've never been turned on by money."

"No. We've asked about you. There's only one thing turns you on, only one thing that turns your head."

"Oh?"

She stood up and walked to the couch at the far end of the lounge-diner. As she slumped down, she appeared to be expecting a reaction. He remained seated.

"Don't make this hard," she said.

"What's going on?"

"My husband is in Cheltenham."

This sounded distinctly ominous, spoken without hint of enticement.

"So he's away."

"If this is what it takes . . ." she threw her head back in an oddly amateurish fashion, like a fifth former trying to be sensual.

He rose to his feet. Slowly, with a sense of confused unease he approached the recumbent woman. With a mixture of fear and pleading she watched him draw closer.

"You've got all night if you want."

Chapter Twenty-Five

Eight steps took Flint from table to sofa. He almost counted them. This was classic James Bond: seduce the woman, win her over to your side, but the routine was being reversed. Earrings dangled over her neck, drawing the eye down to where the necklace pointed the way that hands and tongues should travel. He'd been a reluctant celibate since the turn of the year and Flint found himself fighting against a million years of male conditioning.

Gwen flicked her head back again, trying some odd, non-sexy flutter of her eyebrows. This was a parody of seduction. Her willingness to sacrifice herself was a complete turn-off.

"Gwen! You're a married woman."

"Does that matter?"

"Of course it matters. It also happens to matter that we don't feel a thing about each other."

"We don't have to." Tears formed in her eyes.

"Yes we do."

He sat at the far end of the couch and drew a tissue from his pocket. "Here. I am positively, definitely, not laying a single finger on you. I don't know why you're doing this, but it's not necessary."

"It's all I can do!"

She turned an angry face away from him. Flint dare not draw closer. He proffered the tissue and it was taken.

He wandered into the white-wood kitchen and started the coffee percolator. A block of five knives stood on the work surface and he was grateful for the way her plans had turned.

With the percolator pop-popping happily, he put a hand and his head around the door of the lounge. Gwen was sitting with her elbows on her knees, cheeks in hand, mascara smudged down her cheeks.

"Hey, Gwen. Bad seduction routine."

"Uh?"

"Ten points for effort, none for sincerity." He smiled, and moved over to her, squatting in the centre of the rug, looking up into smeared eyes. "No hard feelings?"

She wouldn't look him in the face. "You must think I'm disgusting."

"I'm confused, but I know you must have a good reason for what you've just done. It can't be my irresistible aftershave, because I don't use the stuff."

"I only want you to go away."

"Read *Gawain and the Green Knight* again," Flint said. "The lady of the castle attempts to seduce Gawain, but he proves true and chaste. Only later does she reveal it was a test of his honour."

Gwen almost laughed through her sobs.

"Chivalry is not dead. Trust me. Tell me what's going on."

"You're destroying us," she said.

"Defeat, yes, destroy no."

"You're playing with words."

She was vulnerable now. Flint might have retreated to save Gwen further anguish, but he needed to press home his advantage.

"The police hold Merlin," he stated. "We have the swords," he told half a lie. "We have a room full of

269

data tracing the fraud from first inception to final tragedy. Gavin killed your mother, didn't he?"

"No."

"As you said, we've got all night. Instead of running through the Kama Sutra, let's run through your family history, and the history of MPP."

"If you like."

He walked back towards the kitchen to collect the coffees, speaking over his shoulder. "That's m'girl. I'm glad I didn't delegate this evening. If you'd tried this trick with Tyrone, he'd have taken up your kind offer."

It was in the small hours that Flint opened the door of the green van and prodded Tyrone from sleep.

"Glad you stayed awake."

"Oh, just closed my eyes for a few seconds," Tyrone said, giving a shiver against the blast of cold air. "So she didn't do you in with the carving knife and stuff you in the freezer?"

"No, she was . . . she was pretty co-operative."

Tyrone would not move the car until told the whole sordid truth. A dirty guffaw greeted the description of Gwen as trainee seductress. Flint ploughed on to retell everything Gwen had told him, plus what he had learned, which were not altogether the same.

"Harry had a cancer scare, apparently, Merlin was correct on that point. What the wretch didn't tell us was that it was a false alarm."

"Lying bastard," Tyrone said.

"He's in good company."

"So we've solved everything," Tyrone said, when the analysis was concluded. "We have one sword, and we know Merlin hid the other and the cops will force him to tell them where it is. So, the theft is solved and we

270

can send the blade back to Italy and the hilt back to Copenhagen rounding off two more crimes. Once the swords are back, the insurance company don't have to pay anything, so they're happy too."

"And Harry?"

"What if it was an accident, like Gwen told you? It only seemed to be part of a plot, because Merlin went off his head and over-reacted. If he hadn't nicked the swords, we wouldn't have become involved."

"Quite. Have you explained the dog?"

After a long gaze out into the night, Tyrone said, "No."

"Have you explained why someone ran us off the road?"

"Accident?"

"That's two accidents, plus the very tragic but convenient death of Charles Evans. Have you explained why Gwen laid on a very poor Suzi Wong act just now?"

"She just fancied a quick bonk while the old man was away. I mean, it's not the first time Doc, you're not Sir Gawain the Chaste."

The analogy was drawn for the second time that night.

"I'm surprised you resisted," Tyrone said.

"Then you know me less well than you should."

"Mind you, she's not much to look at, is she?"

"That's hardly the point! She's a sensible, middle-class married woman who would no sooner have an affair than you would vote Labour. She was trying to buy me off – crudely, as it turned out, her heart wasn't in it."

"If she'd been ten years younger, and single, and a bit better looking?"

"And a darned sight more convincing, yes just possibly

271

I might have stayed for breakfast, but she was going through the motions."

"It could have been a test, like Gawain . . ."

". . . and the Green knight, yes, that's just possible, but is a mite too subtle. She was trying to seduce me in order to protect Gavin."

"Yes," Tyrone said.

"Which scotches all you've just said about accidents."

After a thoughtful pause, Tyrone reluctantly agreed. "Of course," he added. "I've always thought it was Gavin who did it."

"Hmm." That now made three people who viewed Gavin as the culprit. Between teardrops, Gwen had admitted fearing what her brother had done.

"So we shop him," Tyrone said.

"No," Flint said. "It's not enough, there's still something missing. There's a whole tangled web linking these people together – friendship, business, family, romance, money – and amongst the mess we've missed something." He let out a long moan. "This is too bloody hard. I'd rather be dating bloody pottery than this." He thumped the dashboard.

Tyrone started the engine and moved off onto the silent streets.

"It's like those accursed Arthurian stories," Flint said. "Arthur weds Guinevere, Guinevere loves Lancelot, Lancelot is sworn to serve Arthur, Morgan hates Arthur, Mordred is linked to him by blood . . . it's messy, it's complex . . ."

"And it ends with a terrific battle where everyone gets killed."

"Yes," Flint said. "We'll try to avoid that."

Ghostly grey Bath passed in the night. Traffic lights stopped them for no reason. No other cars passed.

"Someone has to tell us the truth," Flint murmured, mostly to himself. "Someone has to tell us the truth." He repeated it, as if it were a mantra or a prayer that needed to be answered. He'd employed the big stick against Gwen, now it was time to swing it in another direction.

"I have to speak to Gavin," Flint stated. "At risk of prompting a showdown, I'll go and visit him first thing tomorrow. He has to play with a straight bat now: we've got him by the short-and-curlies if he doesn't co-operate."

The idea of another confrontation with Gavin exhausted his last shred of energy. "Before all that I need a couple of hours sleep and one of Mrs Hudson's enormous breakfasts."

"Mrs Bates," Tyrone corrected.

"Elementary my dear Doctor – you know what I mean."

Breakfast was survived; muesli, egg, beans, tomato, veggi-sausage, croissants, fruit juice, coffee and wheat-germ toast. Mrs Bates deserved a six-star rating in the bed and breakfast league, and her guests told her so. As she was spoiling the two archaeologists with her attention, she told them the latest sheep-mangling horror story, then tried to discover what 'her doctors' had been doing until three that morning.

Tyrone put on his combat gear, Swiss army knife and all. Flint donned his usual jacket and jeans, sleepy after the late night and hung about by a sense of anti-climax. It would almost have been better if Gwen had ambushed him with the meat cleaver, or tried to lace the Bordeaux with poison; he'd been prepared for both, and the mystery would have been solved. As it was, the unsolved problem formed a pressure-point in

273

his skull, threatening a headache. Flint packed his evidence into Tyrone's briefcase then waited in the hall until his assistant thundered down the stairs to join him.

"Ready for the joust?" he asked.

"Yep. Go for it!"

The door of the bookshop tinkled open, then tinkled closed. A small cash desk was squeezed behind the window display, a stand of secondhand paperbacks faced it on the opposite side of the doorway. The remainder of the shop was cut into three by a pair of floor-to-ceiling bookcases, running back into semi-darkness.

Gavin was atop a ladder, feeding a hardback classic into place. He looked down at Flint over a pair of reading glasses.

"Hi there," said Flint, braced for the inevitable frosty glower of disdain.

Gavin gave a little nod, then turned to continue sorting out his top shelf. "I hear you had dinner with my sister last night." The words struggled out, as if he were speaking around a duck bone in his throat.

"Yes, it was . . . it was very pleasant. I assume she told you about it."

"Yes," Gavin said heavily. "She told me all about it."

"All?"

"Yes."

"She's protecting you," Flint said.

"She thinks I killed mother."

"And did you?"

A pair of books exchanged places on the shelf.

"Of course not."

"Not even as a mercy killing – I know she had cancer. Gwen said you'd talked about it."

Gavin looked his way. "We discussed it, idly, you know, how we couldn't see mother in pain, how we couldn't just sit and watch her die. But I didn't kill my mother, and neither did Gwen."

"So did she kill herself?"

"If you must label me as the culprit, then that is the way I killed her. We argued, you see, during the afternoon and we argued that night. Mother stayed home instead of going to the conference so we could thrash things out. She wanted to drop the court case; she wouldn't see the logic behind my press launch, then you arrived . . ."

"Me? Yes, I thought it would turn out to be my fault," Flint said, with a heavy dose of sarcasm. "I'm not a free agent, I'm a pawn."

"Only obeying orders?" Gavin looked over his shoulder and half withdrew a biography of Rudolf Hess from the opposite shelf. Flint felt an involuntary shudder. Gavin slid the book back into place.

"What was the game with the sword?" Flint asked. "Did you steal it?"

"I bought it," Gavin confessed. "From a man I know in London."

"Intact? Or did you collect the pieces and fit them together yourself?"

"The latter – well, I know another man who performed the handiwork."

Gavin came down his ladder, then slid it along to the end of the bookcase. He wiped dust from the cuff of his purple cardigan.

"Why?" Flint asked. "Why play a practical joke on your poor old mother. She was dying – that was just cruel."

"When mother was given three months to live, I thought it would be a kindness to let her fulfil her life's dream. She died convinced she'd found Excalibur. She died happy."

Flint found this incredible, but refrained from saying so. He'd heard so many far-fetched stories in the past month, that another piece of fiction could easily be accommodated within his collection. Was Gavin truly the devoted son who had granted his mother her ultimate wish? "It must have been inconvenient when she survived longer than three months and lived to see people expose the hoax for what it was."

"Oh, the prognosis was wrong and whatever gimmickry they used on her worked wonders. There was always a chance of a relapse, but by then the die was cast."

"You never told her what you'd done?"

"The philistines are taking over the world. CDs yes, videos yes, books no. How many people have been in this shop since you came in? None. How many people have come in this morning? One."

"Me? So you're going bust too."

"I'm five months behind with the rent. There's stock I can't clear —"

"And MPP?"

"I knew a woman —"

"Alison Wright?"

"She had a business in trouble, I had a business in trouble, we had the means to bail ourselves out."

"So Alison was in on the fraud too."

"No, no, no, it was all my own work."

"But she didn't ask too many questions?"

Now the truth began to show beneath the layers of grime. Gavin had seen an avenue to make it rich, solve his problems and win the favour of a lady.

"Alison is a competent lady, but she's no antiquarian."

Gavin continued to heap blame on himself. "She wouldn't know one sword from another."

"I tried asking her about it and she told me to piss off."

Gavin gave a wry smile. "Did she? Got a lot of spirit, Alison."

Flint had never seen him in this mood, deeply sober, lacking the boorish aggression so evident on their previous meeting. Gwen's attempted sacrifice had produced unexpected side-effects. Gavin was now defending her as vigorously as she had defended him, and with the same disregard for himself.

"Why didn't you just wait until your mother died? You'd have had the insurance, the property —"

"But she wasn't going to die, and I wasn't willing to place my hopes on her dying! She was my mother, remember that. And as for insurance, well —"

"You would have made an effortless amount of money if you'd lost the sword and claimed on the insurance."

"Insurance, insurance. It wasn't my bloody idea to insure the thing. It was worthless, I knew that."

"The replica cost five grand."

"No it didn't; that was just some clever invoicing to cover the cost of buying the original pieces."

Gavin had dug his way into a hole, progressively, even stupidly. Each step may have seemed logical, carrying little danger in itself, but once he had been committed, his only route was down, deeper into conspiracy and fraud. The whole affair was tragically farcical.

"Have you told the police any of this?"

"No."

Of course not. "So why are you telling me?"

"Because Gwen asked me to. If we can get that damnable insurance company off our backs, people will leave us alone. I'm cancelling the whole show, I'm withdrawing my claim for the stolen swords and I'll have MPP liquidated. I hear you even had that idiot Merlin arrested. Are you content?"

"Almost."

It had not quite been the final, apocalyptic battle to close the saga, but the destruction had been wholesale and if not dead and bleeding, the whole cast of characters had been wounded in their hearts or their pockets. It was a kind of justice.

"So you won't tell the police what you know?" Gavin asked.

"Perhaps not," Flint said.

"And you'll leave Gwen alone?" Gavin had softened his tone, making an effort to avoid conflict. "I'm glad you didn't . . ."

"So am I," Flint smiled, finally recognizing that Gavin could hold noble motives, after all. Perhaps it was himself who had played the role of chief villain in the eyes of the protagonists.

His eyes lighted on a heavily foxed Leo Kessler paperback entitled *The Hitler Werewolf Murders* and he bought it for a pound. He found the gall to wish Gavin well, then jogged back to the car park where Tyrone sat. He tossed the book through the open window. "Light reading for you."

"I've had a call." Tyrone tapped his mobile phone. "From Stephanie."

Flint climbed into the passenger seat and slammed the door with the necessary force. "Passionate?"

"Official – we have to report to the police station."

"Report – that sounds ominous."

"I said we'd go immediately you came back."

*   *   *

278

Another drive lay ahead. The Mendips were crossed once again, north to south, the traffic into Devon and Cornwall heavy on the bank holiday weekend. An hour later, at Bridgwater police station, Tyrone parked next to a familiar multicoloured 2CV van. It was propped up on a jack, with its back wheel removed and Merlin was busy about his repairs, pausing guiltily as the archaeologists drove up.

"Hi," said Flint, his firm expression lending irony to his cheerful greeting.

Merlin bobbed down behind his bonnet and pretended to be occupied. He was left to his work, and to his plans, Tyrone muttering many of his character-killing insults as they walked into the police station.

After announcing himself at the desk, Flint was immediately called into an interview room to confess before D.S. Chaff and her superior. His amateur detective work was humbled; he was asked to tell the police everything he had learned, about the thefts, the possible fraud, the postulated murder. Inspector Roper was in uniform, and Chaff had dressed in a smart but sombre ladies' suit. Such dark shades added to the oppression of the bald room, making Flint instantly gloomy and squashing his spirit.

"And now you expect me to interview all your cast of thousands?" Chaff concluded. "Is it you writing the book about Hollywood Epics, or is it Boy Wonder out there?"

"It is I."

"I have to be frank with you, Dr Flint," said the Inspector.

"Jeff, please."

"Dr Flint you are treading very dangerous ground. What you are doing is bordering on harassment."

279

"Of who?"

"Would you like to see the list? Actions for slander are being talked about. Who allowed you to take the law into your own hands?"

"Ah, that's politics. I'm an anarchist you see, I'm not keen on laws, whilst Tyrone believes that laws should be rigidly imposed, but only on other people."

"I am being serious. There is no solid evidence behind your accusations."

"So Merlin didn't confess."

"Mr Barker denied stealing the swords, he denied burying them, he denies breaking into the Abbey, he denies knowing anything about a dead dog, a dead sheep, a car crash or the death of Lady Dunning."

The hawk-nosed Inspector paused.

"Well he would, wouldn't he?"

"Go home, Dr Flint," the Inspector added, deeply irritated by the whole exchange.

"Don't you even want to see the fax from Copenhagen?"

"We're not investigating war crimes."

"How about fraud?"

"The insurance company have informed us that the claim for the swords has been withdrawn."

"Attempted fraud?" he asked in his meekest voice.

"Go home, please. Stop wasting all our time."

Chaff smiled for six seconds as Flint stood to his feet.

"Well thanks, folks, nice knowing you."

It was a sad and chastened Flint that left the interview room. He battled against a sensation that he was unused to: the possibility that he had been wrong, completely wrong.

"Well?" Tyrone asked.

"I think your chances of a romantic candle-lit dinner with the delightful sergeant have declined to zero."

"Miserable tart."

"Now, now, let's not get bitchy. Whatever she did for you, I hope you enjoyed it."

"Uh?"

"You told her everything, the day you went to Glastonbury Tor."

He shrugged. "I got carried away."

"But I promised Gwen and Gavin that we'd keep the police out of things if they played ball."

"They lied to us, so we can lie to them! I've just been trying to talk to that creep Merlin, smiling all over his greasy little face. The cops are letting him go. All he needs is two new tyres and a tax disc and his van is legal again. That was his excuse to walk away from me. He's going to the garage."

"So we've got what? An hour? Then our last witness vanishes."

Tyrone narrowed his eyes, with his jaw set in a cruel snarl.

"Remember what he did to me in the CCL toilet?"

"I shall never forget it."

"Well, I followed Merlin to see how far he was going, but I stopped off at a home brew shop down the high street."

"Are you suggesting we get drunk?"

"No – we get even." Tyrone's face spread into a broad, evil grin. "In fact, we're already even."

Chapter Twenty-Six

The 2CV still stood innocently in the police station car park. Flint hardly dare approach it. At times he'd seen books on SAS ambush and sabotage techniques lying on Tyrone's college desk. He suspected there were ways in which brakes could be made to fail, or fuel tanks explode on a turn of the ignition.

"What the hell have you done?"

"His petrol gauge doesn't work."

"So?"

"He fills up every two hundred miles. His clock reads 74,467; I bet he filled up at 74,400. Remember how brainy he pretends to be."

"And is."

The compliment was shrugged away. "So I went to the brew shop, bought a demi-john and a siphon and I emptied his tank."

"In a police station car park?"

"Nobody gave me a second look: if anyone had asked, I was helping out with the repairs."

"But what was the point? It was evil."

Tyrone shook a finger, pleased with what he had done and what he planned to do. "Pure revenge is futile, this was revenge with a purpose. When I followed Merlin, the first thing he did was go to a phonebox. Now who was he phoning?"

A number of names ran through Flint's mind.

"More pertinently: where will he go when his van is fixed and who will he be meeting? He came south, but not to meet us. He went to Charles Evans' funeral, but scarpered when he saw we were there. He needs money – you're always saying how little people get on the dole. How is he going to buy new tyres, a tax disc and fifty litres of petrol?"

Tyrone was right. Tyrone was forgiven. If he had compromised affairs by opening his mouth to Chaff, he had now atoned.

"He won't get far – a few miles," Tyrone said. "He'll probably head for the M5 and we'll find him on the hard shoulder. Then we've got him all to ourselves."

It was time to wait. Tyrone sat in the UNY-DIG van, out of sight down a side-street, reading *The Hitler Werewolf Murders*. Flint found himself a bus shelter and stood where the queue should be, part watching, part listening for a distinctive French engine. All the time he was watching, he was thinking. He had missed something, something crucial, something that Chaff was unaware of. The truth was there, flitting around like a moth in the dusty corners of his brain. Just one sharp jab with a pin and it would be fixed, motionless, for all to admire.

Technology never endeared itself to Flint. Either it refused to work, or worked to the detriment of all he had grown used to in his thirty-five years. His reliance on cars, computers and mobile phones was depressing. Taking out one of Tyrone's toys, he unfolded the earpiece, stretched out the aerial and posed: using a mobile at a bus stop had to be the height of pretension. It was time to report, and time to discover.

Matt Humphries was drawn from a meeting. Flint

283

launched into the conversation with gusto to hide his apprehension.

"Good news, at last."

"You've found the swords?"

"MPP are withdrawing their claim – the swords need no longer trouble you. In any event we now have documentary proof that we're not dealing with the true Excalibur."

"It's a fake?"

"Not strictly, but it has a fraudulent pedigree. It was fabricated from stolen property, worth a few thousand pounds at most."

There was a pause, then genuine pleasure flooded across the airwaves. "Well done. Well done."

Now it was time, the moth was close, almost stationary, now it was time to raise that pin. "Before I wrap up, and post off my invoice, can I ask a few little questions?"

"Sure, sure," Humphries was positively bubbling with joy.

"Why are you involved?" Flint asked. "This isn't your region . . ."

". . . it is now."

Of course. Euan's fears had been solidly based. "What about Euan Trepennick?"

"Shown the back door, if you don't mind the sick joke."

What joke? thought Flint. It was hardly funny. "So you never cared about the swords, or the money. This was just a piece of office politics?"

"I'm a company man, Flint. I want the best for Northern Consolidated and Trepennick has been on his way out for years. I mean, who wants to buy insurance from a bloody queer?"

Jab! There it was, yet it took Flint a few moments to

recognize his capture. Automatically, he reacted against the bigotry. "Euan told me that people don't buy insurance, it has to be sold." As Flint spoke the words, the facts meshed together and the truth was beautifully displayed.

"I'll catch you later, Matt. I've just suffered a brain-storm."

A total solution was at hand, he was sure. One piece of prejudice, plus a slice of Tyrone's intolerance, added the final string to the web. Pull one strand and the web would quiver, but Flint was certain now who sat at the centre. People had made statements, offhand and unrehearsed, true and partly true, but all had been too clever to voice a blatant lie. Now another lie was going to trap them; it was open season on the gullible.

Another hour and a half elapsed before the 2CV rattled past with its new tyres and tax disc and its engine guzzling sludge from the bottom of its fuel tank. With his legs aching and his mind buzzing with possibilities, Flint took care to watch the direction it travelled, marked the point at which it turned.

He sprinted back to the UNY-DIG van, where Tyrone was half-way through the paperback.

"West," Flint panted.

Tyrone frowned. "Not the M5?"

"If you had a van like his, would you brave the M5? He's a hippy like me, he hates traffic, he's taking the scenic route to Cornwall, so let's move."

The A39 runs west from Bridgwater towards the resorts of the north Devon coast. Dead ahead, the sun glared into their eyes. It was later than it seemed. Some miles ahead lay Exmoor, before them lay the Quantock hills, purple in the growing gloom, blotting out the sun now and again as they crossed the levels and grew closer to the high ground. Soon they were driving along the foot of the hills, with sheep fields rising on the left. From the distance of half a mile ahead, they could see the road curving to the right and a vehicle was stationary before the bend. Tyrone was driving and he slowed down. The vehicle on the grass verge was a very dead 2CV van, its bonnet open, a figure walking around it. Merlin's powers of divination had clearly been defeated.

As the green van pulled up alongside, the logo UNY-DIG and the rampant trowel proclaimed who drove it. Merlin took one glance their way, then dodged behind the 2CV. He was over a stile and running into the sheep field before Tyrone had turned off his own engine.

Tyrone sighed. "We've done this before."

"Are you fit?"

"Yep: here we go."

It could be a long chase. Merlin had started at a sprint, his sandals flapping as he scattered the sheep before him. Flint and Tyrone were wearing trainers and set a more measured pace up the grassy slope.

"Just jog," Tyrone called back.

Flint tried to just jog, but steadily, Tyrone's longer legs and high-protein diet began to beat Flint into third place. Merlin had been slowed to a walk by the time he reached the crest, silhouetted black against a fiery western sky. He disappeared over the skyline as Tyrone made a determined rush to make contact. Flint was dizzy and panting by the time he came to Tyrone, stationary on the spot where Merlin had vanished. The sun was tickling the western horizon. Patches of woodland lay to both sides, with a lane crossing the shallow valley ahead.

"You need to eat more meat," Tyrone panted.

Flint slapped the back of his hand against Tyrone's

stomach. "You need to diet," he panted back. "Where is he?"

"Hiding – he was only . . ." Tyrone drew in breath, "he was only a hundred metres away. And he lost this."

He waggled a sandal with grim satisfaction. Hands clamped on his waist, fighting against the stitch, Flint looked for a hiding place. A stream-line in the valley bottom was too far for Merlin to have run in so short a time. A stone shed stood to one side of the field, almost shouting the words 'hide here'. Flint took a few steps towards it.

"Avoid obvious cover – that's what they teach you in the SAS," Tyrone said.

"But Merlin's not in the SAS."

"But he's not stupid – not completely."

"OK." Flint nodded towards a hedge off to their right. Tyrone immediately broke into a run towards it. Flint followed, as fast as his lungs would allow. The hedgerow was ten yards thick, almost a small copse. They pushed through trees and shrubs which grew thick at the edge, but at its centre found a sanctuary open to the sky. Flint burst from the vegetation, then slipped and fell into something warm and noisome.

The smell was familiar, the texture was familiar. The scent of blood joined the sticky-wet ooze of death. A dark stain smeared his hands and the knees of his jeans. One gut-wrenching look confirmed he had slipped on a string of offal which led from tree to tree. Wool was snagged on branches and a familiar smell of fresh carrion hung all around. One metre from his nose lay a body.

A black figure rose from vegetation on the far side of the clearing, finger on lips. Flint stopped. Merlin was kneeling amongst the bushes, still with finger on lips. They both looked towards the body of a sheep, another dead sheep, dismembered and disembowelled. Little wonder the smell had been so familiar.

Tyrone blundered from a bush and he too halted at the sight. Merlin made shh-shh noises. Cautiously, they advanced to where Merlin knelt, his chest heaving with exertion. He raised a finger and pointed towards the next field. Dumbly, silently, the three of them pushed a way through overhanging branches.

Out in the field, in the semi-darkness stood a black shape, swishing its tail from side to side. The Beast of Exmoor watched the hedge for a few moments, then heard a sound, or spotted motion with its cat's eyes. In an instant it turned and ran with leaping, feline grace, across the field and into the far wood.

None of them said anything for a whole minute.

"The world is a stranger place than we know," Merlin said under his breath.

Reality seemed to have taken a pause for thought, and it was a few moments before Flint stopped looking for the cat and his mind snapped back to the present. "Games up, Colin," he said.

Merlin seemed rueful rather that alarmed, he turned up his nose and asked for his sandal.

"Amazing, wasn't it?" he said.

Flint cast another look over the deserted field. He was one who scorned myths, ancient and modern; he would demand to see evidence before he believed. Without evidence, folk tales were simply stories to frighten children. As darkness claimed the Quantock Hills, popular fantasy had become fact.

After crawling out of the bushes, Merlin was given back his sandal. At the edge of the field was a lane and they followed this back downhill. "What did you do to my van?" he asked.

"No harm done," Tyrone said, and he explained.

"That was clever." The victim sounded amused by the trick, not angry or surly at being ensnared.

"So where is the midnight rendezvous?" Flint asked.

To avoid games, where one asks 'whatever do you mean?' and the other replies 'you know what I mean', Flint came straight out with the facts: all of them. He told Merlin about the sword, its fabrication, Gavin's scam, Gwen's fears, Humphries' plot and Harry's gullibility. He explained Merlin's own role. He guessed where he was going and who he was meeting.

"You're going to dig up the real sword and hand it over – that was the deal, wasn't it?"

"Yeah."

"Presumably, you buried it at Arthur's tomb, Mark II," Flint stated, "the one near Camelford."

"No," said Merlin, hands in pockets, "Tintagel."

"Ah well, that was going to be our second guess. Are you on our team now?"

It was growing too gloomy to read his expression.

"We can keep this in the family, or I can get on the mobile and call the police right now and have them meet us at Tintagel." Secretly, Flint knew that Chaff wouldn't come. She had pushed out her neck as far as she was willing.

"The police let me go," Merlin said, with jaunty confidence. "They've closed the case, they won't come."

Jeffrey Flint was a calm man, not given to violent outbursts, but one came, unbidden. He grabbed the loose arm of Merlin's sweatshirt.

"Use your bloody brains Colin! Why did the state waste all that money on your education? Stop playing the court jester and wake up! You can't go on like this, you can't keep up this act forever. The real world might be a crappy place, but it's where we all have to live. Carry on like this and you'll end up in a lunatic asylum. Call me boring and conventional, but you need a job, you need somewhere to live, you need to clean yourself up and take some responsibility for your actions. God knows what Harry saw in you!"

He released the arm, then quietly, Merlin stated a truth.

"She was my mother."

Chapter Twenty-Seven

For the second time in one month, Flint wiped dead sheep off his hands, but could do little about the soiled jeans. He doubted if he could ever eat kebab again without thinking of raw mutton.

Tintagel Castle, on the north coast of Cornwall, lay at least three hours' drive away. The green van was not noted for its speed, nor Flint for his aggression on the road, so Tyrone took the wheel again. First he drove back towards Bridgwater, then took the M5 Southbound.

Merlin was a different Merlin to that seen at the Nottingham fair. Flint called him 'Colin' repeatedly and Colin emerged slowly from behind the mask.

A voice from the dark void in the rear of the van told a little of his life story. Academics on foreign jollies had been known to let their hair down. Put Lady Harriet Dunning onto a North Sea ferry bound for a conference in Stockholm, supply her cabin with a full duty-free allowance, admit one steward ten years her junior. Result? A distinguished lady in her early forties, with husband absent in Germany and with a surprise child. Harry's physical stature could hide a pregnancy for four or five months and when the shock finally struck her, she had ample money to hide herself in a northern hospital until delivery day. A childless couple in Hull were only too happy to adopt, if a little money came their way, and if the boy was the natural son of the father.

"We had to keep silent about it. There's a clause in the will – I inherit twenty thousand pounds if I don't tell anyone the truth. I think I've botched that now."

"Only if we broadcast your confession."

"My first mum, the one I knew in Hull, couldn't have children, she had something wrong down there. It must have been that tumour, the one that killed her. My second mum was nice, and when she left, I thought she'd take me with her but Dad told me the truth, so I stayed with him."

"And that's when you made contact?"

"No, I avoided Harry, until everything went wrong. I didn't like Maggi, she tried to be mum three, but she already had two other sons. Harry had two children too, plus a granddaughter, so nobody wanted me."

Outside the van, an unlit motorway night was made darker by the bulk of Exmoor. A whole horde of beasts could be lurking out there, but Merlin's horrors lay deep in his psyche.

"So it was all change for the City and you were going to make it on your own?"

"Yes – I thought that was what I'd wanted."

"Then after your breakdown, you started reading your mother's books and became obsessed by Arthur?"

"Yeah, kind of."

"And Colin was reborn as Merlin?"

"It was something to do."

"You should get yourself sorted out."

"Yes."

"Go back to college."

"I hated it."

"Ah, but he wouldn't hate archaeology, would he?" Flint said to Tyrone.

"No."

"Not the way we teach it, and we're only an hour up the road from your dad's place."

"You'd have to wash . . ." Tyrone said between his teeth.

Flint dug him in the ribs, but Merlin had missed the line.

"Give us a try; treat this as your interview. We've got another two hours to kill."

Time remained to kill as a hundred and seventy miles passed in the night. England never seemed so big. Exeter was a brilliant show of lights to the right and a black slash in the sky was the river Exe to the left. Traffic began to thin out as they reached the A30, skirting a black and bleak Dartmoor. As roads grew smaller, and the night grew later, it was if civilization and the modern world was receding. The Okehampton bypass was notorious by day, calm by midnight. In the back of the van, Merlin was slowly abandoned and Colin T.Barker began to take over once more. He told jokes, he was funny, he knew traveller's tales to match any digging yarn that Flint could retell. Darkness suits the introvert.

Most tourists would pass Camelford without a thought, but armed with Harry's Arthurian guidebook, one could hunt amongst the trees for the place where a carved tombstone lay abandoned by a stream. Arthur's Tomb, it was called, even if the inscription suggested it belonged to a Roman named Latinus, son of Magirus. Then again, the ghost of Harry argued, Arthur had been a Roman. As they passed the place, Flint gave Merlin a last chance to confess that he had misled them once more.

"Tintagel," he said, with a jaunty confidence. "You'll see."

On reaching the coast, Tyrone parked beside the old Tintagel post office. Merlin had timed his rendezvous for four in the morning, long before the castle opened, but giving enough light for the task in hand.

Waiting proved cold, and tense, and tiring. Flint was aware of sleeping only five of the past thirty-six hours. Tyrone's stomach rumbled and he complained about it at intervals. Wholly used to life on the road, Colin/Merlin curled up in the back of the van and went to sleep.

As he dozed, Flint thought back to Boorman's *Excalibur* and the scene at Tintagel. Half awake and half asleep, he became Uther Pendragon, riding across the mists to the castle to ravish Igrain. Merlin was played by Merlin and awaiting her rape in silence lay Gwen, bidding him advance with her eyes. In the background lurked the Beast, but surely, that wasn't in the film?

The beep-beep beep-beep of Tyrone's watch alarm jerked him awake.

With a rough thump, Tyrone woke the sleeping Colin.

"H-Hour, stand by yer beds!"

Merlin mumbled something about a toilet.

"Find a tree," Tyrone growled.

Just before four, a car cruised past. In the growing light of sailor's dawn, it had that sleek, new look of a fleet vehicle. It would be fitted with all the extras to ease the miles between business meetings and sales conventions.

"That's him," Colin said.

"Off you go, then," Flint said. "We're counting on you not to let us down."

Colin gave a promise, then left to walk to the

castle. Twenty minutes passed one by one, with Tyrone drumming the dashboard, stating and restating his distrust of Colin. He broke off only to search the glove compartment for a Mars Bar he was sure he'd put somewhere.

"It's time," Tyrone said.

The sky was growing bright as Tyrone started the engine and the UNY-DIG van rolled towards Tintagel castle, chosen by Mallory as the birthplace of Arthur, despite the fact that it was built six hundred years after the event. Oddly, eerily, archaeologists had found traces of a sixth-century monastery beneath the castle. As much as scholars tried to kill Arthur, he would not lay down and die.

Slowly, as if not to break the silence of dawn, the UNY-DIG van approached the one other car in the car park: a sleek red Ford. It had one occupant: a square-backed figure too immobile to scale slopes or skip over perimeter fences in the half light.

Euan Trepennick looked their way. It took more than an instant for him to realize the game was up. He started his engine in a rush and stamped on the accelerator. In a whirr of tyres worthy of Hollywood, the Ford lurched forward. In seconds he'd be speeding away from the lumbering van.

Tyrone stamped on his own accelerator. Euan had to swing in a circle to reach the exit. Tyrone could cut the circle.

"Are we insured?" Flint yelled.

"Yes."

"I always hated this van."

Flint braced himself for the impact. Green van hit red car between driver's door and front wheel, deflecting the Ford into a granite pillar where it was brought to a halt in a shower of headlamp glass. There was a second, lesser impact, as the back of the Ford recoiled into the van, then both vehicles stalled. The seatbelt wrenched Flint's shoulder.

"Yee-hah!" Tyrone cried.

Flint was a foot or so away from where Euan Trepennick was touching his forehead. Neither car had been travelling at more than fifteen miles per hour; the impact had been little worse than a session at the dodgems.

Tyrone was the only one with a free door, and had escaped the wreck within seconds of the impact. Flint crawled across to the driver's door and joined Tyrone, who was already needling Euan as the insurance man crawled out of the ruin of his car.

"Bang goes our no-claims bonus," Flint said.

"Bloody idiots, you bloody idiots." Euan swung his legs into the passenger footwell, but Tyrone prevented him from opening the door. Euan touched his forehead again.

"Are you trying to kill me?"

"It's called revenge," Tyrone said. "*Lex talons*: Eye for an eye, car for a car."

"What?"

"Roman law."

"Where's Merlin and Ivor?" Flint asked.

Euan strayed an eye towards the castle. Tyrone opened the rear door of the car, reached across the driver's empty seat and removed the ignition keys. It may have been immobilized by the crash, it may not.

"You stay here." Tyrone jabbed a finger at Euan as he again tried to open the door.

Euan nodded, the downcast mark of defeat on his face. Tyrone pulled himself out of the car, bringing Euan's walking-stick with him.

"Stay!" he commanded.

He and Flint jogged across the car park and clambered over the perimeter fence. From somewhere behind them a voice challenged the intruders and threatened to call the police. All well and good.

The castle of Tintagel once stood on a narrow promontory, but the isthmus had been cut away by the sea and most had collapsed, with what was left being undermined by 'Merlin's Cave'. On what was now almost an island crowned by ruins, two figures could be seen moving around. Shortly, they came into plain sight, clattering down the walkway which links castle to shore. Ivor was carrying the bundle, Merlin carried the digging tools. Tyrone and Flint were already on the walkway, climbing in the opposite direction. Ivor stopped a dozen steps away, Merlin just behind him.

"Game's up, Ivor."

With Tyrone at his side, Flint was aware of his own blondness, and of Tyrone, the archetypal blue-eyed Anglo-Saxon. Arthur and his Britons had defeated the Saxons in a dozen battles. Now two dark-haired, dark-eyed men stood defending the bridge against the blonde northerners. Step, by step, by step, Ivor advanced down the walkway. Sacking fell to the ground, and for the first time in fifteen centuries, Excalibur was raised in anger.

Chapter Twenty-Eight

Ivor's angelic face had been exchanged for that of a devil. His teeth were bared, slightly parted, with vampiric menace. He advanced down the stairs one at a time, the sword-tip leading the way.

"Get back!" he said.

Flint respected the blade. He'd seen the lovely Tania use the replica to cleave a box and didn't want to see the original tested in anger. He moved down the staircase smartly, fearing to lose his balance. Ivor was with him all the way.

"Get back." Ivor kept coming forward, holding the sword in both hands, its dull point on a line with Flint's nose. It was no longer sharp, but it was a piece of iron as long as an arm and as heavy as a cannonball. It had to be respected.

Ivor gave a short thrust and Flint retreated onto the flat ground. At the end of *Morte d'Arthur* the armies are reduced to a pile of corpses, with just the king, one knight and the pretender left alive. Arthur and Mordred ran each other through with their weapons, and then there was one . . .

A slight, fragile artist continued to press his enemy back with threats and with a wavering blade. Flint recalled the flashing blade at the Medieval Fayre, the gory end of the Arthurian saga, the power of the sword over the word.

"It's not genuine," Flint panted. "It's worthless, it's stolen, it's not worth all this drama!"

He stopped retreating. In an instant, the sword lifted above shoulder-height, in another it swung forwards and downwards with skull-cleaving power. Tyrone had never fenced, but he leaped forward into the path of the swinging sword, walking-stick raised. Flint threw himself backwards and landed rump-first on the grass. There was a dull crack, then the blade tumbled towards him.

Ivor hardly moved. He stood frozen, looking at the Saxon hilt he held in his hand. The Byzantine blade was on the floor, Merlin rushing to pick it up, issuing short gasps of despair.

Tyrone waggled the walking-stick towards Ivor's nose.

"Good English Ash," he said. "None of yer Italian rubbish."

"'Seek for the sword that is broken'," quoted Flint, getting to his feet, "Sorry, wrong fairy-tale, but equally believable."

Merlin was silent in his despair, cradling the blade.

"Corroded right through," Flint said, jabbing a finger towards the broken tang.

Ivor dropped the hilt. "So what are you going to do now? Beat me up? Isn't that what thugs like you like to do?"

Tyrone tapped the walking-stick across the palm of his hands, as a headmaster handles a cane. Ivor was not far off the mark, so Flint intervened quickly, laying a hand on Tyrone's eager grip.

"I think we'll wait for the police."

"Must we?" Tyrone said, enjoying his moment of power.

"Engage your brain."

"It was him driving that van wasn't it? He's the one who tried to kill us."

"Me?" Ivor asked, trying to regain that cherubic innocence.

"Euan was the only other person I told about meeting Charles Evans," Flint said. "But you were standing next to him when we made the arrangements. You feared that Charles might tell us that Euan had agreed to see Harry the night she died. And you thought Euan had killed her."

"What wouldn't you do to protect someone you loved?" Ivor asked.

Flint's mind flitted across time and space. To a suntanned blonde travel courier somewhere in Greece; to a dinky, headstrong crime reporter; to Tania, vibrant and lively, plunging into some shipwreck half-way across the world. What wouldn't he do for someone he loved?

"I wouldn't try to kill anyone."

Myths have deep, unseen roots but their branches grow, blossom and sprout new branches of their own. Take one twig and one cannot see exactly from which part of the story tree it sprang. Take several twigs and one cannot choose between them on grounds of authenticity. Flint had heard several versions of what happened the night Harry died. None of them were the same, none rang true as the definitive account.

The single policeman who had arrived at the castle had taken Ivor away. D.S. Chaff had been summoned, and Tyrone awaited her arrival down by the crippled cars. Merlin could be seen as a black silhouette, seated quietly on the outer works. Perhaps now he'd seek therapy, even return to his home and the real world.

Euan and Flint sat high on the windswept ramparts of

Tintagel, the sun now bobbing amongst thin cloud over Bodmin Moor. The ex-insurance man had regained his walking-stick, deeply notched by the impact of history. Its distinctive rubber heel explained the curious round marks visible in the forensic photographs at the scene of Harry's death. Euan and D.S. Chaff would have much to talk about.

"Sorry about your car," Flint said to Euan.

"I'm afraid it's no longer my car. Direct your apologies to Matt Humphries."

"It was the only way to be sure you wouldn't escape."

"Where to? And why?"

"Suspicion of murder."

"Murder? No one's been murdered, Dr Flint."

"Convince me; tell me what really happened. I've worked out most of the picture, but the corners need shading in."

"No one is going to believe me; no one would have believed me at the time. I don't think even Ivor believed me. It explains what he did."

"I'll believe you. I've spent a lifetime sifting facts from the dirt; I can tell a tall story from sound narrative."

It was some time before Euan's tale began. He may have been sorting it into logical order, editing it, deciding where to begin. "I came from public school into the Royal Marines; a boy's world into a man's world. You're a womanizer, Flint, but when I was young, women . . ." He strained as if the thought was painful. "Women had an almost artefactual quality. Wives were something one owned, one showed off at dinners, someone to write to, but . . ."

"You preferred men?"

"The company of men," he said, in a relaxed tone.

"One met young ladies of course, very beautiful ones, but I was in a world they could never share."

"Some of my oldest friends are gay," Flint said.

Euan understood what he was saying, he nodded his head, putting his eyes down onto the gravel path. "It's not easy, is it?"

"No; that's what sank you in the end; a homophobe comment about Ivor, another about yourself and I was able to put one and one together. It's no crime in my eyes, but I imagine it's what forced you out of the Marines."

Euan slapped his left leg. "No, it was this. I suppose one could boast if one had been shot by a sniper whilst winning the MC, but this was an accident, not even on active service. I was rock-climbing in Wales; I slipped and shattered my bones into shards; in the old days, the surgeon would have had my leg off in a jiffy, but they saved it – most of it. My left is now an inch shorter than the right and I'm all held together by rivets."

"Compensation?"

"No – and no insurance. Don't you think that's the cruelest irony? Once I was back on two feet, a friend of mine invited me into the business – I was able to get into the firm whilst it was still run by decent types; when Humphries and his sort were still in short trousers. To occupy my mind I delved into folklore, which was how I came to join the Pendragons, and how I met Harry. She sold me King Arthur and I sold her my policies."

"And Ivor came in where?"

"I met him at one of Harry's parties, a year ago. I think it was when she officially joined MPP."

"So you and Harry went back a long way, but what about Charles Evans?"

"I knew Charles before Harry – he was a master at my school."

"Many people think he killed Harry to stop the lawsuit."

Euan employed that pained face again. "No, I was going to stop the suit. That's why I met Harry that Friday night; to persuade her to meet Charles during the conference and make up.

"Harry was tied up all day, preparing for the conference and having some god-awful row with Gavin; I managed to speak to Ivor, but I spoke to Ivor most days. When she didn't come to the opening session, I rang her at home and she said she'd meet me by the jetty. It was a warm night, considering the season, pleasant moon. She usually took her dog for a walk before bed. I'd even accompanied her on some nights, when I stayed as a guest. She'd had her old dog then, a collie, a fine, sensible animal."

"Why didn't you just go to the house?"

"Because Gavin would know what I was up to: I'd been *persona non grata* for the past three or four months, since I'd taken Charles' side. It was Gavin that put her up to suing him in the first place; it was another one of his failed money-making opportunities."

"And Harry was alive when you met her?"

"Very. I came armed with a plan, but we found ourselves at odds within minutes. She'd been arguing with Gavin on and off all day and was very strained, not in the mood to compromise at all. She walked out onto the jetty, changed the subject, then started talking all about this sword and her fame and her discovery. I'm afraid I lost my temper then, telling her that once she'd made Excalibur public she'd have to sue half the historians in the country, as everyone would try to disprove her story. I overplayed my hand and things became very heated . . ."

"So you pushed her in?"

303

"No, no, it was that dog, that darned stupid dog. It attacked me. We were on the jetty, in the moonlight, twenty or thirty feet out into the lake, arguing. That stupid dog began barking and leaping around. Harry tried to restrain it, then the next thing, she was in the water."

"How deep is it by the jetty?"

"Deep enough, she may have even hit herself on the woodwork. The dog was going absolutely crazy, I held out my stick for Harry to grab, but the dog just bit into my arm and I lost my grip."

"So you killed the dog."

"It was reflex, the old commando training."

Flint had once been attacked by a dog. The urge to kill the beast could be understood. He recalled the gloves worn by Euan at Harry's funeral, presumably to cover dog bites and scratches. He remembered Euan's crushing handshake and knew those broad shoulders still held a soldier's power. Everything was making sense now.

"Did you make another attempt to save Harry, once the dog was dead?"

"Yes, I waded in, but, the water was cold and I was wearing my car coat and she was in her long boots. And with this . . ." He indicated his leg. "I swim like a brick. I couldn't see Harry at all, she'd stopped making a noise, she'd stopped struggling very quickly. I splashed around for a few minutes until I found her, but getting her out exhausted me. I tried to revive her, but I was breathless. It seemed to have been hours since she'd first fallen in. She was dead, and she still held my stick in her hand."

"So you went back to the house?"

"No."

"You ran away?"

"Yes."

"Why?"

"Put yourself in my shoes. Put yourself in policemen's boots. You know what was happening at MPP, you know about the writ against Charles . . . at least there would be a scandal, at worst —"

"They would say you killed her?"

Euan nodded. "That stupid dog, if only it hadn't been for that dog. I threw its body into the lake. I thought perhaps they'd assume Harry was trying to save the dog. It might stop them asking questions; there was nothing to be gained."

"Except clarity. Gwen thought Gavin had committed some kind of mercy killing, Gavin thought she'd committed suicide because of my investigation, and they both dreaded Merlin becoming involved . . ." Flint stopped, remembering the newly-established bond of trust with Merlin. His parentage should remain secret until he himself wanted to reveal it.

"It would have been better for Ivor if you'd simply come clean at the start."

Euan shook his head. "Poor Ivor. I only wanted the best for him."

"Ivor thought you'd killed her," Flint stated. "To him, it must have seemed just another facet of your little plot. With Harry dead, you could write out three insurance claims. That would save Ivor from bankruptcy, wouldn't it?"

"You see what I mean, about no one believing me?"

Euan was right; Flint was still sceptical. "So Ivor tried to ram us off the road in a stolen van to protect you?"

"You'll have to ask Ivor."

"So the death was accidental, but there was a scam at the back your mind when you talked Gavin and Harry into insuring the sword – half a million, wasn't it? You'd bide your time, then arrange for it to be lost, and bingo,

Ivor would be solvent once more. It would be a nice way of getting revenge on the company that was about to sack you. Was it you that hired Merlin to swipe the swords?"

"No, no, no. We were going to wait to see whether the Arthur Roadshow succeeded. Merlin simply pre-empted our plans; it made us look guilty, before we'd done anything."

"So why try to recover the sword today? You knew it had no value, surely."

"We had our doubts."

Flint told him about Gavin's scheme to assemble an identikit Excalibur from stolen parts, then milk the publicity for all it was worth.

"I suspected Gavin's motives," Euan said, "But never the sword itself. All the experts supported what Harry and Gavin said about its date. It was ancient and still valuable, even if not *the* Excalibur. What made up my mind was that you – of all people – were turning the county upside-down to find it. Once it was clear that Humphries had won and that MPP would go to the wall, we had nothing left, except the sword. We contacted Merlin through Harry's solicitor and persuaded him to atone for his sins."

"You were going to try and flog it on the black market?"

Euan looked Flint in the eye, for once. "No, were going to return it to Gavin. Once the sword was back, I thought people would grow bored and stop asking questions."

It was time to stop asking questions. Whether the police would believe Euan's story and whether they would take action against Ivor or Gavin remained to be seen. Frankly, Flint hardly cared. An Italian museum would receive a broken sword blade, and a Saxon hilt would be returned to Copenhagen. Matt Humphries would become manager, South-Western region and UNY-DIG would receive a handy cheque to pave its way to solvency. MPP would be liquidated, with Alison, Ivor and Gavin shouldering the debt. Some won, many lost and Merlin's future could not be predicted.

Flint could just see the patch of disturbed turf where Merlin had re-excavated the sword. It reminded him of how he should be spending his time.

The green van stood outside Bridgwater police station, its front wing held in place by masking tape, its left headlight covered with a polythene bag and its bumper suspended by string. Flint had hoped for a write-off.

"I'll drive a bit faster next time," Tyrone promised.

Flint winced then held up a finger to his lips. Detective Sergeant Chaff emerged from the police station with a heavy wooden box in her arms.

"Your toy gun."

Tyrone received the Bren gun case with a smirk. He'd never won a kiss, or words warmer than a rebuke, but Chaff still charmed him.

"Why does someone want to own a machine-gun?" she asked, feigning a scowl.

"Cult of weapons," said Flint. "They have a strange fascination, for some people."

"Well," Chaff said. She formed a soft knuckle and tapped Tyrone on the breast. "See you boys."

"Fancy lunch?" Tyrone said, on impulse.

She laughed, then paused. "OK, as I'll never see you again. There's a café down the High Street, we can all —"

"Not me, thanks," Flint said. "You two go on your own, I've got something to do. Catch you later, Tyrone."

307

"See you, boss."

He agreed a time and rendezvous, then Flint got into the battered van. Chaff leaned into the window.

"Drive carefully."

He drove, carefully, to the village where Lady Dunning once held court with her round table of helpers. Gavin knew the replica sword was worthless and neither he, nor the insurance company cared that it lay in the back of the Green Van beside the Bren gun.

Flint parked in the lane, on the spot Euan had chosen to park on the night Harry died. Here there was a gate, held closed by blue string. A rutted track led down to the boathouse, where Flint stopped at the lake's edge. It was a fine spring afternoon, with hardly a breeze to disturb the water. Birdsong was alive in the woodland along the far shore.

It was a rich and beautiful world, he thought, but just a little short on happy endings. King Arthur never existed, but he should have done. Why couldn't there be magic, and mystery and romance and chivalry? Modern life called out for a hefty dose of each.

With bundle under his arm, Flint walked out onto the jetty, thinking of Harry and of obsessions. The past was always best viewed at a distance, it could not be wished back. Legends should be left unscrutinized; they fall apart like frail manuscript when handled roughly.

A dramatic sunset would add poetry to the drama, but the sun was still high behind a mask of hazy cloud. Flint unwrapped the bundle and took the replica sword by its handle. He raised it in his right hand, remembering Harry's words on a day which now seemed so distant:

"How far could you throw a three-pound sword?"

He hurled it spinning across the pool, but no hand

arose to catch it. The replica Excalibur slashed into the water and vanished.

One day that sword would be found again, perhaps in a few years or perhaps many centuries into the future. The discovery would give someone a good story to tell. Flint waited for the first ripples to reach the jetty, then turned and walked back to shore.